SHE WAS HIS NOBLESSE OBLIGE....

"When one inherits an estate," Lord Dearborne said suavely, "he inherits the responsibilities as well as the income of the estate. But sometimes a responsibility can also be a pleasure." His hand lifted and cupped one light lock of hair that had been curling against Elizabeth's breast. "Do you mind very much being my responsibility?" he intoned in his husky whisper as he leaned languidly close, too close.

"I...I'm not sure." Elizabeth bit her lip, unable to complete her thought. Her head began to buzz and hum. Dear God. What was happening to her? "I don't know you...."

"We could remedy that, couldn't we?" He raised his eyebrows slightly. "Today is your lucky day, foolish one."

Also by Laura London:

THE WINDFLOWER

And in the months to come, look for:

THE BAD BARON'S DAUGHTER
THE GYPSY HEIRESS
LOVE'S A STAGE
MOONLIGHT MIST

A
HEART
TOO PROUD

Laura London

A DELL BOOK

Published by
Dell Publishing
a division of
Bantam Doubleday Dell Publishing Group, Inc.
666 Fifth Avenue
New York, New York 10103

With love—to Laurel, Jane, and Jill

ISBN: 0-440-13498-6

Printed in the United States of America

One Previous Dell Edition
New Dell Edition
February 1985

10 9 8 7 6 5 4 3

Chapter One

When one of the twins said that I looked like a shake-rag after a full day's dusting, I was able to laugh with her, knowing full well that I would get no scolding from Mrs. Goodbody for my grubby appearance. Indeed, how should I look after a berry-picking expedition on a warm summer's day? For though I am normally neat as wax (as Mrs. Goodbody often says with pride) I am also quite capable of becoming a deal more bedraggled than my younger sisters.

And play had been the order of the day. Mrs. Goodbody had shoved the children and me firmly out the door that morning, baskets and wrapped lunches under our arms, telling us to rush and get the mayberries before the birds had them, just as she had every year since I can remember. As always, too, we had eaten as many as we had picked, or so it seemed, then spent the rest of the day wading in the stream, hunting for lucky clovers, or lying in the grass feeling the sun burn warmly through our now stained muslin gowns. At such times I would think, Who could ask life for more? Then I would think of my uncertain future and a slight shiver of fear would pass through me; I would quickly force the unwelcome thought from my mind. Much better, it was, to think of the past, of my childhood filled with security and simple pleasures.

It may surprise you that one left an orphan at the age of eight could honestly say that she had passed a happy childhood, yet such a person am I. My parents

died as they had lived, with calm dignity and faith,
laying no burdens on the living. For all that I had
loved them, they did not carry part of me with them
to the grave. Do not think me heartless, for they
would never have wished it. In fact, my twin sisters,
now thirteen years old, cannot remember either parent;
for their arrival in the world had been the occasion of
my mother's departure from it and my father had out-
lived her by only two years.

Before his death, Father had been private secretary
to Admiral Barfreston and we had lived in a cottage
on the admiral's estate, Barfrestly. After Father's
death, Admiral Barfreston had continued to let us remain in the cottage, even sending his own housekeeper,
Mrs. Goodbody, to live with us, providing her with a
modest portion of the estate's revenue for our care.

Admiral Barfreston had been a kind though absentminded guardian. When we did attract his occasional
notice, he would toss us a sixpence and tell us to be
good children. Unfortunately, we must have slipped
from his erratic memory at the crucial moment when
he made his will. Thus we had been left unprovided
for when he died that September. This time I was old
enough to understand the implications of being left
penniless and unprotected and I'm afraid that I embarrassed Admiral Barfreston's austere lawyer with a
hug of gratitude upon learning that we could remain
on at Barfrestly, at least temporarily. "Temporarily"
had slipped into weeks and weeks into months and it
seemed that we would go on forever just as we always
had.

On the admiral's death, the estate had passed on to
a distant cousin, the notorious Lord Nicholas Dearborne, Marquis of Lorne; Admiral Barfreston had
never married and had not even a nephew to receive
his property. And as for Lord Dearborne, they said he
was so wealthy that his tenant farmers lived in houses
as big as Barfrestly Manor. A gentleman of Lord

Dearborne's exalted degree was hardly likely to visit a small and ramshackle estate like Barfrestly, the admiral's lawyer had told us. He would probably leave the whole affair to his man of business, who would eventually sell the place. Dearborne himself was a leader in London society, a close personal friend of the Prince Regent, and "indifferent, arrogant, and dangerous." So Mrs. Goodbody said, and she had that personally from the innkeeper's wife, who had it from Lady Peterby's maid, who had spent one whole season in London attending to her mistress.

There were other things said of Lord Dearborne, too. Once I overheard Squire Macready's stableboys in whispered gossip, and went to Mrs. Goodbody for an explanation. What was a Paphian? She had stiffened like a fence post and snapped that the evil goings-on of London dandies were not for the innocent ears of young maidens.

When other sources failed, my sisters Caroline and Christa were there to provide enlightenment. They are inveterate eavesdroppers and often have the gossip. Lord Dearborne, they pronounced, spent time with wicked women. When I questioned them further I was relieved to discover that they were mercifully in ignorance of exactly what it was that he did with the wicked women. If truth be told, I had somewhat of a confused idea myself. Even though I am six years older than the twins, I don't often play big sister to them; our relationship is more that of beloved playmates.

And so it had been on this warm June day as we returned home from the orchard, our hearts full of goodwill and our baskets brimming with berries, little dreaming that today something would happen to interrupt forever our present peaceful lives.

Once through the orchard you can look across the now tangled jungle of a garden that Admiral Barfreston's mother had lavished such care upon and see, rising above our cottage and other outbuildings, a large timber-framed mansion set between rows of chestnut and silver birch trees. It had been closed up since the death of Admiral Barfreston, and even before that only a few of its many rooms were in use.

The tireless twins raced up the weedy path to the cottage, eager to show off our harvest of fruit just as I noticed Cleo disappearing around the corner of the mansion. Cleo was the twins' spaniel pup and unfortunately, we've not yet been able to convince her that chickens are not placed on earth for the sole purpose of being chased around for the entertainment of wiry young dogs. As there were almost certain to be hens scratching about in front of the house at this time of the afternoon, I decided to make haste to the front yard to insure that no damage was done to the estate's prime egg producers. As I rounded the corner of the house I stopped short in astonishment.

There, in the driveway, was the most magnificent carriage that I had ever seen. Up until then I had thought Mrs. Macready's shiny barouche the height of elegance, but now I saw there was a level beyond. Beneath a fine coat of recently acquired travel silt, the carriage's satin-smooth sides gleamed and sparkled with colorful inlay. An elaborate crest in black and red was emblazoned on its door and it was drawn by a perfectly matched team-of-six in a silver-studded harness. Several bewigged liverymen, formally garbed in matching red and black uniforms, were standing at attention. Not being one to call a pigeon a peacock, I must admit that I gaped like a yokel. I was so engrossed in gawking at this equipage, which compared favorably with my imaginings of Cinderella's coach, that until he spoke I didn't even notice the stylishly dressed young man standing not four yards from me.

"Sweet Jesus, Nicky, will you look at that? I swear I'd have spent less time in London lately if I'd known the Kentish milkmaids had become so devilishly beautiful."

Startled, I looked around me for the beautiful milkmaid, then gasped as the young man walked over to me and slid an arm firmly about my waist, pulling me close against his chest. Looking into the hard features above me, I recognized Lord Lesley Peterby from Petersperch; the Peterbys' acres marched with the squire's. I had not had any social intercourse with the Peterby family, for I'd as likely chat with the Archangel Gabriel, but I had several times seen Lord Peterby riding through the countryside on his visits to Petersperch. If the Marquis of Lorne was notorious, Lord Peterby was so disreputable that his name wasn't even mentioned (at least it wasn't supposed to be). He was, as they say, not received locally, and spent most of his time in London where they are more broadminded. Lord Peterby was reputedly the despair of his well-liked and respectable mama, and was popularly credited with having driven his long-suffering papa to death with his dueling, gambling, and preoccupation with low company.

Before I had time to collect my scattered wits, Lord Peterby had reached his other hand up to the collar of my gown, pulling it carefully aside to caress the base of my neck.

I heard the twins come racing into the yard, their voices shrill with excitement. "Mrs. Goodbody, come quick! There's a London dandy in the yard and he's trying to steal Lizzie's virtue!"

At that Lord Peterby let out what in a less elegant person would have been a yelp, and released me with such suddenness that I fell back to sit down hard on the drive. I saw then that my release was not due to the twins, but to Cleo, who had rushed across the yard to sink her sharp teeth firmly into His Lordship's ankle in a gallant effort in my defense. Of course, I should have done then what any other girl with the least pretension to gentility would have done: fainted. Regrettably, one's spur-of-the-moment responses are not so easily controlled, and it was not my gentility that won the day, but my sense of humor. Lord Peterby's unsuccessful attempts to free his polished Hessians from Cleo's determined attack brought my choked laughter bubbling to the surface. Once, when the sexton's wife had reproved me for laughing during choir practice, the vicar had told her to let me laugh, "for Elizabeth's laughter charms like moonbeams on water." But Lord Peterby certainly looked in no mood to appreciate its charm. Caro scooped the wriggling Cleo into her arms where she barked indignantly at being snatched from the best sport she had seen all week. Her excited little face made me laugh all the harder. So there I sat—a crumpled heap in the dirt, shouting with laughter as Mrs. Goodbody came running across the yard. Jolly tears streaming down my face, I looked, I fear, as vulgar as a barmaid in a Rowlandson etching.

Though Mrs. Goodbody could see that I had not been hurt, there was no diminution of her white-hot wrath. "How dare you, young good-for-naught?" she rounded on Lord Lesley Peterby. "Do you think this is London? No doubt there are the sort of women there who would welcome your insulting advances, but this is Kent, my lad. Decent women live here. If you ever so much as touch my lamb again, I will take a full account of your actions to your mama—who is a fine woman, well you know it, and would never sanction such rakings in her own village." I'll bet it's been a while since someone threatened to tell his mother on Lord Peterby, I thought to myself. "And what's more, I will bring an account of your behavior to the Marquis of Lorne," continued Mrs. Goodbody, obviously determined to brazen it out in fine style, "who now owns this estate!"

Whatever Mrs. Goodbody had planned to say next

was interrupted by a titter from inside the coach. There was a movement of one of the satin window curtains and then it was pulled aside to reveal a previously hidden occupant.

If this carriage was Cinderella's coach, the feminine occupant could easily have passed for Cinderella herself. Her smartly coiffed blond hair cascaded onto a slender, creamy neck which shone with jewels. And her gown! The neckline was so low that it later led Christa to remark, to Mrs. Goodbody's horror, that she'd been afraid "they" would fall out. Dragging my eyes away from the amazing décolletage, I saw that it would be impossible, as well, to find fault with her face. Long and surprisingly dark-lashed brown eyes, wonderfully pink cheeks, and bright red lips combined to make her look rather like an exquisite china-head doll. Mrs. Goodbody can snort and say "pretty is as pretty does" but to me, uninitiated into the mysteries of rouge pots and mascara, she was unquestionably lovely.

The vision shook a ringed finger at Lord Peterby and gurglingly reproved:

"Here now, Lesley, don't be handling Nicky's inheritance before he has had a chance to examine it himself."

Lord Lesley began shaking the country dust off his trousers, and flicked an imaginary speck from his embroidered waistcoat. Mrs. Goodbody was still drawn up like a bow ready to be sprung, the light of battle in her eye.

"Now don't go aiming at me again, my good woman. You can see the chit is none the worse off," observed Lord Peterby drily, glancing at my laughing countenance.

"No thanks to you!" snapped Mrs. Goodbody. "Now take yourself and your . . . lady friend off before I take it upon myself to inform His Lordship of your

conduct here. He would welcome no debaucher on his
lands!"

The lady in the carriage tittered again, then said:

"A-ha, Lesley, that you cannot deny. Nicky has
never liked another man poaching on his preserve.
Have you, Nicky?" She leaned even further out of the
coach as she spoke and fluttered the sooty lashes at
another man, who had been leaning his long, graceful
body against the shadowed side of the coach, his arms
folded negligently before him. I had not noticed him
in all the excitement; he stood in a shadowed position;
but as he straightened and stepped into the sun I saw
immediately that he was not a man who could go long
unnoticed in any company.

He could have posed for a Greek god in a Botticelli
painting. The sun shafted off his red-gold hair, which
fell in shining curls to brush his broad shoulders. His
beautifully molded features were set in an expression
of sardonic indifference, and the clear blue eyes that
swept briefly over us were the coldest I'd ever seen.
Instead of being robed in classical tradition, the Botticelli god wore riding clothes so expertly fitted to his
slender, powerful frame that even my inexperienced
eye could judge them as having been made by no
provincial tailor. Even his name was Greek; "Nicky,"
the lady in the carriage had called him. I think it
means something to do with victory.

"You are Mrs. Goodbody?" asked the stranger
curtly.

"Aye, 'tis," assented Mrs. Goodbody warily.

"I wasn't aware that you had any daughters." He
was frowning slightly.

"Daughters? To be sure, I have not—the Good Lord
didn't see fit to bless Joe and me with youngsters of
our own and Joe's been gone these fifteen years now ...
Daughters—you think Miss Elizabeth here . . . ?
I should say not! Why the very idea! Miss Elizabeth is
quality! She's here under the protection of Admiral

Barfreston, sir." Mrs. Goodbody spoke with such conviction that I half expected the admiral's shade to appear forthwith, rapier in hand, to offer me protection. The thought made me giggle.

The golden-haired man raised his eyebrows slightly and came over to stand above me. Reaching out one long, shapely hand, he grasped my elbow and dragged me easily to my feet. I flushed under his insolent gaze which played over my body with the dispassionate appraisal of a cattle judge on fair day.

"She's quality, I agree," sneered the hateful stranger. He turned to Mrs. Goodbody. "But I was under the impression that Admiral Barfreston was a man in his eighties . . . ?"

For a moment I was afraid that Mrs. Goodbody would pop out the buttons of her dress, with such rage did her bosom swell.

"Nothing of the sort, sir! The admiral was a fine Christian gentleman, and Miss Elizabeth's father was employed by him as a secretary. When he died, orphans they were left—poor little Elizabeth only eight years old, and Caroline and Christa not out of nappies. And the admiral supported the dears like his own. These are good, innocent children, sir, and know naught of evil." Mrs. Goodbody stopped, as though a thought had suddenly occurred to her. "Might I ask your name, sir?"

"Nicholas Dearborne," he said shortly.

Poor Mrs. Goodbody. To say that she was dismayed would much understate the case. My sister Christa, who was supposed to know naught of evil, didn't help matters by pointing at the lady in the carriage and piping:

"Then that must be a wicked woman."

Mrs. Goodbody shot her a look that boded ill for the miscreant twin, though I saw Lord Dearborne's lips twitch in spite of himself. You had to admit that the man had presence, but I cared not for his arro-

gant, commanding air. I imagined he would throw the
lot of us off what was now his property with no further ado. He certainly looked capable of doing so. If
that was intended, however, he gave no sign of it but
calmly began to question Mrs. Goodbody about the
condition of the manor house. How long since it had
been in use? How much work was necessary to make
it habitable? How many servants were needed to op-
erate it? Could she acquire servants from the village?
It seemed Milord was coming to stay for a time!

When he announced that he was bringing along his
ward, it was too much for Christa. She had obviously
decided that since she was already in trouble, there
was nothing to lose by questioning the marquis further.

"Mr. Marquis, sir? Is your ward a boy or a girl?"

"He's a boy," said the marquis, indifferently.

"Is he an orphan?" she pursued.

"Yes."

I'm sure she would have asked more if the more
cautious Caro hadn't dug her elbow into her sister's
ribs and told her to hush.

The lady in the carriage again leaned out and said
petulantly:

"Do hurry and complete your domestic business,
Nicky darling. I vow I'm eager to relax and refresh
myself in that excellent inn Lesley has been promising
us."

"One moment more, Cat," said Lord Dearborne,
over his shoulder. "Mrs. Goodbody, Lord Barfreston's
solicitor will call on you this evening and he has been
instructed to advance you whatever sums you need to
make the manor livable. Hire whatever help you find
necessary. Just don't economize. The place looks half
eaten by dry rot and I've no desire to wake one morning with the ceiling collapsed."

"Oh . . . Your Lordship, the girls here . . . ," began
Mrs. Goodbody.

"I'll discuss that with you when I return next week. In the meantime you may continue as you see fit." One of the marquis's grooms brought up a handsome Arabian stallion and the marquis swung himself lightly into the saddle. To my surprise, he brought the mincing stallion alongside me. He reached down and carelessly flicked my cheek with one long finger.

"Don't look so dismayed, sweetheart," he drawled. "I daresay something can be arranged."

I felt Mrs. Goodbody place a protective arm around my shoulder as we watched the visitors depart. Somehow I knew that I would dream that night of cold blue eyes.

Chapter Two

It may surprise you to learn that I, dependent upon charity as any pauper in the workhouse, am actually the granddaughter of a duke. But I am more fortunate than my grandfather was, for it is better to be poor and face that honestly than to be poor and grow monstrously in debt pretending to the life-style of a feudal baron. Grandfather was too encased in pride to admit that the revenues of his lands could no longer support him in the luxury that had been the lot of his family for generations. It must be from him that I inherit my ability to view the future with tranquil optimism. This characteristic gives my nature a buoyancy welcome in stressful times, but can as easily become a weakness. And so it was with Grandfather. He ignored the rapidly worsening state of his finances until his creditors lost patience and announced that he must bring his ship about or sail no more upon the River Tick. Grandfather panicked and fled the country, abandoning not only his debts but also his sixteen-year-old son, who later became my father. The moneylenders, taking revenge through the only avenue open to them, threw my father into debtor's prison. I can only imagine what he suffered there because he discussed those days with no one. I knew only that he contracted jail fever, leaving him with the damaged heart that finally caused his death.

It is to Admiral Barfreston that Father owed his last happy years. The admiral, the duke's last loyal friend, convinced the duke's creditors to drop the charges against my father. He then brought my father to Barfrestly and employed him as his secretary, a post that was never more than a polite fiction.

My mother was a governess on the Peterby estate when she met my father. She taught French to Lord Peterby's older sisters—Lord Lesley was only in the nursery at the time. The vicar, who prides himself on having introduced my parents, says that my mother reanimated the gentle shell my father had become. Her gifts of joy and laughter were a healing balm to my father's broken spirit. That is the way I remember her, laughing with such delight that all the world rejoiced with her. I love to watch the twins at play, for they are so like her they bring her back to me. She was French, and had borne her own measure of grief. Though she had been sent from France before the Terror reached its peak, her own parents' heads had been part of the gruesome feast of Madame Guillotine.

Nevertheless, it was my own trials that beset me as I walked to the church the next morning. We'd had little enough claim on the admiral, and we had none at all on the Marquis of Lorne. News has wings and the whole parish knew every detail of Dearborne's visit before we had even entered the churchyard. Mrs. Blakslee, the innkeeper's wife, was the first to identify my Cinderella as Lady Catherine Doran. She was the marquis's current mistress, as Mrs. Blakslee, who hadn't been born yesterday, could judge from the sleeping arrangements.

"My Fine Lady made sure that her bedchamber was right next to Lord Dearborne's. Shameful, I call it! The very name of womanhood dragged through the dirt! And my John was the one to see that hussy sneak into His Lordship's room, bold as a mare in season!"

Mrs. Plumford, the sexton's wife, gave a snort. "Possibly, but I fear we must ask ourselves if these are meet matters to discuss on the threshold of the Lord's house, and in hearing of such tender ears as well." That last was said with a significant glance in my direction.

"Oh, Amelia, you and your prudish pecking. Do tell, Mrs. Goodbody, have you seen the solicitor yet?" queried Mrs. Coleman, the apothecary's lively wife.

"To be sure. Last evening he called at the cottage. The purse isn't skimpy for fixing up the estate, and that house is going to get the cleaning I've been itching to give it all these years. Can you spare Jane to give a hand?"

"We'd do well to have the extra shillings. But understand that when that rakish Lord Dearborne arrives I want her straight home. My Jane's virtue is worth more than all the money in the Bank of England." She leaned closer to Mrs. Goodbody. "Has mention been made of providing for your three dear lambs?"

I broke gaily into the conversation: "I don't care if he tosses me off his lands on my ear. I've an education, thanks to the kind offices of the vicar, and I'll become a governess like my mother was." This show of bravado was as much to convince myself as my listeners. I longed to chase away the apprehension that tapped at my shoulder like an unwelcome stranger.

"I'd like to know what matron would put a gal your age in a responsible position like the care of children?" sniffed Mrs. Plumford.

Privately, I wondered the same thing. But I said, "Oh, the mysterious ways of the adult world. They won't hire you unless you have experience, but how will you ever get experience unless you are hired to begin with?" Mrs. Goodbody's frown informed me that I'd been pert. I hastily begged pardon, for I don't like to give anyone offense.

There was a stir of interest in the assembled throng as two men alighted from a gig that had just pulled into the churchyard.

"Who can that be with old Dr. Lindham?"

"Why, 'tis his new assistant, a Dr. Brent, I believe."
Trust Mrs. Plumford to know all the doctor's business.
She was a small-scale hypochondriac and commanded
Dr. Lindham's services more than anyone else in the
village.

Dr. Lindham threaded his way to our circle with
the new assistant in tow. Bowing, for he liked to think
of himself as a lady's man, he presented "Dr. Brent,
who's come to relieve my old bones from handling all
the complaints of you charming ladies."

We charming ladies greeted the sally with the obli-
gatory giggling disclaimers as Dr. Brent took the hand
of each lady in turn. He was a harsh-featured man in
his late thirties with an air of calm self-possession.
There was a vaguely military air about him, though
I'm not sure whether it came from his ramrod posture
or the thin, undisfiguring scar that ran across his left
cheek. His dark hair was graying slightly at the temples and I remember thinking that he looked too distinguished to be a mere country doctor.

He bowed over my hand with practiced grace. To
my surprise he did not release it immediately, keeping
it prisoner in his own a moment longer than courtesy
permitted.

"Charming," he breathed. His smile-softened eyes
caressed my face with surprising intimacy. What in
the Creator's name! I almost snatched my hand away.
Dr. Brent's behavior had been as overfamiliar in its
subtle way as Lord Peterby's. Or so it appeared to me,
but I have no experience with masculine attentions
and perhaps refine too much on a simple compliment.
I was left with a feeling of unease and could only be
grateful when the sexton opened the church door and
called us into worship.

Unease was to be my close companion that week.
Like an uninvited guest it hovered beside me, defying

my efforts to banish it. I was grateful for Mrs. Goodbody's practical comfort. She kept me busy until I
dropped into bed at night, so tired that sleep came as
soon as I drew the quilt to my chin. Had I been given
time to mope I assuredly would have done so, for at
the time I thought that this uncertainty was the most
difficult thing that life could hand me.

On Monday morning the attack began. Armed with
buckets and brushes of every description, under the
ruthless generalship of Mrs. Goodbody, we marched
upon the manor house determined to clean or die.
And our valiant little regiment had won a heroic battle by Friday afternoon. My own assignment, the admiral's favorite sitting room, looked fresh as a spring
hay crop. For all that the carpet was threadbare in
spots and the draperies yellowed, at least the detestable marquis could not sneer that his new house was
dirty.

I stepped back for a satisfied view of the gilded
mirror that I'd just polished and suddenly noticed my
face reflected back at me. I'd never seen my face in
any mirror before save for a handglass that Caro had
won by tossing balls through a hoop at last year's
church fair. The glass on that mirror was so badly
warped that it made my nose look perched between
my eyebrows, a vastly comical effect. The sitting-
room mirror's glass was flawless though, and I could
see every detail of my face. How curious it is that I
should look so unfamiliar to myself. I suppose that's
because I'm used to being on the inside looking out
instead of on the outside looking in.

I recalled the strange behavior of the doctor and
Lord Peterby with their male assessments of me as
"beautiful" and "charming." The thought disturbed
me as I studied the face of the girl in the mirror with
detachment. Hair the palest blond curled riotously
around an oval-shaped face. The violet eyes appeared
huge above the other small features, glowing lumi-

nously against the white skin that would never tan.
Ruefully I remembered Olivia's wry catalogue of her
features in *Twelfth Night*: "Item: two lips, indifferent
red; item: two gray eyes, with lids to them."

I turned away, wanting no closer acquaintance with
the pale young woman in the mirror. It is unnerving
to think that there is part of me, unseen by myself,
that is exposed to all who look at me. I heard the reassuringly normal voices of my sisters in the hallway
and called them in to me, longing for their cheerful
nonsense to distract me from my unsettling introspec-
tion.

"Have you no mercy on the handiwork of poor
Arachne?" I asked Caroline, gently brushing a cobweb
from her hair.

"We've been cleaning up the servants' quarters for
the marquis's London servants. There were hundreds
of spiders! Mrs. Blakslee says they'll be snottier than
their master." She grinned. "The servants, not the spiders. Just think, he's bringing a cook, a valet, and two
grooms. Barfrestly will be tricked out as fine as the
squire's place."

"Who's Arachne?" asked Christa impatiently. She was
not one to let things go unexplained.

"Why, she was a lady who lived in Greece long ago,
who made such beautiful woven cloth that she became known all over Greece for it. But she became
conceited and bragged that she could weave better
than the Goddess Minerva herself."

"Did Minerva punish her for being proud?"

"Indeed she did. She put her finger on Arachne's
forehead as a mark of shame. Poor Arachne went mad
from the misery and hung herself and would have
died if Minerva had not pitied her and turned her into
a spider to spin forever."

"What a horrid story. Was Minerva always so cruel?"
wondered Caro.

"Ah, I can tell you stories of her that will turn the

very blood in your veins to ice water." I made my voice low and breathless as I settled myself down on the faded carpet.

"Yes, Lizzie, do! No one can tell a tale like you." Christa shivered in delighted anticipation and flopped down on her stomach to gaze at me with her chin nestling on her upturned palms. Caro lay on her back with her head resting on my knee, her wheat-colored curls spreading across the skirt of my apron. Thus we sat as I spun the enraptured pair a yarn of ancient gods and heroes. By the time my fancy has played with mythology the plot little resembles the original and if my sisters ever aspire to classical scholarship I fear they will have volumes of material to unlearn.

". . . and then Cupid and Psyche lived happily ever after," I finished. I had put my hand out to stroke away the hair fallen across Caro's forehead when a slight movement drew my attention to the doorway.

There stood Nicholas Dearborne. Even through my alarm I was struck by the impact of his incredible male beauty. It was as if one of the heroes from my fractured mythology had somehow overcome the boundaries of space and time to join us. Whatever he thought of our trespass was not revealed as he studied me. I think that if he had not been blocking the doorway, I would have risen and scampered through it like a frightened fox. With great relief I heard Mrs. Goodbody's firm tread in the hall beyond.

"Good afternoon, Your Lordship. Joe Hawkins fetched me from the dairy to tell me you was come." She stepped into the room and quickly took in our confused embarrassment as we stumbled to our feet. "Your Lordship won't mind the girls, I'm sure. They were just finishing up their chores and will be running along so as not to bother Your Lordship."

Taking hasty advantage of Mrs. Goodbody's tactful dismissal, I gathered my cleaning rags and followed the twins out of the room without a backward glance. What had the marquis thought, coming into the library to discover my sisters and me thus? Probably, he thought we were making pretty free of his newly acquired house. Milkmaids in the parlor; what next? I wondered dejectedly if we were to be evicted from our little cottage and if poor Mrs. Goodbody would be given the unhappy task of telling us. I believed that it would be even more painful for her than for us.

I climbed up the well-scrubbed stone steps into the cottage and took refuge in the accustomed task of preparing dinner—a boiled neck of mutton.

The twins came in carrying a bucket of water between them just as I was testing my crusty buns for doneness.

"Watch what you're doing, Caro. There, now see what you've done, sloshed water all over my skirt. Say, what's that smell?" Christa plunked down her end of the bucket to lift the lid of the cooking pot and sniff cautiously. "Ugh, mutton again?"

"You should thank the Lord for what He provides, my girl," said Mrs. Goodbody. She ducked her head slightly to pass through the low doorway and came over to give me a motherly kiss on the cheek. "You can put your mind at rest now, Elizabeth, the admiral didn't forget you children after all. Before he died, he told his solicitor that he wanted his heir to continue to support you so that you could remain here as you always have!"

I was too relieved even to speak and sank down limply onto a convenient three-legged stool. Caro continued to set the table with childish unconcern and asked Mrs. Goodbody casually why the solicitor hadn't told us all this before, just after Admiral Barfreston's death, because "then Lizzie wouldn't have had to worry herself about it like a toad on a hot stone."

Mrs. Goodbody answered her before I had time to refute so unflattering a comparison.

"Well, perhaps the solicitor didn't feel that he could reveal that to us before he discussed the affair at length with the marquis. Not wanting to raise false hopes, you see? To tell the truth, girls, I didn't want to query too closely, not wanting to tease His Lordship. Lord Dearborne has been more than generous. Why, he's more than doubled the allowance the admiral made for you!"

"I hope that means we can have something besides mutton for dinner once in a while," said Christa, unimpressed. "Did you find out anything about the orphan—you know, the one that is the marquis's ward?"

"His Lordship stayed the last few days at Petersperch and rode over here on his stallion. A nasty brute that stallion is, too, so Joe Hawkins says."

"That's all very interesting, Mrs. Goodbody, but what about the orphan?" pressed Christa with a lamentable absence of manners.

"I was coming to that. The boy will arrive tomorrow in the coach from London, the one that's bringing the marquis's London servants."

"Oh, I hope the carriage is that lovely one that was here before, with the wicked woman in it," said Caro.

"You're not too old to have your mouth washed out with soap, young lady, and so it will be if you've a mind to continue talking piggish," admonished Mrs. Goodbody with unruffled placidity. "Oh dear. In all the bustle I forgot to check up on the room for Master Christopher."

"Is that the orphan's name? I wish we had known earlier, then we could have made a sign that said *Welcome, Christopher* or some such thing."

"Never mind, Christa," said her twin, consolingly. "The room looks perfect as is. You don't have to worry about a thing, Mrs. Goodbody, because Christa and I did the thoroughest job on his room. We even repainted that set of toy soldiers that's been up in the attic all these years, and Joe Hawkins put new straw ticking into our old rocking horse. Christopher will be so surprised tomorrow!"

Regaining my power of speech, I tried to express to Mrs. Goodbody a thought that had been floating hazily in my mind ever since she had entered the cottage.

"Mrs. Goodbody, isn't it . . . wrong for us to take money from someone we're not related to? I mean, strictly speaking, we weren't related to the admiral either, but that seemed different. Mrs. Plumford says . . ."

"Now don't be tellin' me what Mrs. Plumford says because that woman never had a teapot's worth of sense in her life, and so everyone in the village knows. The idea! A sexton's wife telling a duke's granddaughter what's proper! Your blood is just as good as the Marquis of Lorne's. Maybe you weren't raised in a fancy house like you ought to have been, around your own kind, but true ladies you are for all that, and so I told My Fine Lordship." It was a picture to command awe, Mrs. Goodbody telling His Fine Lordship that three country wenches in berry-stained gowns living in his back cottage were "true ladies."

The potatoes boiled over then, which is always a real conversation silencer, and we were eating dessert before Christa brought up the subject of our new benefactor again.

"I wonder what a man like the marquis is doing at Barfrestly. He's got much nicer houses to live in than this, they say. Why come here?"

Mrs. Goodbody shook her head, frowning. "I don't know—perhaps it's to fix up the place before he sells it. He did mention something about men coming from London to do some work here. At any rate, it's not for us to speculate about how the marquis spends his time—so don't go popping your nose into his affairs,

Christa. Now promise, pet—we don't go snoopin' into the marquis's business, all right?"

Mrs. Goodbody paused in the act of serving out the mayberry pie, remembering another piece of good news.

"It's to be new clothing from London for you girls! The marquis has had orders sent to some hoity-toity dress shop in London so you'll be dressed as is fitting for your station. Lord Dearborne says it is high time you were dressed as proper young ladies."

What the marquis had actually said, as Mrs. Goodbody confided to me long afterward, was:

"For God's sake, get that chit out of those rags before one of my friends mistakes her for a scullery maid and gives her a toss in the nearest haystack."

Chapter Three

Red sky at night, shepherd's delight;
Red sky at dawning, shepherd's warning.

I don't know what color the sky had been at dawning
but by the time I had risen from my cot the heavens
had taken on a grayish ombré. The rain came on and
off all morning, collecting in the worn ruts in the car-
riageway to make hundreds of silvery looking glasses.
Lifting our long skirts to keep the hemlines dry, my
sisters and I made hasty progress down the front drive
during a pause in the deluge. We had decided to await
Christopher's arrival in the gateway cottage where Joe
Hawkins, the coachman, lived with his nine cats. "It's
like having eighty-one cats, for they each have their
nine lives," Joe would say with his huge wink. Since
Cleo wasn't very sociable with felines we left her at
home to comfort Mrs. Goodbody during thunderclaps.

I sat musing by the window while the twins played
hide-and-seek with the cats around the heavy old furniture in Joe's parlor. We were prepared to wait all
day for the coach if need be, but shortly after one
o'clock we heard the rumble of carriage wheels like
thunder from afar. A few moments later, the carriage
pulled through the gate, rain steaming off the horses'
backs. The looking-glass puddles were shattered into
crystals by the stamp of powerful hooves.

The twins and I pulled woolen shawls over our

heads to keep off the halfhearted drizzle and followed the marquis's impressive coach up the drive to the mansion. We watched from a wary distance as Lord Dearborne gracefully descended the front steps. The coachman pulled the team to a stop, and out stepped—a handsome adolescent boy. His friendly open face was glowing with affection as he looked up at the marquis.

Lord Dearborne smiled back; a warm, rich grin that penetrated through the coldness of his eyes, softening them. I felt my breath catch in my throat.

"Lord, who would think the old crosspatch could look so chummy?" Caro whispered to her twin, *sotto voce*.

"'Lo, Uncle Nicky," said the youth.

"Lord, brat, every time I see you you've grown another inch. I hope this wet weather hasn't dampened your young spirits any."

"No, sir, I'm in excellent gear for all that it's plaguily damp. I confess to one or two bad moments back on your drive, though. I feared the potholes in the lane were going to tip the carriage over into that jungle of undergrowth. I've never seen such a place for rack and ruin. I hope you know what you're doing, coming here."

Lord Dearborne lifted his hand, rumpled his ward's hair lightly.

"Have faith, halfling," he said. Mrs. Goodbody joined us, puffing from her quick walk from the cottage. The smile remained with Lord Dearborne's mouth as he turned to her, though his eyes became distant.

"Mrs. Goodbody, may I present my ward, Christopher Warrington." And Christopher Warrington took her hand just as though she was some great titled lady, which warmed me to him right from the start. Having a little boy to fuss over had its charms, but those paled into insignificance compared with the prospect of having a lively friend of one's own age.

"To be sure, Your Lordship," stated Mrs. Goodbody. " 'Twill be a fine thing to have a lad about the place. But Mr. Warrington must meet my dear charges. They've been looking forward to your coming, like Christmas."

I stepped forward, eager to waste no more time in establishing friendships with this handsome boy whose kind brown eyes were smiling down into mine.

"Why, you must be as old as I. And quite six feet tall in the bargain," I said, shyly. "It would take a rocking horse big as entered Troy to hold you."

"It has been a few years since I rode my last rocking horse," he said with a puzzled grin.

Caro and Christa came to my side, giggling. Christa told him:

"We were expecting a jam-faced tot to mother. Wait until you see how we've fixed your bedchamber. There are toy soldiers and an old kite, along with the restuffed rocking horse. We'd even planned to take you on a picnic by Townsey Mill House tomorrow if this bothersome rain clears."

"I am not so ancient that I can't appreciate a good picnic. Especially in such charming company." His smile took us all in and visions of jam-faced tots were banished unregretted.

That was the last we were to see of Christopher that day. The twins and I had planned to walk to Squire Macready's stables with Jane Coleman if the weather would cooperate. Indeed, before the hour was out, the determined sun began to push aside the sulky rain clouds and Jane's cheerful, freckled face poked around the cottage door. One of the squire's huge plow horses had just that week foaled and we spent a long while peering between the bar gates of the hay-lined box stall in the corner of the stables, full of admiration for the proud mother and her frisky, dappled colt. It was almost dusk by the time we trudged back to the cottage.

When we returned we found that Mrs. Blakslee's predictions about Lord Dearborne's London servants had been borne out. The French chef was especially difficult. His name was Henri, and he stated that the kitchen, with its old and wheezy stove, was fit only for the cannibal feasts of a wild tribe of aboriginies. Or so Mrs. Goodbody told us when she returned for a short time in the evening to assist in seeing the twins to bed. Mrs. Goodbody said only the presence of His Lordship's valet, Roger, made the experience bearable. He was, said she, "a fine gentleman, very proper and distinguished." Chuckling warmly, Mrs. Goodbody bid us goodnight to hustle back to the kitchen and help poor Henri clean up his mess.

After she had gone, I lay in bed, listening to the happy chatter of the twins as they hugged each other under the covers in anticipation of the morrow's picnic. Then their talk grew quieter, with sleepy comments coming less and less often, until their slow rhythmic breathing informed me that they had fallen asleep. The chatter of the crickets took up the conversation where they had left it, with the night birds adding faraway high cadenzas. Unable to sleep, I left my bed and walked to the window where the curtain billowed quietly like a sail in the warm night breeze. The sky had cleared, the clouds having spent their tearful sorrows and moved on. The full moon made it nearly as bright as day, with the light of the distant stars adding silvery highlights to the warm glow from the windows of Barfrestly. As I watched, many of the lamps in the mansion began to blink off, leaving only a dim glow in the library, where I supposed Lord Dearborne and Christopher to be enjoying their after-dinner brandy and talk, and one in the kitchen, where Mrs. Goodbody was likely enjoying a late-night discussion of London downstairs happenings with the new servants.

On a whim, I pulled an old cotton gown from the wall and threw on a light shawl to protect myself from the still dampness of the night. Stirring as I was with inexplicable longing, I wished to be out in the spacious coolness of the evening. I made my way out across the moonlit garden, my bare feet sliding softly through the wet grass. As I stood in the breeze in the middle of the grounds the night sounds played a concert of which I was the only patron.

Then to my surprise I observed what appeared to be a man standing directly underneath the window of the library!

After some reluctance to vacate my front-row seat, I decided I had better investigate, and I was nearly going to call out to the mysterious form when it vanished into a shadow. This warranted closer investigation. It didn't occur to me to be afraid; I had never been in danger in my life. When I reached the spot under the library window I found nothing but a decrepit ladder draped helter-skelter with old washrags, probably left there by some lately industrious servant who had planned on resuming his labors there on the morrow. I poked at the ladder and laughed at my fancy, and turned to resume my place at the opera when a scrap of conversation floated from the open library window above my innocent head.

"I'm glad that you decided to bring me out here, Uncle Nicky. Anne is all at sea right now, what with her husband being posted to Europe. Lord, you wouldn't believe all the fuss and botheration. Now that we're out of black gloves, I daresay that Anne would use every spare minute to drag me to Almack's and a mass of other devilish places, expecting me to do the pretty to a lot of stiff-rumped dowagers and their die-away daughters."

The speaker was, without doubt, Christopher Warrington. I heard Lord Dearborne laugh softly at Christopher's morose tone.

"Somehow I can't picture you eschewing female companionship." He paused, and when he spoke again, his voice had become curiously gentle. "Give yourself time, Kit."

"Yes," Christopher said quietly. "Uncle Nicky, have you come any closer, yet? Since coming to Kent, I mean?"

"Little things happen; nothing dramatic though." I wondered briefly what Lord Dearborne could be trying to come closer to and was suddenly struck by a flash of guilt. Here I was, eavesdropping, "pokin' my nose" into Lord Dearborne's affairs against Mrs. Goodbody's emphatic prohibition. I was about to tiptoe stealthily away when I heard Christopher speak again:

"I know what your business is here, but what do you do here for pleasure in this season?"

"Ride mostly."

"So," Christopher's voice sounded amused, "have you succeeded in mounting the beautiful violet-eyed filly you have stabled in the back cottage?"

Eavesdroppers never hear any good of themselves. How often I had heard Mrs. Goodbody say that to the twins, and how crushingly true it had just proved to be. I am the world's worst sinner. My sisters had been stealing apples all along from the Squire's orchard and the one time I went along, unwillingly, we were caught. And now I had been paid off again. I'd never before eavesdropped on a conversation, purposefully or otherwise; and while the twins had been getting away with it for years, on my one transgression I became the victim of humiliation. A mortified blush fanned my cheeks. If only I had stayed in bed where I belonged I might have been spared this mortification. I decided to return thence, where I would be safe from such punishing temptation.

To avoid waking the twins I tiptoed over the threshold, but I heard Christa whisper, "Is that you, Lizzie?"

"Yes it is, pet. Go to sleep now."

"Lizzie, Cleo was scratching at the door so I let her out. But when I called her she ran off toward the big house."

"Don't worry then, Christa, I will bring her back. Go to sleep now."

I retraced my steps back toward the house, calling softly for Cleo. I decided to look toward the side of the house, where Cleo liked to dig for field mice in the weeds. But when I arrived there was no sign of the errant puppy.

Suddenly there was a scrape and a rattle and something dropped in front of me, seemingly from out of the sky. When I bent down to pick it up, it turned out to be a piece of shingling from the roof. Ladders don't knock off shingles, and Cleo can't climb walls, I thought to myself nervously. I looked up toward the roof.

No doubt about it, there was a man, or the form of a man, standing on the roof. He, or it, was facing away from me and was moving laterally, silently, across the edge of the roof. I resolved to follow it at a safe distance. It would do no good to call for help until I was sure I had seen what I thought I had. I began walking, keeping the form in view some paces ahead of me, until it disappeared at the corner of the house. Had it flown off into the air like some wild ghost? Or if it was a man, had he only crossed to the other side of the roof? I walked on a little farther until I too had reached the corner of the house.

Cleo was digging underneath the lilacs there. I was very glad to see her.

"Cleo," I said, "help me find the scary ghost." My voice sounded unnatural and brave in the night. Cleo looked up and then continued with her worrying.

I bent closer to remove the object from her teeth, then held the thing curiously. In stunned horror I realized that what I held was a human hand! In the instant that this knowledge hit my consciousness another hand came to lie lightly on my shoulder and the scream that poured from my throat was a lusty one indeed.

"There's no need to shriek, you foolish child. I'm not going to hurt you." Not five minutes ago I had thought that if I never saw the Marquis of Lorne again it would be much too soon for me. Now I almost wept with gratitude.

"A hand," I gasped rather incoherently.

He stretched out an impatient arm to help me to my feet and I tried again.

"There's a hand under the lilac bush."

He went then and looked where I had pointed. I heard him curse softly under his breath as he pulled me roughly to my feet. With one sinewy arm about my shoulders he half dragged me across the grass to the kitchen door with Cleo running at my heels. He called Mrs. Goodbody sharply and thrust me into her arms as she came running.

The next morning I woke puffy-eyed and headachy. The events of the evening before had kept me away from my cot far beyond the usual hour. And being the discoverer of a dead man does not induce the most restful of slumbers, I assure you. The hand under the lilac bush had been connected to the body of a man with a broken neck. Henri, the French cook, had whipped his last soufflé.

Mrs. Goodbody had taken one glance at my wan face at breakfast and sent me back to bed for the balance of the morning. When I woke the second time I felt better and didn't wince when I heard a determined rap on the cottage door. I pulled down my quilt and rose.

"Yes?" I called.

"It's Christopher," came a masculine voice. "Your sisters are eager to picnic and Mrs. Goodbody said that I should come and wake you."

"Oh, thank you," I returned, though I felt shy. After what I had heard last night outside the window, I was embarrassed to face Christopher. At least he didn't know that I had eavesdropped. It was some consolation.

Yet it didn't seem proper to go off merrymaking the day after someone had died right here on our very grounds, and I said as much to Christopher as I tied the frayed ribbons of my second-best bonnet under my chin.

"Don't be a goose," replied Christopher, sounding muffled but sensible through the door. "Henri was related to no one here—I daresay you hadn't even met him. What happened is a shame but we can scarcely mourn a man none of us knew. Uncle Nicky will do what's proper for Henri's remains, you can be sure of that."

I doubted that very much. Last night the Marquis of Lorne had shown little inclination to trouble himself with the business. When the squire, who is justice of the peace, arrived to examine the particulars of the matter last night, the marquis had suggested with freezing boredom that surely the matter could be handled as expeditiously as possible. Squire Macready, as cringing a sycophant as any you will find, had hastily agreed. He had no sooner listened to my sketch of the night's events (my eavesdropping carefully omitted) than he had pompously pronounced it obvious that Henri had been attempting to gain entry to Lord Dearborne's bedroom "for the purposes of robbery" when he had fallen to his death. It was clear to me that his opinion owed more to his desire to accommodate Lord Dearborne than to his own convictions.

"'Lizbeth, are you going to dream away the whole

day? Come on," yelled my sister Caro peremptorily. I grabbed up a worn coverlet to sit upon and stepped out, squinting in the bright sunlight. The twins were standing, impatiently shifting about, with an over-sized picnic hamper between them. Christopher stood nearby, his stylishly cropped brown hair tousled by the breeze. He gave me a smile that was at once so boyish and warm that my reserve melted away and I cheerfully took his proffered arm.

"Good morning, everyone," I said.

"'Tis afternoon, slug-a-bed," teased Caro.

"So it is," I said. The sun streamed down from Olympian heights as we walked lazily to the back meadow, the twins merrily scattering a small herd of lambs. A meadowlark piped from somewhere in the woods to the west and the pungent odor of clover mixed with trampled sheep dung. We passed next to a low forest of brush and a bramble bush reached out to grab a bite from my gown. The thorns had just put out leaves to disguise their small sabers. One must tread warily past them.

Finally we reached the shade of our favorite elder tree. Its branches leaned over a twinkling stream bor-dered with reeds. Spreading out the coverlet on a comfortable cushion of moss, we sat down and I gave the twins and Christopher an account of my nocturnal adventures. Afterward Christopher whistled, but re-spectfully gave his considered opinion that I should let be.

"Well, of course I'll let be. There's nothing I can do. But here is a man dead and all Lord Dearborne can think is how he's being kept from his bed. It was cal-lous, Christopher, and I don't think the full story has come out."

"And what was a cook doing on the roof?" returned Christopher with a knowing air. "Making soup from starlight?"

"But Christopher, that's the point. I'm not sure that

it was Henri on the roof. I could barely make out that it was a man, much less the man's face. When I tried to explain that to the squire he looked at me like I was a chair with its springs popping out. I tell you, he'll never properly investigate because Lord Dearborne does not want the matter pursued. The squire dissolved into a slithering jelly in front of Lord Dearborne," I finished in disgust.

"If Uncle Nicky doesn't want the thing looked into then there's an end to it. He never does anything without a good reason, I promise you. How do you think that he got to be one of the most important men in the War Office?"

"Influence!" I said firmly.

"You're far off there. M'father always said that Uncle Nicky was one of the brightest young men in government. Said he had a knack for organization combined with a quick eye for detail. That's the kind of men they want running the country. Damn, girl, your country's in a state of siege. Do you think they'd want a bunch of titled nodcocks minding the store?"

"Quick eye for the ladies, too," shot in Caro, who had been busy untangling her fishing line. "The innkeeper's wife said it was musical bedrooms when he stayed there with Lady Doran."

Christopher raised his eyebrows meaningfully at me, but as I rarely discipline the twins I remained silent.

"The innkeeper's wife ought to be ashamed of herself repeating fudge like that around a little poppet like you," growled Christopher.

"I'll wager that she didn't know she was repeating it around Caro," I said, casting a shrewd eye over my unrepentant sister. "Besides, if people don't want to get talked about then they ought not to do things that people will want to talk about."

"Of all the prim . . . What do you expect a man to do, live like a monk?" asked Christopher indignantly.

I was coyly silent for a moment and then replied as prissily as I possibly could, "Happily, I know nothing of men or the way they live. Surely that you would have the indelicacy to raise such a subject to me shows that you have no regard for my sensibilities. In short, sir, I find you shock-ing!" I quickly buried my head in my hands to hide my laughter—the sight of his mortified face had been too much for me.

"Elizabeth! I beg your . . . so sorry . . . pray do not be upset. Why you imp, I believe you're laughing." He pried my fingers away from my mouth. "You *are* laughing." Christopher smiled down on me dazedly, like one charmed. He sat down next to me, and then, becoming aware that he was still holding my fingers, released them hurriedly.

"You oughtn't to look like that, makes a fellow feel like he's been hit over the head with a two-by-four. Nor blush like that either, has the same effect."

Caro finished untangling her fishing line and walked over to the stream to drop it in. "Is there to be an inquest, Lizzie?"

"Yes. Next week at the Tenterly courthouse. And the squire says that I will have to testify."

Christa looked at me with awe. "Won't you be afraid to speak in front of all the people?"

"I'm more likely to grow puffed up with my own importance, from all the attention, like poor Niobe, who suffered a most painful fate."

My sisters deserted their fishing rods to come and sit across from Christopher and me. "Tell us about Niobe, Lizzie, c'mon, do . . ."

Chapter Four

The twins and I spent most of the next week getting
to know Christopher, who seemed as pleased in our
company as we were with his. By the second day we
were calling him Kit, and by the third we had exchanged stories of how we had lost our parents. Christopher's mother had died in a runaway carriage when
he was seven. The loss of his father was still raw—
Christopher told us bleakly that he had been shot by
housebreakers only six months ago.

In spite of his loss, Christopher was as open and
unaffected as Lord Dearborne was cold and withdrawn. Not that I saw much of the marquis; he stayed
only a few days before returning to London to more
sophisticated amusements and, so Christopher averred,
his government responsibilities. To Christopher, Lord
Dearborne was all things. Kit plainly worshipped the
man, to no degree less than did Squire Macready. It
was Uncle Nicky this and Uncle Nicky that with Kit.
I thought glumly that there was at least one bone I
would have picked with Uncle Nicky if I had the
chance:

The marquis had sent workmen from London to un-
dertake long-needed repairs to the estate. They were
rough city-bred types who seemed to be everywhere,
turning up at unexpected places. They were near the
gatehouse when we took Christopher to see the new
litter of kittens. One man came to hammer in the stables when I was feeding the old cob a carrot, and the

same man went into Tenterly with us on the day of
the inquest, saying that he needed to purchase some
more building materials. In short, I got an uncanny
feeling of being spied on. I should have been glad to
have the men there making those repairs to the neglected buildings of Barfrestly—but I wasn't. I felt tiny
fingers of resentment prodding at me. Before Lord
Dearborne's arrival we had done very well, thank you.
There had been no pesky workmen, no corpses in the
bushes, and no coldly mocking blue eyes to disturb
my dreams.

I decided that, perhaps, my unaccustomed tension
was due to the upcoming inquest over Henri's death. I
had been assured and reassured by everyone from
Mrs. Goodbody to the squire that there was nothing
to fear, that I would merely have to tell my story of
the events immediately leading to the discovery of
Henri's body and then answer a few simple questions.
Still, Caro had read me well in guessing that I was shy
at speaking before so many people. There is something unnerving about being the center of attention at
a legal proceeding.

Fortified with an egg-and-bacon breakfast and a
new Sunday bonnet, I set off for Tenterly in Lord
Dearborne's elegant carriage, Christopher and Caro
on either side of me and Mrs. Goodbody and Christa
across from us. Riding in this magnificent equipage
had gone a fair way toward reconciling me to the trip.
What lady could fail to be pleased by a ride in a carriage out of a fairy tale? My sisters leaned perilously
out the window to shout greetings to passersby and to
laugh at their expressions of awe at seeing those Cordell gals riding in such splendor.

I had laughed that morning as Mrs. Goodbody had
packed a bottle of smelling salts in her reticule, possibly on the conviction that the inquest would leave me
with a fit of the vapors. If the truth be told, however,
there was a moment in the inquest when I was afraid

that I might really end up requiring the services of that ominous little brown bottle.

As I sat on the stand giving my testimony, having sworn on a Bible to tell the truth, my narrative reached the point where I had seen the shadow and walked to investigate under the library window. The squire interjected, "and did you hear anything just then?" I of course took him literally for a moment and, blushing to the roots of my hair, I thought he wished me to recount the humiliating conversation between the marquis and Christopher concerning myself. I would rather have eaten all the ribbons on my new Sunday bonnet.

But I had sworn on the Bible to tell the whole truth, so it was either relate the conversation or go to hell! Thinking that never again would I be able to hold my head up in Tenterly, I closed my eyes and started to speak. Mercifully, the squire's voice interrupted me to clarify that he only wondered if I had heard any footsteps or noises on the roof at that point. Saved by the donkey's bray!

There were several others that gave evidence after me, including Roger and the coroner, though no new evidence came forth. After only eight minutes of deliberation the jury returned with a verdict of death by misadventure, just as the squire had predicted. Henri had been French and as we were at war with France, people were only too ready to believe anything bad of a Frenchman. I have no patience with that type of national prejudice, but what could I do? I knew nothing that would exonerate the poor chef from the posthumous charge of attempted robbery. I had never even met the man.

I was glad to leave the musty courtroom behind and step into the fresh breezes that blew upon Tenterly's High Street. Here, surrounded by half-timbered houses, pubs, and small shops, one can see the tall spire of the church tower. It dwarfs everything around it into insignificance, which is not such an unpleasant feeling sometimes.

Christopher, the twins, Mrs. Goodbody, and I went to the White Lion for tea. We sat down and got cozy after Mrs. Goodbody had quieted the twins, and began talking over the events of the day. My mind was wavering in and out of the conversation, when I heard Caro speak, in her forthright way, to Christopher.

"Why, Kit," she said. "Whatever are you looking at?"

Christopher was indeed staring intently out the window, even rising into a half-crouch, suddenly oblivious to what was taking place around him.

We were all growing very much alarmed, and I turned to look out the window myself, thinking I was missing some momentous occurrence. Perhaps the Prince Regent himself was passing by the inn with his entire entourage and I was missing it. But no, it was only Dr. Brent, standing and talking to one of the workmen from the estate, out in the road.

"Who is that man?" said Christopher. "That straight-backed, distinguished fellow standing in the road? He looks familiar to me."

"Why, that's only Dr. Brent," I told him. "He's not half so distinguished as he looks."

"Who is Dr. Brent?" he said, still staring out the window.

"Only the new assistant to Dr. Lindham in the area," said Caro disparagingly.

Christopher appeared to relax. Just then Dr. Brent turned, observed us all gawking at him through the window, gave us a huge smile and wave, and walked into the inn to stand beside our table. He was indeed a forward gentleman.

"Elizabeth, Mrs. Goodbody, and the dear little girls," he said, his eyes twinkling. "And this must be the new guest at Barfrestly I have heard about—a sturdy young man to hold the walls up while the marquis is away."

Christopher extended his hand. "Christopher Warrington is the name, Dr. Brent. Pleased to meet you." Whatever had made Christopher feel ill-at-ease had vanished when Dr. Brent presented himself, and they soon fell into an easy banter. I was surprised at how well they hit it off until it occurred to me that what I was seeing was the well-mannered interplay of two determinedly charming people, and that all they did have in common was their late residence in London. Dr. Brent had taken his medicals there and Christopher had lived there with his family. I supposed this was London manners in action. I was surprised at the skill with which Christopher handled sociable small talk and it brought home to me that, though I was an aristocrat by birth as he was, our differences in upbringing were pronounced. He had been raised to his station, where I had been raised to be a simple country girl, polite in my way, but perhaps a little too direct and obvious. I felt like an openmouthed bumpkin as I followed the banter between Christopher and Dr. Brent.

"I heard you had some excitement at your house lately?" said Dr. Brent. His face was solemn but his eyes were twinkling in a way I did not really find amusing considering the ordeal I had been through. "Miss Elizabeth looks rather petite to be confronting housebreakers, trespassers, and things that go bump in the night."

That last remark brought my chin up. Though his face was solemn I could detect a real note of mockery in his eyes. "I don't think the entire story of the cook's death came out in the inquest," I said defiantly. It seemed to me that his eyes narrowed slightly, but perhaps he was only squinting at a sunbeam deflected from outside. I could detect no change in his easy manner. He leaned his hands on the table, bent forward, and looked intently into my face.

"Tell me, Miss Elizabeth, what is the real story of what happened that night?"

"I'm not sure," I retreated. "It just seems to me that people were too easy with their judgments because the cook was French."

His smile widened perceptibly. I stifled an unlady-like desire to grind my teeth. I had already felt behind in the conversation, and now my ego was really bruised at being made sport of like a foolish child. I longed to recoup my stock in this entire enterprise.

"I just don't consider the case closed, that's all," I declared ringingly, with much more bravado than I was actually feeling.

"So you are setting yourself up in competition with the Bow Street Runners, Miss Elizabeth?" said Dr. Brent, smirking.

It did nothing for my temper that I could think of no very clever comeback to this snide remark. Why was the man so obnoxious? We teased in my family, yes, but only for fun, not to humiliate. Caro's hand stole underneath the table and softly patted mine. Christopher, reading my frustration and distress, changed the subject, and kept the conversation away from me until the coach arrived to take us back to Barfrestly.

As we rumbled down the road in the big carriage, Caro patted my hand again and spoke. "Never mind that horrid Mr. Medicine-Menace, Lizzie. He was just trying to show off, making fun of you like that."

Mrs. Goodbody clucked mildly. "I'm sure he meant no harm, dears. Gentlemen," she proclaimed importantly, "will have their jokes."

"Well," I retorted, "if that's an example of their jokes, than the less I see of 'gentlemen,' the better!"

I hummed as I poured water into the old porcelain washbasin the next morning. My good mood sprouted like spring flowers after a May rainfall. I realized that

I had put the inquest and all that went with it behind me. God bless the Fates for restoring me to my accustomed serenity. I think that because I feel pain so deeply when it strikes me, some merciful natural balance prevents me from feeling it for too long.

That day, Caro, Christa, and I were to begin work on our annual theatrical production. Every year since my twelfth birthday I had written and directed a play as a parish fund-raising activity. It was presented on the same day as the church bazaar, and I must admit that it is usually one of the bazaar's most popular attractions. Though our modest productions could never play Drury Lane, to the people of our parish who hardly ever see a show of any kind, they are a source of much enjoyment. The whole parish eagerly inundates us with ideas and suggestions that are often as humorous as they are impractical.

This production was to be the most ambitious since three summers ago when we had put on "The Plagues Visited Upon Egypt and the Subsequent Exodus of the Hebrew People to the Promised Land." We had decided to pull out all the stops with a play so grandiose that it would, we hoped, leave our audience in a state of rapt amazement. We planned to enact "The Battle of Hastings Culminating the Norman Invasion of England in the Year of Our Lord 1066." Unfortunately, the only thing in scarcity for our productions were those few souls fearless enough to risk forgetting their lines and embarrassing themselves before the village. So far we only had a scant half-dozen ferocious Norman invaders. I was stuck with the role of King Harold. No one else wanted to be the loser. Jane Coleman was to be the lachrymose Queen Edith. She showed a regrettable tendency to giggle when the news of her husband's death was brought to her by the wounded messenger (Christa). The role of William the Conqueror was yet unfilled because every potential applicant had declared that the part had too

many long speeches to memorize. I was beginning to
think that I would have to cut out some of my most
cherished declamations. I had taken particular care in
writing William's part, for I have always felt rather
sorry for him. The only way that I can account for this
strange partiality is that he is an unpopular figure in
British history and I have what Caro says is a maudlin
tendency to sympathize with the underdog. I brought
the problem up to Christopher as we walked down
the lane together.

"So here I am, having to choose which precious
lines will go. I feel like a poor mother who has to decide which of her children will go to work in the city,"
I told him in melancholy accents.

"Why cut any lines? Right at your doorstep is an
actor willing to do lengthy speeches all day if only to
please you, little Elizabeth," Christopher said solemnly, with teasing eyes.

"If you mean Mrs. Goodbody, I can assure you that
nothing would induce her . . . Why I believe you
mean yourself! You must be jesting!" I was amazed.
Hazy as my notions of the proper behavior for young
bluebloods were, I knew that nothing could be more
shocking than for one to appear in a public theatrical.
So I told Christopher, who laughed so hard that he
almost fell into a ditch.

"What a peagoose you are, sweetheart," he said. "If
it's proper for you then it can hardly be too scandalous for me." I replied huffily that I had only been
trying to protect his reputation, but saw that this only
threatened to set him off again.

"Well, it's true for all that, Christopher. I don't have
a reputation to lose. As far as society is concerned I
am nobody. If your guardian heard that you were
going to act in public he would think it an unbecom-
ing prank and yank you out by the ear."

I had expected a grin to answer this sally, but to my
surprise he grew quiet. After a minute he said, very

gently: "Elizabeth, don't go saying you're a nobody because it ain't true." He paused reflectively and his face brightened. "Damn if I don't set out to prove it to you, too."

Considerably intrigued, I teased him to tell just how he meant to set about this mysterious task, when we were interrupted by mischievous Cleo who had flushed a partridge from the underbrush beside the lane. There was a great deal of commotion as the twins tried to retrieve the triumphant puppy before she damaged Mother Partridge's hidden nest.

We were on our way to the village to pick up a large piece of lumber that the blacksmith was donating to the production. It was destined to become the historical vessel that carried the invading Norman army to the English shore.

The village is more accurately called a hamlet. It nestles in a valley's dip about half an hour's brisk walk from Barfrestly Estate and rejoices in the name of Mudbury. You may laugh, but it is surely no worse than being called Broughton Poggs, Bumpstead, or Sparrowpit, which also number among England's more than thirteen thousand villages. Mudbury is a hamlet of such great charm that I think it picturesque, and I have lived close by it all my life! A tidy row of whitewashed cottages cuddles cozily about the little church with its Gothic stone cross. Separated from the buildings by a trim yew hedge, there slopes a wide piece of common land, now bright with marsh marigolds.

As the lane turns abruptly into the village, we were hailed by my friend Jane Coleman, hanging out a washing on a clothesline behind their cottage. After introducing Christopher to Jane, the twins took him across the village square and then disappeared behind a stone-built barn where the blacksmith carried out his trade. Jane and I sat together on the overturned clothesbasket to chat in the sun while they were arranging the transportation of our lumber. Fine brown curls frame Jane's sweet freckled face, which reflects its owner's quiet strengths and the graceful humor that she applies to everything she does, from frying bacon to being my friend.

Jane had gone into the cottage for another basket of wash when, to my exasperation, I saw Cleo come tearing around the side of the barn in hot pursuit of an angry young duckling. So intent was I upon catching the miscreant spaniel that I didn't hear the drumming of hoofbeats until the horse was almost upon me.

The large bay stallion had been running hard. A dash of foam from its slavering mouth landed on my sleeve as it reared to stop only inches from where I was standing. It was close enough to blot out the sun. Thank God English boys learn to ride almost before they learn to walk or this country girl would have been but a memory. I was conscious of a snarling, adolescent male voice.

"What in hell do you mean running under my horse's hooves, you paper-skulled twit? You could have been trampled!" The boy dismounted and angrily shook his riding crop in my face.

At that moment, Christopher rounded the corner of the barn, took in the scene, and ran up and punched the other boy in the face without a by-your-leave. Good for you, Kit, I thought as the reckless young rider landed in the dirt. But he was up in a flash and they were into it deep, all arms flailing like windmills, a donnybrook in the middle of the dusty road. Before too long, there was a gaggle of spectators, with the twins carrying on a running commentary, and the old village men gazing on speculatively, laying bets as to the outcome. The young rider's anger had changed to fear under Christopher's well-trained onslaught; he was definitely getting the worst of it but refused to yield before such a crowd. Boys are funny and I shall never understand them. I was beginning to get upset.

I saw Lord Peterby riding up the road on his mincing thoroughbred and I hailed him to stop and put an end to this scene of what looked to me to be incredible violence.

"It's really too bad that Dearborne isn't here to see this," he said. "He taught the boy much of what he knows. However I love a mill though, I suppose it isn't proper for them to carry on so in the village square."

Lord Peterby swung himself down easily from the saddle, entrusting his reins to the blacksmith. He walked up to the milling pair, and, placing a firm hand on each wilted collar, pulled them apart.

"Take a damper, you two, or I'll have you fighting in the pigsty." They turned and looked at him; Lord Peterby was apparently known to both combatants, even though they themselves had never met.

"He was insulting Elizabeth, Lord Lesley," said Christopher hotly. "He was raising his crop at her and he called her disrespectful names."

"Insulting her? She ran in front of me and shied my horse!" said the unknown rider, pointing at me with a bloody finger.

"Ah, *chercher la femme*," said Lord Peterby, casting his eyes heavenward. "Whoever is to blame, the matter does not warrant dueling pistols at dawn, would you say, Master Jeffrey? Sir Christopher of the Roundhouse Right?"

The boys shook hands, apologies were made all around, and Lord Peterby made us known to Christopher's erstwhile opponent, who turned out to be Jeffrey Macready, the squire's oldest boy. To my amusement, the two really began to hit it off, making plans to go and have target practice the next morning. Fisticuffs one moment and friends the next!

Lord Peterby remounted, advising Jeffrey to do the same if he wanted to get home in time to clean himself up before luncheon or his father would know he'd been brawling. He added that he would have accompanied us home if he were not on the way to an appointment. As he spoke he ran his eyes over me in the fashion that puts one forcibly in mind of the Wolf's first view of Little Red Riding Cape. I was grateful that he had urgent business elsewhere.

"My goodness, Kit," said Caro on the way home, as we four struggled with the lumber. "If we knew you were so ferocious we would have taken great care before this not to tease you so much."

Ferocious indeed. By the time we had reached the house, Christopher had a horrible shiner, which closed his left eye and quite discolored his entire face. With his black eye and torn clothes he looked not like a member of the aristocracy, but a blind beggar who should be sitting by the roadside soliciting contributions.

"Poor Kit," I said with heartfelt sympathy. "That must be very painful."

"It do sting a bit." He winced.

"If you want to go and get cleaned up, I shall bring you a piece of meat for poultice to keep down the swelling."

"That sounds good," said Christopher, walking in the direction of his room. I followed him after a bit, knocking on the door of his room with meat in hand.

"It's Elizabeth."

"Yes, come on in." His jacket was draped over the bedpost. He was standing by the washbasin cleaning his face; there was a rent in the sleeve of his shirt.

"If you are to be my knight-errant, at least let me mend your armor for you." He shrugged himself out of the shirt and handed it negligently to me. It was then I saw the jagged red scar on the left side of his chest, just below his collarbone.

"Christopher, how on earth . . ." I looked up at his face, and reached out and touched the wound.

He hesitated. "It's just an old wound."

"It's not old, it's recent. Tell me how this happened. Who did this to you?"

He looked uncomfortable, and said, "I'll tell you then, but you can't repeat it to anyone."

"I'm listening."

"I was with my father when he was shot and, as you can see, I caught one of the bullets myself. The men came while we were asleep; the memory is very hazy to me even though it happened just months ago. My father died that night, and they tell me I nearly died myself. I already told you my father worked in the War Office with Uncle Nicky. It seems they were after something other than mere plunder because none of our valuables were taken. Our library was left in a shambles; Father's books were ripped apart violently, the bindings all slashed and destroyed, the pages strewn about the room."

"Aren't you afraid they'll try and kill you again?" I asked, my voice tight with horror.

"I don't know why they would. I certainly don't remember anyone's identity. I suppose the shock must have wiped it out of my mind because I don't recall anyone wearing a mask, either. And I don't know a thing about what the men might have been after. But Uncle Nicky is having me guarded; that is why I am here and that is why he suddenly hired that crew of rough-looking laborers. Among them are my bodyguards."

Chapter Five

The next day was a rainy, gusty Kentish day, and I lay
in bed past time to get up, listening to the drops thud
against the ground outside. It would turn the countryside an even deeper green, and the grasses would
sparkle like a thousand jeweled ladies. Or a thousand
polished daggers. I shuddered. It was an ugly story
that Christopher had told me yesterday, but it hadn't
frightened me so much as it had filled me with a wild
righteous fury. I wanted to see the killers brought to
justice. That such men had only to pull a trigger to
cause so much grief and misery!

A tiny breeze set the curtains aflutter as Christa
came into the room. She had seen Christopher set out
for target practice with Jeffrey—rain or no rain—and
his eye looked much better. I wondered if Kit had
been followed by one of the workmen-bodyguards.

Today we would begin work on the Norman man-
o'-war for our theatrical. We had planned to set up in
the barn and paint, saw, and hammer madly away.
Caro pointed out that we had better hurry our project
along—if it rained any more we might need it to sail
away to safety from the deluge, like Noah. The twins
and I decided to meet later in the barn. First I had to
finish some research in the library at Barfrestly
Manor.

I try to make my productions as historically accu-
rate as possible, unless it suited my fancy to do otherwise. The admiral's main library was always a trea-

sure trove of information, full of old maps, charts, books, and treatises. Where else could I have learned that a muslin band soaked in liquefied cat's dung makes an excellent depilatory (give me the hair any day) or that King Jamie had a marvelously odd fondness for young boys? I pulled a tattered wool shawl over my head and dashed through the garden, letting myself into the manor by a side door. Once inside, I dried my wet pattens on my hem. Better to dampen my skirt than one of the admiral's old carpets.

I stepped into the library, leaving the door ajar behind me, and then walked over to the window. The soft, moist breeze swept in from the outside and ran around the corners of the room like a sprightly child. I always felt at home here; this is where I spent much of my time on days like this. This had been my special room. The admiral had allowed me the run of the place because he knew I liked to read, and I tried to show my gratitude by keeping the books in good condition and airing the room. The admiral didn't use the room much himself as he had a small study stocked with his favorite books, which were of a highly technical military and nautical nature.

I paused a moment in reverie about the old admiral. He was always described as eccentric, but I thought of him as interesting. He liked to relive his battles, and whatever you wished to converse with him about, he would always manage to lead the talk, in ways subtle or direct, to his experiences with the fleet. His last big commission had been with His Majesty's fleet in the war with the American colonies, and we were always hearing about the damned Yankee Doodles. He was nearly stone-deaf, probably from the din of battle, and used a speaking tube which never seemed to work very well. In his last years, therefore, he was lost at sea, tossed on the roaring storm of his own memories, never to come back to port. On a stormy winter night, when the wind would rattle the shutters and howl from the Channel, he would climb up the ivy on the side of the manor as ably as if he had once again been a twenty-year-old midshipman sporting in the rigging, and he would step out onto the roof. I used to see him there when I was a child, stalking back and forth with his garrick topcoat on, his hawklike face splitting the gale, shouting orders and obscenities to the imaginary topmen breaking sail in the black clouds above his head. I admired him for that, but it always caused a great commotion among the servants for fear that he would try to walk the plank and end up on the ground below with a broken neck. Like poor Henri.

I put down the book I had been reading and shuddered. Like poor Henri. I had seen someone walking on the roof, and Henri had been found dead immediately afterward.

I felt a sudden urge to complete my reading in our cottage in the company of Mrs. Goodbody. As I rose to my feet I heard the sound of firm footsteps in the hallway. The library door was thrust open, and Lord Nicholas Dearborne, the Marquis of Lorne, strode into the room and grabbed me by the wrist.

"What are you doing in here?" he demanded. I hadn't even known he had returned from London. As before, his physical attractiveness hit me like a blow beneath the ribs, leaving me feeling slightly giddy. My attempt to free my wrist from his fingers caused them unconsciously to tighten their hold so that I felt shackled by iron.

"Do you always gape like a startled sheep whenever anyone asks you a question?" he snapped, cutting the carpet from under my dignity.

"I think you've broken my wrist," I managed to gasp, stupidly. He released me. Staring resentfully at the marquis, I rubbed the mistreated joint.

"Sir," I began, attempting to restand my poise on its tottering foothold, "Admiral Barfreston allowed me free access to the library and I didn't think to ask your permission before I used it again; that is, now that it is yours. I didn't even know that you had returned to Barfrestly." My voice was quite steady. "If you don't wish me to use the library, you have only to say so—I'm aware that my sisters and I are at the mercy of your generosity, thus making your wishes of paramount concern to me." This hadn't been delivered with quite the degree of crushing scorn that I had intended, crushing scorn not being something at which I particularly shine. To my humiliation, I felt a blush rise to my cheeks—the curse of fair skin.

The marquis frowned and ran a careless hand through his shining hair.

"You are not at the mercy of my generosity, as you so quaintly phrase it. By supporting you, I am merely fulfilling my obligations to Admiral Barfreston."

Far from mollified, I tried to match the coolness of his tone as I answered, "That's what Mrs. Goodbody told us, but that is not everyone's opinion. There are some people who feel that it is improper for me to receive support from someone whom . . . I have no claim on." I saw Lord Dearborne's lip curl sardonically. "Like Mrs. Plumford," I added, wanting to be specific.

"And who is Mrs. Plumford?" asked the marquis. He crossed his arms and leaned a shoulder casually against one of the tidy bookcases.

"She's Mr. Plumford's wife." The marquis's smile deepened. I could tell that he thought he was dealing with an idiot. "Mr. Plumford is the parish sexton."

"Perhaps Mrs. Plumford is uninformed on the finer points of British law concerning inheritance. When one inherits an estate, he inherits the responsibilities and liabilities as well as the income of the estate," Lord Dearborne said suavely. "In supporting you I am merely carrying out the wishes of Admiral Barfreston, in accordance with the law."

I believed him. Whatever Mrs. Plumford might know about the finer points of British inheritance law, to me they were an uninteresting enigma. What the marquis said was so, must be so.

"Do you mind very much having me for a responsibility?" I asked, looking up at the marquis. The hard-temper lines around his mouth relaxed as he reached out his hand and with one long finger lightly traced the curve of my cheek. The color seemed to darken in his eyes as he regarded me thoughtfully. Very gently, his exploring fingers traveled down to stroke the sensitive skin at the back of my neck; it felt as though it melted at his touch. In fact, time itself took on a curious liquid quality.

"Sometimes a responsibility can also be a pleasure," he said languidly. His hand lifted and cupped one light lock of hair that had been curling against my breast. I looked down to where his hand played, and felt a strange tightening in my throat as he caressed and stroked and swirled the lock of hair, where it lay. My head began to buzz and hum; exotic sensations seemed to be washing into my body. It was as if the room had turned into a voluminous honeycomb and we were being drowned in honey.

"Do you mind very much being my responsibility?" His words penetrated slowly and softly through the thick haze that had engulfed my consciousness, as though the pound-pounding of the surf on a seashore had formed itself into a language which only I could understand. Lord Dearborne was the sea, the earth, and the spring honey, and I would be drowned and washed away whether I responded or not. There was no one to save me.

"I . . . I'm not sure." Dear God. Why must I stammer and speak in monosyllables? What was happening to me? I lifted my head to his, causing a tear to drop unbidden down my cheek. I blinked back further tears, hoping against hope to find the answer in his eyes. There was no answer there, only an immense azure sadness. I searched his face briefly, and abandoned the quest as the search became its own justification, as my eyes came to rest finally, inevitably, on his lips. He had asked me a question. I lifted a hand, experimentally, and placed it near his mouth, a thrill paralyzing my wrist as I felt his soft breath. His arms were around me now, and he was pulling me fully against him.

"I don't know you . . ." I bit my lip, unable to complete my thought.

"We could remedy that, couldn't we," he said. His lips were very close to mine. Suddenly, unbidden, Christopher's words came back to me, just as they had been spoken in this room. I was the violet-eyed filly. I disentangled myself from him, pushing weakly against his chest.

"I'm afraid," I whispered.

He raised his eyebrows slightly, slipping his fingers to steady my chin.

"Are you afraid?" he said, looking at me strangely. "You ought to be, little flower. Beauty is a dangerous gift for an innocent like you. Today is your lucky day, foolish one." Lord Dearborne picked up the book I had been holding on his entrance to the room and handed it to me. His voice was curt and impatient as he said, "You may come into the library whenever you wish but run along just now."

I ran.

Neglecting to collect my shawl, I slipped quietly out the back door. The rain touched my shoulders like cat's paws and I shivered involuntarily, though it was not cold. The rain was pouring out of the sky, sending fine mists curling from the leaves of the trees. Foolish one. But not so foolish that I didn't understand the implications of Lord Dearborne's actions. And not so innocent that I couldn't recognize lovemaking when I was its object. Unfortunately, I was not so clever as to

meet these very improper advances with the treatment
they deserved. I should have screamed, fainted, and
cried. I should have called for Mrs. Goodbody. I
should have done anything but stand there while the
marquis touched me in a fashion I was convinced
would be repugnant to any gently bred lady of sensi-
bility. I reflected gloomily on my lack of femininity.
Why had I become so confused and passive when
Lord Dearborne touched me? Because he was a practiced rake, I told myself severely, resolving to avoid
him as much as possible in the future. I made my way
toward the old barn where a light burned through the
slats.

The twins were there, working on the boat. Christopher was there also, sitting on a mound of hay, Joe
Hawkins's ancient fowling-piece next to him.

"Lizzie, wherever have you been?" chorused the
twins. "We've been looking everywhere for you. We
thought you had gotten washed away in the flood."

"I believe she *has* been washed away," said Christopher. "Come and get dry. 'Lizbeth, you look like a
wet rag."

I sat next to him on the hay. Taking off his coat, he
flung it over my shoulders and patted my wet hair
with a piece of toweling. A drop of water ran down
my nose, pausing a moment before leaping off into
the dry dust on the barn floor. I sneezed.

"How was your target practice?" I wondered. "Did
you hit the target?"

"Twice," said Christopher, regretfully. "Only twice.
But then Jeffrey didn't hit it at all. But I did hit the
bull's-eye in entertainment terms, Princess. Squire
Macready is having a ball this weekend and your
humble servant here is going to escort you."

"Banbury tales won't mend torn sails," I remarked
tartly if obscurely. "The Macreadys would never in-
vite me into their sacred portals. Why, the squire
won't even let us in to see his thoroughbreds—

probably thinks we'll contaminate them with our vulgar peasant ways."

Christopher grinned and pulled from his pocket a card of invitation, addressed to me. The envelope was perhaps a little shopworn from such a close acquaintance with the inside of Christopher's pocket, but the contents, in an elegant gilt scrawl, confirmed Christopher's words. I was bereft of speech.

"I can't understand it," I said, studying the invitation with awe. The Macreadys' social ambitions were the byword of the village, and I could readily understand what a social triumph it would be for them to have Lord Dearborne and Christopher on the guest list. I could well imagine that the marquis would become "Dear Lord Dearborne" to Mrs. Macready and that for months to come she would regale her friends with the story of his visit to her house. But why had she felt impelled to include me in the invitation? I sighed and decided "impelled" was probably the right word. Christopher looked like a mischievous kitten climbing a curtain. I wondered if this was part of his plan to show me that I was not "nobody." I folded the invitation, stuffed it resolutely inside my tight sleeve for safekeeping, and looked up at Christopher.

"There's no purpose to discussing it further because it will come to nothing anyway. There are a million reasons why I can't go to this ball," I pronounced dampeningly.

"Fiddle!" said Christopher. "Name two."

"I have nothing to wear and I don't know how to dance."

"Paltry details. I'll teach you how to dance. Tolerable dancer, m'self, not wishing to boast," boasted Christopher.

"And are you a tolerable dressmaker, too? I can barely sew a hem. Forget making a new ball dress."

"Well, you can forget making a new ball dress," Christa retorted. "Lord Dearborne came back from

London last night and what do you think he brought with him?"

"Trouble!" I said shortly, my encounter with the marquis fresh in my mind. I saw Christa's eyes widen and hastily turned the subject before she could seek elaboration on my remark. "I hope that he's brought a new cook. Poor Mrs. Goodbody trembles at the thought of cooking for Lord Dearborne."

"Well, he did bring a new cook, but that's not all. Our new clothes are here; Robert carried the trunks over to the cottage this morning and Mrs. Goodbody hardly knows where it's all to go. It's beautiful stuff, too. Mrs. Goodbody says you can tell it's made in the finest shop—and there are good dresses made of real silk! Think of it, Lizzie—you and real silk." Christa paused for a moment, apparently overcome by the power of her vision of me in real silk.

I suppose that these revelations should have made me feel more grateful to Lord Dearborne. But I remembered his curt tones and the fingers that could be so gentle one minute and hurtful the next. Did he think that because he gave me dresses he had the right to insult me? "Startled sheep" still rankled. The less I saw or heard of Lord Dearborne, the better for my peace of mind.

"Right, sweet, you've given two reasons for not going to the ball. You said there were a million reasons. What are the other nine hundred ninety-nine thousand nine hundred ninety-eight?" said Christopher.

"How did you say all that without one stumble, Kit?"

"Hidden talent. No need to worry 'bout how to go on at the ball. I'll stick close to you and play the mentor. Don't be obstinate."

"I was hoping that you'd talk me into it." I was laughing now. "All right, mentor, I have complete faith in your ability to prepare me for any situation that might arise at a ball."

"Such touching naïveté," Christopher said, chucking me under the chin with his fist. "M'sister would be horrified if she knew I'd taken it 'pon myself to ready a young girl for her come-out in society."

Christopher was true to his word. That week, the lessons I received from him would have done credit to the strictest duenna. In fact, it did cross my mind that there was quite an astonishing scope to his knowledge of feminine behavior. Once, as he was teaching me the stops in a quadrille, he told me:

"Lord's sake, 'Lizabeth, don't bend over so far. Your gown will gape so at the bodice that people will see clear to your waist."

"Christopher Warrington!" I said, shocked to receive this sophisticated tip. "Where did you ever . . . ? I mean, how do you . . . ? You know, something like that would never have occurred to me."

"Don't know how I know, must have heard about it somewhere." His eyes twinkled. "And 'course I know that it would never occur to you. That's why I told you, m'dear. A greener girl I've never met in my life."

By Friday night, Christopher was so pleased with the progress of my dancing lessons that he pronounced me "graceful enough to please the severest critic."

"Of all the bouncers! Just after I trod on your toe, too, during the last country dance we practiced. And you know that half the time I forget the steps and wind up curtseying to the wrong side."

"Dash it all, Elizabeth, you're so lovely that there ain't a fellow alive who'd notice if you dance the whole set standing on his instep." He grinned. "Oh, don't color up so. A girl must allow one compliment per dancing master, at least."

As for the trunks of clothes that came from London, I can only say that they contained a wardrobe of which the most stylish young London lady would be proud and, yes, my silly Christa was able to gaze at the spectacle of me in real silk. To me, the cheerful donner of many a hand-it-down and make-it-over, this was heaven. I won't describe all the dresses that arrived, though; what could be more tedious than a catalogue of someone else's wardrobe?

I thought of seeking out the marquis to thank him for the outlay of what had obviously been a very generous sum of money; but somehow, I couldn't. What if he tried to touch me again? Perhaps I should have slapped his face, that morning in the library. Christa, an avid novel-reader, had once assured me that was the proper treatment for overly familiar gentlemen. Wryly, I remembered the strength in Lord Dearborne's grasp, the bright hostility of his gaze. Had I slapped him, I don't doubt that he would have retaliated in a very unpleasant manner. I decided against thanking him—Mrs. Goodbody had already done it once and he would probably just treat me to the rough side of his tongue anyway.

The night of the ball arrived too soon. I was to have more attendants to prepare for that night than Queen Caroline needed on the day of her wedding. Actually, it was only the twins, Mrs. Goodbody, and Jane Coleman, but Janey and Mrs. Goodbody were so solicitous and attentive, and the twins were so wild and underfoot, it seemed as though I were getting ready in a marketplace. Four times Janey tried to put my hair up before she was satisfied with the effect. The first three tries looked as though I had a recent narrow escape from a pack of head hunters—not that they would have wanted a head looking like *that*.

Yet with all the trouble of getting ready, I was set to go a full ten minutes before Christopher was to call for me. The assembled multitude had chosen a gown for me from the London arrivals which they deemed appropriate for a country ball: a willowy creation of coral pink sarcenet with tiny puff sleeves and a narrow buoyant skirt trimmed in a double pleating of winter-white ribbon. Caro's contribution was a pair of white rosebuds from the garden to ornament the low bodice. She forgot to excise the thorns from the sprig and I was nearly maimed for life. I wondered if this was what they meant by the hazards of fashionable life.

Too agitated to await his arrival, I ran up to the manor to show Christopher my finery. Roger, Lord Dearborne's valet, met me at the door and, after paying kindly tribute to my new gown, informed me that Master Christopher could be found in the library. I tripped excitedly down the hall and pirouetted through the door. Christopher was standing by the window; his mouth dropped open when I entered. I saw it. I was silly with excitement.

"Oh, Kit, I had so much fun getting ready. You should have seen the first way Janey did my hair with the topknot askew and hanging over my right shoulder. Isn't this gown a dream? And look at this, real satin gloves. But do you think this bodice shows too much of my bosom? I recall that you said when women bend over that they . . ."

Christopher was laughing and at this last he raised delightedly scandalized eyebrows and clapped one hand over my active mouth.

"I can see one area I've definitely neglected. That's one thing you can't talk about in public and I hereby declare this public. Now make your curtsey to Uncle Nicky; no young lady on her social debut should omit her courtesies to a marquis. No, sweetheart, he's right behind you. Won't she make the ladies go green, Uncle Nicky?"

Uncle Nicky? Christopher had pulled me around to face Lord Dearborne before I knew what was happening. The marquis was regarding me through eyes as critically slitted as Kit's were openly admiring. I wondered if he disapproved of Christopher's taking me to the ball; perhaps he thought I should have stayed put in my cottage like a good little milkmaid.

Both Christopher and the marquis were dressed in fine evening clothes, worn with the natural confidence of the wealthy and well-bred. Christopher looked almost as much an Adonis as the marquis. I felt like a dandelion in a daffodil garden.

"No need to take your lip between your teeth like that, infant, I won't eat you," Lord Dearborne drawled, coming forward to take my hand.

"Lord, yes, Elizabeth. You look as if I'd suddenly grown a pair of horns and a tail," Christopher said.

"I'm sorry, Kit, it's just that I never thought that you were good-looking before. Now what have I said to make you go into whoops? Christopher Warrington, if you don't stop laughing at me this minute, I'll stab you with one of the thorns from my rosebuds."

"I've learned to be wary of young ladies with thorns in their rosebuds," said Christopher, with a wink at Lord Dearborne. "I'm a wretch to tease you, Elizabeth, but you see it's no secret to me that you've never paid attention to the way I look, one way or the other. And now, to my chagrin, you do notice and disapprove." He made a mock-sad face and held out his arm to me. "Well, then, since you're not disposed to admire me, I might at least have the honor of escorting you to the coach. There's no quicker way of putting Uncle Nicky in a temper than to keep his horses waiting."

Thus I left to my first ball.

The setting sun played through the curtains of the carriage, glazing the cranberry velvet of the interior with a deep red fire. I was sitting next to Christopher and the marquis sat across from us. I felt the sun hit the side of my face and it was a touch too bright, so I turned a little from it. The velvet, as velvet will, made a change of color when rubbed the wrong way. To pass the time, I tried writing my nickname in the pile.

L-I-Z shone in the sun. When I raised my eyes I saw the marquis looking at me. I turned to Christopher and said hurriedly:

"I expect there will be many people there tonight I've never met before."

"Does meeting new people make you nervous, m'dear?"

"No-o. Well, perhaps it does sometimes. It depends on how they act toward me. Janey said that Mrs. Macready hired extra help from the village because she was having houseguests. Did Jeffrey tell you who they were?"

"Godfrey Woodman, for one. He's a friend of Jeffrey's. Fancies himself a poet. Lady Doran stays there as well. Did you know that she is some sort of cousin to the squire's wife, Uncle Nicky?"

"I believe they have mutually discovered a family tie," agreed Lord Dearborne drily, relaxing against the coach's seat.

"I've seen Lady Catherine once before, Kit," I said. "She came to Barfrestly in this very carriage. Of course I didn't know that she was Lord Dearborne's betrothed until later. And this carriage. I never thought that I would ride in anything like it or wear such lovely clothes or go to a real ball. It's just as though I were a real lady."

Christopher frowned. "Back up a little, Elizabeth. Figuratively, I mean. What did you just say?"

"Um, about being like a lady?"

"You are a lady, sweetness. Before that."

"I said I never thought I'd ride in a carriage like this."

"Before that," pursued Christopher patiently.

"Did you have too much wine at dinner, Kit? I was talking about Lady Catherine. I said I hadn't known that she is Lord Dearborne's fiancée."

"Right," approved Christopher. "Wherever did you

get a foolish idea like that? She's no more Uncle Nicky's fiancée than she is mine."

"Mrs. Blakslee said, when Lady Doran and Lord Dearborne stayed at the inn that she . . ." I stopped. Lord Dearborne was regarding me with a fascinated air and Christopher's hand flew to his brow. Perceiving that I had erred grievously, I tried lamely to correct my mistake. "I mean, since she was staying at the same inn as Lord Dearborne I thought that meant they were engaged to be . . ." My voice trailed off into unhappy silence. I think that I remarked earlier that I am the world's worst sinner. Some people gossip like magpies in the morning and never fare the worse for it, and I hear one snippet of scandal and blurt it out in the presence of one of the parties concerned.

"First Mrs. Plumford and now Mrs. Blakslee." The Marquis of Lorne tipped his bicorne to the back of his head with the tip of his cane. "The village goodwives should take care who is listening before they let loose with their on-dits. Kit, I salute your courage in endeavoring to shepherd this lamb through the weedy pastures of society. Careful her bleat doesn't bring the wolves down on you."

Christopher grinned at his guardian. "My lamb will melt the heart of the hungriest predator."

"Perhaps she will," returned the marquis, lightly. He reached out his hand to give one of my springy ringlets a good-humored tweak. "Keep a guard on your artless tongue tonight, my pet. Discretion is a valued accomplishment." The smile that accompanied his words was so attractive that I began to understand the reasons behind Lady Catherine's midnight ramblings at the inn.

The rest of the ride was spent with Christopher regaling me with anecdotes about the many elegant horses that were, he assured me, stabled at Lord Dearborne's principal estate in Sussex. Upon learning that I had never so much as sat on a horse, he promised that he and "Uncle Nicky" would procure suitable animals and teach my sisters and me to ride. Gratified though I was, I dismissed his promise from my mind, thinking that it was mere civility. How much I underrated Christopher.

Walking through the squire's ridiculously overdecorated hallway, I clutched Christopher's arm a trifle tightly. The squire and Mrs. Macready came forward to greet the marquis and Christopher with the same gobbling enthusiasm a pair of tom turkeys might bestow on a fresh scattering of grain. I was perfectly satisfied, not to say relieved, with the degree of tepid courtesy in the Macreadys' welcome for me. I had never quite convinced myself that Christopher hadn't forged my invitation.

Jeffrey Macready broke away from a chattering crowd of well-scrubbed, tony young people and bore Kit and me off to join them. I was introduced to so many people at once that I didn't absorb their identities, though some of the names were familiar as local land-owning gentry. I was gratified with their friendly acceptance of me, but wondered if it was just good manners or if Christopher's introduction of me was entrée enough. After a few minutes of conversation, the musicians picked up their instruments and the dancing began.

The room whirled around in the soft yellow candle-glow as about thirty couples performed. Jeffrey claimed my hand after Christopher and, later, in the most gallant fashion, several of Jeffrey's friends asked me to dance. The music made time pass alarmingly fast; I was afraid the sparkling melodies would be over before I had time to savor them fully. Dancing, listening, exchanging smiles with my partners, I wished it would all last forever. Once Christopher passed me in a movement of the dance and gave me a wink and nod. I saw, far on the other side of the ballroom, Lady Doran and the marquis dancing together.

They made a stunning couple. Lady Catherine was wearing a gown of clinging silver silk which sent dazzling, mobile reflections from the candles. And the marquis—well, you never really notice what he's wearing—it's the general effect, like a thoroughbred at the racetrack.

A young man named Godfrey was about to ask me for another dance when Christopher appeared, more or less requisitioning my company. He said I looked flushed, what I needed was a glass of lemonade and a breather. He led me to a divan by the wall, sitting me next to Jeffrey's younger sister, Cecilia, and then disappeared in search of the refreshment.

"Miss Macready, Christopher tells me that you are cousins with Lady Doran," I said politely. Cecilia giggled and rolled her eyes expressively.

"Oh, yes, indeed, my dear Miss Cordell," she replied, fluttering her pudgy hands as she spoke. "Why, Lady Doran never cared two pins about us or our relationship until Lord Dearborne inherited the old admiral's estate. Poor Mama had been trying to get Lady Catherine's attention for years; for all that she's as fast as she can be, she moves in the highest circles. Dear me, she's been the talk of the town ever since she was widowed two years ago, though so careful never to make an open scandal, until now. Mama says she's as indiscreet as a Covent Garden strumpet over Lord Dearborne. That's why she's come to stay with us." Cecilia gave another one of her warbling giggles. "You see, Miss Cordell, she admires our geographical position."

Now how was I supposed to respond to that? Kit, where are you? The last thing I wanted to hear was more gossip about Lady Catherine. And so I told Cecilia, who nodded in good-natured assent. As an alternative, she suggested we gossip about Lord Dearborne. Snapping her ivory fan and blinking her sparse eyelashes like a chicken in a windstorm, she warmed to her theme.

"Oh, and he's the most sought-after rake in London. Why all the women he's had! Last summer was the most ravishing opera singer—the toast of the demi-monde. I saw her once in Hyde Park dashing along in her lovely white carriage with lovely white horses and liverymen all dressed in white." I wondered if the liverymen had been lovely, too. "They called her the Snow Queen. She was supposed to be irresistible to men, but even she melted away under the heat of the marquis's boredom, you might say. Hee-hee, Snow Queen, melt away, you get it?" I forced a smile. "Anyway, Lord Dearborne up and gave the fair Snow Queen her marching orders in the most peremptory way, they say. She was simply wretched and wouldn't sing for weeks. The Prince Regent himself went to beg her to return to the stage. He's too fatally attractive. Lord Dearborne, I mean, not the Prince Regent." She shrieked so loudly in appreciation of her own humor that I wondered with horrid fascination if she would expire on the spot. When she had recovered herself sufficiently to talk again, she leaned over to me conspiratorially.

"Now, my dear Miss Cordell, you know that I wouldn't dream of repeating confidences shared between friends. You live so near to Lord Dearborne. Tell me, has he ever tried . . . ?" She left the sentence delicately unfinished, but I felt the color flame into my cheeks. To my fervent though unexpressed gratitude, our *tête-à-tête* was interrupted by the fatally attractive one himself. Lord Dearborne strolled leisurely up to us, oblivious to the many covert glances that followed him across the room.

"Your pardon, ladies." He spoke with such obvious *ennui* that it must have forever dispelled any notion in Cecilia's head that he had ever tried . . . with me. "Miss Cordell, may I drag you away from your companion? Lady Peterby begs that I bring you at once for an introduction."

Thankfully, a summons from Lady Peterby was the local equivalent to a royal command. I made good my escape on Lord Dearborne's arm. However formidable Lady Peterby might be, it was tarts to table scraps better than being grilled about Lord Dearborne by Cecilia.

Lady Peterby, as it turned out, was all friendliness and warmth. As I reached her side, she extended a pair of exquisitely gloved hands to draw me to the settee beside her. The merest trace of a French accent filled her voice with fascinating lilts.

"Ah, my poor child, forgive me for having sent for you in such a fashion, but I saw that unsuspecting young Warrington left you with that horrid Macready chit. Then when I saw your cheeks brighten like holly berries I was sure that girl was treating you to some of her dreadful store of . . . anecdotes. Naturally the color is most becoming to you, but I thought you might prefer to hear no more. No, no, my dear child, there is no need to thank me. Pray dismiss the whole incident from your mind. Cecilia is a notorious rattle-pate with less sense than a molting hen. Now tell me how you go on? You must know that I was very fond of your dear mother. Perhaps you know that she once did us the honor of staying with us?" The truth was that Mama had been too proud to take the hospitality that Lady Peterby had offered and stayed at Peters-perch under the condition that she tutor the Peterby daughters in their French. My mother and Lady Peterby had lived in the same province in France before the Revolution, though Lady Peterby had left France to marry Lord Lesley's father long before the Terror was more than a gleam in M. Danton's eye. My mother had often told me of the many kindnesses shown her by the gracious Lady Peterby when she had arrived in England, friendless and without means.

Indeed, I discovered that Lady Peterby had the most tactfully unobtrusive sympathy and found it frighteningly easy to confide in her.

"And so now you find yourself in the guardianship of Nicholas Dearborne, yes? Ah, he is a good boy at heart, with good intentions, although he does not always live up to them. I've known Nicholas since he was a little one. His father was a cousin to my husband—though a distant one. If he doesn't behave well toward you then you must come and tell me and I will beat him for you with my cane!"

Lady Peterby shook her silver-tipped walking stick so threateningly in the air that I gave a peal of laughter. She was crippled, poor lady, from a hunting accident years ago, and though she couldn't get around very well by herself, you would hardly notice the handicap, so charmingly did she bear it.

"Ah, now there is a laugh that will turn heads," said Lady Peterby. "So like your lively mama, I can see. Oh, I suppose you must dance with this Godfrey Woodman, here. He is planting himself beside the chair to gain a dance with you and will obviously not be got rid of until he has it."

The rest of the evening passed in a delightful haze. I left with a very favorable opinion of balls; everyone had been kind and friendly (except the squire and Mrs. Macready who treated me as tactfully as a pair of nesting swans who have discovered a cuckoo in the nest). I wondered again how Christopher had managed to secure an invitation for me and taxed him with it in the carriage on the way home.

"C'mon, Kit, tell. Mrs. Macready would never have invited me of her own free will. How did you talk her into it? Threaten to whip Jeffrey in another bout of fisticuffs?"

"No, all I did was to have Jeffrey tell his mother that I couldn't accept an invitation in which you weren't included. That brought her around quick enough, I promise you. She thinks that I might pay court to Cecilia."

"You wouldn't!" I exclaimed involuntarily.

"Lord, no. Have you got windmills in your head? Pay court to that simpering, twittering half-wit?"

He looked so indignant that I hastily begged pardon. "And you know, Kit, I had the best time, so I'm glad that you got me invited," I said placatingly. "Now I'll always be able to say that I've been to a real ball. It's not every cottage dweller who is privileged to attend a ball at the squire's place and hobnob with no less a personage than Lady Peterby herself! She said the kindest things to me. My head was quite turned by it."

Christopher only sniffed. "Like to know why she shouldn't say kind things to you. As for the Macreadys, it's they should be privileged to have you at their ball. You come from a damnsight better family than they do, 'scuse my language. It makes my blood boil that a bunch of provincial nobodies like the Macreadys think they can play the patricians over you."

"What a disgusting thing to say. Boiling blood—ugh!" I wrinkled my nose. "How do you think I did on the dance floor?"

"Looked like an angel," my erstwhile dancing master commented simply. "How did you manage to keep Godfrey Woodman's rapt attention for so long? The fellow hung on your every word—which is amazing considering the time he's spent perfecting his poetic sulk. It's the first time I've ever seen him show any interest in any female other than . . . ahem. What allurements did you offer to keep him at your side?"

"None. That is, I don't consider a discussion of the symbolism of Clytië to be an allurement. Not precisely, at least."

Lord Dearborne raised one elegant eyebrow. "What an odd education you've had. One usually doesn't find young girls with a grounding in the classics. Their mamas are content to rear them to paint in runny watercolors, speak unintelligible French, and pluck on poorly tuned harps."

Christopher gave me a tolerant grin. "That's what comes of receiving an education under the tutelage of a harebrained old scholar like Mudbury's vicar. Elizabeth is so well grounded in the classics that the poor girl is almost more pagan than she is Christian. I believe she prays to Zeus when no one is listening."

"Just because the poor vicar forgot to remove his nightcap before services Sunday morning is no reason to say he's harebrained. It might have happened to anyone." I bristled in defense of my beloved mentor.

"I daresay," said Christopher skeptically. "But what about last evening when Mrs. Goodbody asked you to read from that book of sermons? Are you going to deny that you said the Lord Jove instead of the Lord Jehovah?"

"No, I'm not. But I daresay that no one else would have noticed it if you hadn't commenced to snicker. And you say I'm un-Christian!"

"So, who *is* Clytië—some overaroused wood nymph, I suppose?" asked Christopher.

"Yes," I replied, "though that's a horridly unchivalrous way of putting it. Clytië fell in love with Apollo, the lord of the sun. She would spend the day lying on the grass watching the sun blaze across the sky. Finally, in mercy, she became a sunflower and eternally tilts her face to the sun's path."

"What a familiar story," said Christopher. "Think of all the Clytiës left gazing at you, Uncle Nicky. How many gardens have you filled with weepy sunflowers?"

"None," said Lord Dearborne. He had been silently gazing out at the moonlit landscape. "Love is a farce, Kit. You'll find it only in bad novels and good poetry.

All those weepy sunflowers want is my title and income."

When is the last time you looked in a mirror, Milord?

Chapter Six

The next morning I was awakened by a persistent patting on my shoulder.

"Elizabeth, Lizzie," Christa stage-whispered. She slipped under the covers with me. "I've got something of the greatest importance to tell you!"

She'd slopped tea on my new shawl, I thought sleepily. "It's all right, Christa, go ahead and tell. I won't be angry."

"It's not an angry thing. It's a make-fun-of thing. That's why I didn't tell you last night when you came home from the ball. I didn't want anyone else to hear about it. You must promise not to tell anyone about it, or they'll all laugh at me. No one ever believes anything I say. So swear an oath not to tell."

"All right, um . . . Certain true, black and blue, lay me down and cut me in two. Now tell."

"I saw a ghost last night. See, you're smiling—I can see that you're trying to hide it but it's definitely a smile."

"I beg your pardon, pet. Where did you see your ghost and what did he look like?"

"It was just before you returned from the ball last night. I took Cleo out for her walk and saw it slipping away through the orchard. Do you remember the old topcoat that Admiral Barfreston used to wear, the one with three shoulder capes? He wore it again last night."

I shivered in spite of myself. "Christa, Admiral Bar-

freston is dead. We went to his funeral and saw them
lower his coffin in the ground with our own eyes.
Sometimes at night, in the poor light, you can think
that you see all kinds of things. It's your imagination
at work. Once when I was out at night I thought I
saw a man standing against the house, but when I
came closer to it, I saw that it was only an old ladder."

"That was the night of Henri's death, wasn't it? I
remember you telling about it at the inquest. Well, listen to this: suppose that Henri didn't fall from the
roof after all. Suppose that Admiral Barfreston's ghost
returned to the house and murdered Henri because he
thought he was a French spy!"

"Of all the lurid . . . Christa, have you been reading those dreadful Minerva novels? First of all, why a
spy?"

"Mr. Blakslee says the countryside is just crawling
with French spies. You know we are only ten miles
from the Channel here. The spies come in at hidden
coves with the smugglers."

"Well, Henri didn't come to Barfrestly with any
smugglers. He came in a perfectly respectable coach
from London with the marquis's other servants."

"I know that, Lizzie, but how is the admiral supposed to know that when he's been dead all this
time?"

I wished that Christa would stop referring to the
admiral as if he were not really dead. It was enough
to give one an attack of gooseflesh. I could see that I
would be unable to convince her that her imagination
had produced the specter, so I switched tactics, dis-
tracting her with a reference to our planned trip to
Dyle.

"Run along now and get ready for our trip today. At
this rate it will be midday before we get away."

My pessimistic remark proved to be unfounded because when we pulled away in the carriage, the dew
had barely dried on the tall grasses around our cot-

tage. The twins, Mrs. Goodbody, and I make an annual excursion to Dyle. Mrs. Goodbody's brother-in-law sails as a fisherman from the port there. Christopher had expressed a desire to accompany us this year, and he was kind enough to procure the use of Lord Dearborne's carriage for the ten-mile ride. It proved to be a definite improvement over former years, when we relied on the bumpy public stage-coach.

As we neared Dyle and the seacoast, the tame farm-land gave way to low-shingled marshes—a gala dappled swirl of sheer blue greens, russets, and pewter. The air grew sly with the scents of salts and fish. My sisters and I listened for the high calls of the shy bittern and marsh hen, two birds which rarely come so far inland as Barfrestly. The weather, for once, was perfect.

Mrs. Goodbody's brother-in-law lived with his large, busy family in a snug whitewashed cottage that poked sturdily up from its nest of trimmed evergreen bushes. Their family had lived there for generations—as long as Lord Dearborne's arrogant ancestors have dominated their thousands of acres, I reflected. I tried to imagine Lord Dearborne in hobnail boots and woolen trousers. I was forced to the unsatisfactory conclusion that he would still look exactly like a marquis.

Christopher, on the other hand, had no airs, no cultivated arrogance to keep him separated from the human race. Kit had something far better than good manners—he was naturally friendly. I watched with appreciation at the way he smiled himself into the good graces of Mrs. Goodbody's sister and ended up with the largest slice of the potato pie that was served for luncheon. We ate outside to the low rumble of crashing waves; the salt smell was fresh and invigorating as it came in on the breeze. Time passed quickly as Mrs. Goodbody's brother-in-law kept us enthralled with tales of the sea, with its invisible tides and hidden coves where mermaids and monsters lurked.

After we had lunched, we walked down to the harbor to view the ceremony which served as an excuse for our yearly pilgrimage, the blessing of the fishing boats and nets. This was an important day for fisherfolk. We joined the large crowd at seaside, so large that it stretched up the brow of the hill by the harbor. The gathering was a colorful sight as I turned to look behind me. It is the custom at the ceremony to arrive loaded down with garlands of flowers which are tossed into the water at a certain point as a way of blessing the catch. Dr. Smithfield, the old vicar, had told me that the ceremony dated from the pre-Christian era when the offerings were made to a Roman fertility goddess, and had only been embellished with Christian trappings with the arrival of Christian missionaries. I wondered what the assembled multitude would think if they knew they were participating in a pagan ritual.

The members of the town council, along with the mayor, were standing on a makeshift platform by the quay. The mayor looked important and solemn in his official robes with his chain of office around his wrinkled neck. The gathering hushed as the parson mounted the platform and made his blessing upon the boat and nets. His voice carried over the crowd, rolling and sonorous like the waves that were washing to the beach, as he recited the ancient prayer.

"Good Lord lead us
Good Lord speed us
From all perils protect us
From the darkness us protect.
Finest nights to land our fish
Sound and big to fill our wish
God keep our nets from snag and break

For every man a goodly take
Lord grant us."

At the finish of the traditional prayer it seemed to
be raining gardens as the flowers were tossed in the
brine. All about me the people were saying, "Lord
bless me" as they rid themselves of their fragrant blos-
soms.

After the beautiful open-air ceremony, through the
crowd were passed baskets full of tiny squares of stale
gingerbread, along with flasks of gin from which
everyone took a swig. When the flask reached our
gathering, Christopher looked at it doubtfully.

"Don't worry," said Caro. "The gin is strong enough
to kill any bad humors which might be hanging about
the flask." Christopher drank and passed it to me. I
permitted myself one cautious sip. Christopher
laughed when I pulled a face. The ceremony was
over.

It was Mrs. Goodbody's intention to return to the
cottage with her brother-in-law and his family to enjoy a leisurely coze, sharing confidences in the inti-
mate way one does with members of one's family.
This left Christopher, my sisters, and me with some
time to savor the attractions of Dyle. As the sea was
too chilly for wading that early in the year, we decided to take Christopher on a tour of the town itself.

Dyle is built up a hillside on a series of terraces that
rise from the smooth stretch of beach. The narrow
high street cuts through the town and ends on top of
the hill in front of the parish church. We took the exhausting trek up High Street to a vantage point below
the church, and turned to enjoy the view. The ocean
was dark blue under the sun, contrasting nicely with
the ochre thatch of the rooftops. It was as if we were
standing on the edge of a great bowl. I was certain I
could make out the outline of the French coast if only
I peered hard enough.

"Lizzie, why are you making that awful squint?" asked Christa.

"She is trying to see France," returned Caro, whose intent, furrowed brow indicated she was undertaking the same project.

"The wind is very strong up here, isn't it, Christopher," I shouted. He was standing on a large rock, pointing at something and shouting back.

"Over there to the south," he was saying. "What are all those grayish rectangular buildings there?"

I scrambled up the rock after him and looked where he was pointing, shielding my eyes from the sun.

"Those are army barracks," I said. "There's a lot of invasion scares on the coast here. Look behind us; you can see the martello towers, and down below, that dark line of water coming out from behind that bluff. That is the Napoleonic Defensive Waterway. The army built it."

"Think that canal's going to keep Napoleon out?" said Christopher, grinning.

"Do you really think we are going to be invaded?" I asked him. It seemed so strange to contemplate.

"No, he's too busy dealing with the blockades and Continental armies to invade this man's island," said Christopher with assurance. "No need to hurry with your French, 'Lizbeth."

"Well, that's comforting. You know everyone who lives near the coast worries about being ravished in their beds by foreign soldiers. Julius Caesar landed his galleys here; so did William the Conqueror. There is always a lot of drama connected with these coastal towns. Just twenty-five years ago, William Pitt sent soldiers here to burn all the fishing boats because some of them were built with false bottoms to hide contraband goods. Mrs. Goodbody's brother-in-law is bitter about it to this day."

"But as we both know, that didn't stop the smugglers," Christopher declared.

"Hell's bells, no," flashed Christa. The twins had clambered up to join us. "The excisemen still fight it out with the smugglers. Isn't that right, Lizzie? And I'll bet plenty of spies sneak over here, too."

"I'm going to tell Mrs. Goodbody you cursed," Caro shot at her twin. "She is going to wash out your mouth with soap." They chased each other across the hillside. I looked at Christopher, suddenly remembering his father may have been shot by spies. If he was disturbed it didn't show.

"C'mon, Christopher, I want to show you the church," I said. We climbed the narrow path up to an even higher level and threaded our way along a row of pollard limes. Far out to the left, in dour isolation, stood the Time Bell Tower, an important landmark. Its huge clock is used to determine the sailing times for ships in the harbor. On a clear day, they say it can be seen for miles out to sea. I dutifully pointed it out to Christopher, who expressed a desire to see it closer.

"Maybe there is a way to climb up inside and look out to sea?" said Christopher hopefully.

"Oh no, it's much too dangerous. Two years ago there was a terrible accident there. A couple of village boys climbed out on the ledge underneath the clock to see a heron that was nesting. They lost their footing in a gust of wind and fell to the bottom and were killed. Now it's kept locked all the time."

We reached the medieval church, pulled open the heavy oaken door, and stepped inside. The interior of the ancient church is colored a deep, ashen gray, the smoky light that filters in through the high clerestory windows falling lifelessly upon the stone walls. The place is almost crushingly claustrophobic. The roof is supported by pillars of pewter-colored marble which adds to the air of dead elegance. I showed Christopher a crack in the side wall which was caused by an earthquake in the last century.

"There's an old catacomb underneath the church," I

volunteered in a whisper. "Below the chancel. It contains old skulls and shinbones that were saved when the graveyard was dug up at some point in medieval times."

"Can we go look at it?" said Christopher. I wasn't expecting him to say that, but I supposed I should accommodate a guest. We began the trek down the center aisle to the chancel. It seemed a very long way. The twins were tiptoeing. When we reached the door that led below, we pulled it open and were at once hit with a wave of chill, dampish air. We each took one of the smelly fish-oil lamps that stood on a nearby table, ready for those who made the pilgrimage into the basement crypt. I felt the need to put on a brave front so I led the way down the mossy steps to the earth-lined passageway below. As we came out of the stair-hall our lamplight filled a cavernous chamber that was lined from floor to ceiling with skulls and long bones.

"There must be thousands of skulls here," came Christopher's voice in my ear.

"Two thousand. At least that's what they said last time they were counted. They've started keeping count of them since Gypsy women started coming here to steal the bones for boiling down to make an infusion against rheumatism."

Christa stood with her arms wrapped around her, rubbing her shoulders to keep out the cold. "They say the smugglers use this place as a hideout. There are millions of tunnels leading through the ground here," she told Christopher.

I suddenly got the most pronounced sensation of being watched. The light slanted crazily off the eyeless sockets of the skulls, giving them an unearthly wavering glitter. "Christa, in the name of Zeus, would you stop carping about spies?" I said with unaccustomed snappishness. I turned around and led the way back up the slippery stairs to the dry stale air of the church. It wasn't until we were halfway down the aisle that I realized dismally that my sash was undone and my reticule gone.

"It must have come untied when I brushed against the wall near the foot of the stairs. And I had my reticule tied to it. It's missing now. I suppose it fell off somewhere near the bottom of the steps."

Christopher volunteered to go down to get it while the girls and I went outside to warm up. I would have liked to accept his offer but I stated firmly that I would run back and fetch it myself. Pride stiffened my backbone and made me call out airily, "Wait outside, I'll be right back up."

My brave words were still echoing from the farthest reaches of the vaulted chancel as I made my way back. I relit an oil lantern and proceeded determinedly down the narrow stairway. It seemed to have grown even colder since I had left. Rivulets of brackish water oozed from the rough sides of the walls and fell into soupy puddles with a tinny, clinking sound. I tried to turn off my thoughts, to concentrate on my search for the missing reticule. As I reached the end of the steps, the object of my search appeared in the circle of light from the lamp. I stepped forward and my body came up against a warm, solid mass. I stepped back quickly and there, in the light of my lamp, glowed a fantastically shadowed face.

"*Sacre bleu!*" The French curse rang profanely. I didn't waste time screaming. I just fled.

I didn't stop until I was encircled by Christopher's comforting arms. I told him what happened with chattering teeth. He looked grim as he let go of me and said, "You three stay up here. I'm going down to investigate."

"No, Christopher, you can't. That man was hiding down there. Don't you see? He's probably a smuggler. If you go back there he's likely to kill you." I was desperate with fear.

Christopher pulled back his jacket, revealing a serviceable-looking pistol held in place by a leather strap.

"Don't worry on my account, Elizabeth. I may not be able to hit the side of a smokehouse with an old fowling piece, but with a pistol I'm a dead shot."

He disappeared down the stairway. After what seemed like hours, he returned.

"There was no sign of him by the time I got down there. He must have gone into one of those connecting tunnels. It would be foolish to try to follow him. I don't know my way around down there so it would give him too much of an advantage," Christopher concluded with reluctance.

"Of course you shouldn't go after him. It's not your business to go chasing after smugglers. That's up to the customs men. What made you go after him anyway?" I asked.

Christopher shrugged. His face took on a guarded look.

"Just an impulse, I guess. That man may have been down there earlier when we went down. I don't like being spied on. It's a dashed havey-cavey business. Let's get back to the Goodbodys before they get worried about us."

I wasn't about to argue with that! He couldn't have been more eager to get away than I was. On the way down the hill he handed me my reticule, which he had remembered to pick up from the cavern floor. As I took it from him I asked:

"Christopher, why are you carrying a pistol? Do you always bring it places with you?"

"Well, no. Uncle Nicky thought it would be a good idea for me to have it with me since the whole thing surrounding my father's death isn't resolved." He was still looking uncomfortable. "I shouldn't have shown it to you. I don't want you to be frightened. There is just a remote possibility that whoever killed my father could take another crack at me. Of course, that's totally unlikely; the gun is the merest precaution," he pointed out a little too emphatically.

I was happy for the sane normal atmosphere of the Goodbody home. They were alarmed at the story we told them but didn't hesitate to endorse our actions. The possibility that the man in the crypt had been another tourist who was just as startled as I was speedily dismissed. No tourist would have been down in that stygian darkness without a lamp to guide him. Also, a legitimate visitor would have followed me, calling out reassurances. No, the man was probably a smuggler, perhaps checking on a cache of contraband brought into port one moonless night when respectable folk were home safe in their beds. There was general agreement that the story of my encounter should go no further than this snug parlor. The "gentlemen," as the smugglers were called, had a longer arm than the law even in these civilized times, and it could be fatally dangerous to provoke them. Besides, the excisemen were far from popular in the neighborhood as their jobs often involved harassing legitimate fishermen as they searched for illegal cargos.

It wasn't until I lay in bed that night that I remembered the oath that the "smuggler" had uttered as I ran into him. "*Sacre bleu.*" How many smugglers in Dyle would curse in French?

Chapter Seven

After the excitement of our visit to Dyle, the next few days seemed sadly flat. Christopher had gone away with Lord Dearborne to spend some time at Peters-perch. Kit had hinted broadly that there would be a surprise for me on his return. So there was that to look forward to, I supposed, making a few uneven stitches in the worn sheet I was darning. My bare feet were cool against the uneven stone floor of the cottage. It had been warm all week.

I wondered what Christopher and his handsome guardian were doing at this minute. Perhaps sitting in an elegant velvet-walled drawing room sipping chilled champagne from crystal goblets. I leaned back against the old elm settee and lifted my feet up onto a nearby chair. Wearily I reached my hand up to rub the back of my neck, when the memory of Lord Dearborne's caress that day in the library came floating, unbidden, into my mind. Hastily lowering my hand, I glanced across the room to where Mrs. Goodbody sweated over her butter churn, to make sure she hadn't noticed the betraying rush of color to my cheeks. I saw with relief that she was still intent on her task. She was attacking the semiliquid butter with such vigor that it set a-tremble the flitch of home-cured bacon which hung from the ceiling. I smiled, thinking how Christopher always managed to knock his head on the bacon whenever he came into the cottage.

I decided to get up from my comfortable place and

add some water to the peonies that I had placed in an old stoneware vase in the middle of the table. The heat had wilted them until they looked like the wives of Henry VIII, making obeisance before losing their heads.

"Halloa," came from outside. It sounded like Christopher himself.

"We're here," I called back, and he entered, promptly setting the flitch of bacon to swinging with a knock of his head.

"Blast!" he muttered.

"Oh, poor Christopher. We've been thinking about moving that bacon for quite some time," I said.

"How are you all?" he said, nodding to Mrs. Goodbody.

"It's good to have you back, young sir," she said heartily. "Elizabeth and I were becoming bored without our young Christopher." Christopher looked pleased.

"You'll be gladder yet to hear I'm back when I tell you what we've brought with us—the primest bits of blood you ever saw," said Christopher with the air of one delivering joyful tidings.

"Kit, I've never heard anyone like you for going on about blood," I told him tartly. He frowned at my response and then laughed, lifting me in his arms and whirling me round and round, threatening to upset every knickknack in the cottage.

"There's never another girl like you, 'Lizbeth." Kit put me down, choking with laughter. "I mean horses, little dunce. Remember I said I'd teach you how to ride. You know, on the night of the Macreadys' ball! Well, so I will. Uncle Nicky's bought us horses to ride. Run and get into your riding habit now. It'll be the greatest sport ever!"

I was about to protest that I didn't own a riding habit when it occurred to me that there was one in the shipment from London. I remembered it particularly because the bonnet that came with it had a teal-blue poke front trimmed with puffs of ribbon and everyone had been dismayed that it was so pretty but there had been no horses to wear it for.

"Go," said Christopher, nudging me imperatively toward the bedroom. I wondered more about the horses as I donned my riding habit. Was the marquis extending his commission more than was customary in this case? Horses were hardly a necessity of life. Perhaps he was doing it to amuse Christopher. It occurred to me that I should look these gift horses in the mouth and place it before the marquis that he was being overly generous. But life is full of things that one should do and one does not.

The twins were already bouncing around on a pair of lively chestnut Welsh ponies at the shouted corrections and instructions of Jason, the groom.

"We picked a very ladylike mare for you," Christopher said. "She had beautiful manners, you'll get along famously with her. Jason, bring out Snowball," he called. Jason disappeared into the stables and came out again leading a delicate-looking pearl-gray mare who pawed the ground and snickered as she was brought over to us. In spite of her delicate appearance, she looked rather large from up close. Too large.

"Might as well begin right away. Come over to the mounting block. That's right, now put your left foot in the stirrup," said Christopher, with the unconcern of someone born on a horse's back. "No, Elizabeth, not like that! All you have to do is slide your foot into the stirrup."

"I am trying to," I said, vexed. "But the horse keeps moving away."

"Right. Well, I'll help you mount. Jason, hold tight on the reins and I'll give her a boost. There now, up you go!"

In a flash, I was on the horse's back. It was a very long way to the ground.

"Hello down there," I said weakly. My vertigo increased as Snowball began turning in circles underneath me.

"Snowball is a weathercock," I told Christopher. "You stole her from the top of the barn."

"No, honestly, I didn't. She only acts that way because she knows you're a beginner," said Christopher, intent on his new role as Job's Comforter. Being on horseback was a strange feeling.

The twins were soon right at home on a horse's back. As for my own case, never was there a more patient teacher than Christopher nor a more inept pupil than myself. I had less grace on the Arabian mare than a farmboy on a plowhorse; moreover, instead of improving as the lessons went on, I merely grew more nervous. Once, in despair, Christopher cried:

"Elizabeth, you'll never be able to ride until you show the horse who's boss."

"I don't have to show the horse who's boss," I wailed. "Snowball already knows that she's the boss—it's a foregone conclusion, she's fifty times bigger than I."

Christopher sighed, patting me on the shoulder with tolerant affection. "I'm afraid you're just too nice to ever be much of a rider."

Apart from riding lessons and the usual chores, the twins and I devoted all our energies to preparations for the Norman Conquest pageant. Christopher's efficient and imaginative assistance made us sure that our depiction of the invasion would be so spectacular as to outdo the real thing. After I had completed the final draft of the dialogue and read it aloud in the cottage, Mrs. Goodbody pronounced it "not half bad," which my sisters and I interpreted as tribute indeed. There had been only one reservation. Mrs. Goodbody felt that a reference by King Harold to "William the

Bastard" was coming it a bit strong and she told me mildly that I could keep or change the line as I saw fit; unfortunately, the look that accompanied her words made it clear that I had better see fit. I wanted to oblige her. But "William the Love Child" . . . ? I was mulling the problem as I lay flopped on my stomach on a worn blanket under a honeysuckle bush near the orchard. It was one of my favorite places for thinking, especially in the summer; it combined quiet with shade and the sweet perfume of blooming honeysuckle. Today I was awaiting the arrival of Christopher and the twins for a Play Committee meeting. I was munching absent-mindedly on an oaten cake left from lunch when I heard the firm tread of leather boots approaching.

"Well, Kit," I called out without turning my head, "what do you think? Shall we have a bastard or a love child?"

The footsteps stopped and I froze as I heard the voice that accompanied them.

"It would seem that the freedom of manners current among modern youth has reached alarming proportions." Lord Dearborne's drawl was lightly spiced with sarcasm.

I flushed, thinking sourly that if we were talking about the freedom of modern manners, the marquis was certainly no one to moralize. I wondered what he would say if I asked him if he had warned the "Snow Queen" or Lady Doran about overfree manners. It was better not to find out.

"It's the play for our parish fête day," I explained. "We plan to put on the Norman invasion of England this year and Mrs. Goodbody doesn't think we should call William the Conqueror by William the Bastard (for all that it's true). But if we call him William the Love Child, it will sound like we're only calling him that because we didn't have the courage to say bastard. If you can see what I mean."

To my surprise, the marquis dropped, with lazy grace, next to me on the blanket.

"I can see that it would be a struggle for a sincere playwright." I couldn't tell whether he meant to be satirical. "Torn between artistic integrity and the limitations of one's audience. I'm afraid you'll have to settle for 'natural son'—a compromise of bluntness and insipidity."

"Natural son." I thought it over and sighed. "I suppose it will do though it still rings like a euphemism."

Lord Dearborne supported himself on one elbow. He was dressed casually, in buckskins and riding boots with his lawn shirt open at the neck. A light breeze gently ruffled his hair as his sapphire eyes scanned me with idle speculation. His new benign attitude put me more on my guard than ever. What a pity it is that my guard is so weak. I returned his look with one of grave suspicion.

"I suppose that you've come out here to tell me something unpleasant," I told him candidly. "I can't think of any other reason for you to come out here and cozy up to me."

"Can't you?" A smile lurked behind the brilliant eyes. "Actually I do have something I'd like to ask you. I meant to lead up to it by tactful degrees but since you're so perceptive I might as well tell you now."

"Pray, do," I requested with dignity.

"It's nothing so terrible, only that I would like you to take one of the servants whenever you leave the estate grounds."

Of all things, I had not been expecting this. I stared at him, amazed.

"But that would be ridiculous!" I said, in rather a hurry. "To begin with, I never go anywhere. Well . . . except Dyle, but that's only once a year. Oh, and I went to the squire's ball, though I doubt if they would ask me again because they only had me on Kit's ac-

count." My God, was I now to be like Christopher,
with spying bodyguards? I felt a nasty tinge of resentment creep up to sit gargoyle-like on my shoulder. I
wasn't used to taking orders from anyone but Mrs.
Goodbody.

"I daresay it's that you don't want me in Mudbury
alone. Now that I can understand—such a den of vice
and iniquity as it is." I could hear the rebellion in my
voice.

"It's a routine precaution. I work in the War Office
and you are my dependent. There's no real danger, of
course. It is general government policy. Your friend
Christopher is used to this sort of thing."

It was all too pat for me. "Your routine precautions
didn't help Christopher and his father much, did
they?" I blurted out.

He seemed to hesitate. "So Kit confided that to you.
Christopher's father was directly involved in military
espionage for the Crown. Unfortunately, this made
him a prime target for Bonapartist agents. Obviously
you don't qualify as a dire threat to Napoleon."

The marquis looked like he had more to say, but he
was interrupted by a long, silvery whistle that
sounded like a cross between a calf's bleat and the
somber honk of flying geese. The whistle was quickly
answered by another. I picked up a long, fat blade of
grass, folded it between my thumbs, and made an
echo of the whistles.

"Do you hear those whistles? Those are my sisters
calling to each other. Grass whistles are our secret sig-
nals. They can be heard farther than a shout," I explained.

A more experienced woman would have been quick
to recognize the sensuality behind the marquis's slow,
lazy smile. I misunderstood. Encouraged by his smile,
I asked him doubtfully if he had made grass whistles
as a child; it was hard to picture Lord Dearborne as a
rowdy schoolboy.

"No, but why don't you teach me," he said with a deepening smile. "It seems like a valuable skill to acquire."

Oh, the traps that are laid for the unwary. I'd been warned before that Lord Dearborne was an experienced rake, but that didn't deter me from taking the bait like a mouse scampering to a cheesed mousetrap. I took a spike of grass between my thumbs, carefully cupping my fingers with the tips touching, and presented my hands to him with great seriousness.

"See, first you must hold the grass like this."

He took my cupped hands gently between his and regarded me quizzically. "And then?"

"Then you bring your fingers to your lips . . ." Oh, stupid, stupid me.

His long fingers slowly removed the grass from my hands and opened my fingers so that they lay palm up in his grasp. He drew both trembling palms to his lips, kissing them softly. These were the first real kisses I had received from a member of the male sex and they had a devastating effect. I melted as butter in the sun. His fingers caressed the sensitive skin of my wrists before drawing them up to his neck, at the same time forcing my shoulders gently down until I lay back on the blanket, passive and stunned. He tenderly lifted a strand of hair from my forehead, brushing his lips lightly across the skin beneath. A moment passed. His voice was a husky whisper:

"I wish that my conscience was either a bit stronger or a bit weaker. My God, you'd be such an easy mark." He cupped my cheek in his hand. "You're so damnably seductive even in all your innocence. There should be a legion of chaperones protecting your virtue. Such a slow learner, pet."

He was right. He was also gone before I realized it. I opened my eyes and I was alone, listening once again to the far-off whistle of the twins. It seemed as though nothing had happened, like he had not been

beside me at all, had not kissed me and spoken to me.
It had been a dream . . . or a wish.

I stood up and shakily brushed the grass from the
front of my gown. Far off over the hill, I could see the
twins running toward me. Christopher would be here
as well. It was time for our meeting.

Later that week, another misfortune occurred
among the staff at Barfrestly Manor. Although it was
not as serious as the mishap which ended Henri, it
was still the cause of considerable alarm. Jason, the
undergroom, while exercising one of the horses,
stepped into a rabbit hole and broke his leg.

Dr. Brent spied me at the cottage door as he was
riding out after attending Jason. Though I gave him
no encouragement, he trotted over to say hello, his
oversized medicine bag bumping clumsily against the
saddle back, where it was secured.

"Well, how's the little sleuth? Still a lover of French
cuisine?" he asked, smiling down at me. Gentlemen
will have their joke.

"I'm doing very well, thank you. Have you finished
setting the undergroom's leg? Will he be all right, do
you think?"

"Yes, he'll do, it was a simple fracture. You would
do well to fill in that hole the horse tripped in though;
someone might have a nasty fall." He favored me with
a patronizing smirk. "Where is your little friend Christopher?" His horse sidled briefly as he reached down
to slap a deerfly from its neck.

"Oh, he's around. I'm surprised you didn't see him."

The smirk intensified and his eyes widened with
unconvincing disingenuousness.

"But how good it is of Lord Dearborne to keep you
here, you and Christopher make such charming play-
fellows."

"The marquis is not being 'good' at all," I retorted,
stung. Dr. Brent had a special talent for touching the

raw places. "My sisters and I are responsibilities of the estate. It's in the will."

"Ah, naturally, it's in the will. Good-bye for now, and give my regards to your sturdy Mrs. Goodbody," he said, turning his horse.

I watched him ride out of sight, down the carriage-way. He had an obnoxious way of putting things; in fact, he could make my hands curl into fists just by the way he said "how-di-doo." It wasn't only the things he said, it was also the way he said them, as though he knew that you fed your share of boiled turnips to the cat or used your church-offering money to buy peppermint sticks. Like the nursery rhyme:

> I do not like thee, Dr. Fell,
> The reason why I can not tell,
> But this I know, and know full well,
> I do not like thee, Dr. Fell.

The marquis instructed Joe Hawkins to fill in the rabbit holes in the pasture, but even with the assistance of my sharp-eyed sisters, Joe was unable to find the offending opening. Jason was put on a stagecoach for another Lorne property, to recuperate under the watchful eye of his mother, who was housekeeper there. Luckily for him, Dr. Brent was able to recommend a replacement as undergroom, because there were now so many horses at Barfrestly, between riding hacks and coach horses, that it was full-time work for two people to care for them.

The play was only a week away now and we were busy with dozens of last-minute tasks. It was necessary for me to go into Mudbury to round up some final props—a rusty old sword from the blacksmith that looked like it had been around since the real Norman invasion, an old hobbyhorse for one of the twins to ride (what's a battle without cavalry?). These

items and others had to be collected and ready in time
for our dress rehearsal.

I set off on foot for the village, alone. I knew Lord
Dearborne didn't want me to go places by myself, but
I had several reasons, good ones, I thought, for ignoring his politely phrased orders. One, it was only Mudbury; two, I was not about to walk around Mudbury
with a servant in tow. Lord, people would think I'd
grown as puffed up as the squire's wife! Lastly, I was
a big girl now, in spite of what the marquis obviously
thought. I hadn't been allowed to go alone to the village until my fifteenth birthday. Mrs. Goodbody always said, "Little ships must keep to shore, larger
ships may venture more." I was a larger ship now and
I wasn't going to give up this hard-won privilege,
marquis or no marquis. I felt the little resentment gargoyle still enthroned on my shoulder.

After picking up the old sword, I stood outside the
blacksmith shop, chatting with the smithy. He was
only too glad for the company and an excuse to pass a
few minutes in the fresh air. The blacksmith was just
in the middle of telling me how lucky I was to ride on
such wonderful horses as Lord Dearborne's when my
eyes widened like harvest moons. I had been idly regarding the passersby, when, incredibly, I saw the
same man that I had smashed into in the church crypt
in Dyle! There was no doubt it was him, walking
hunched over down the other side of the road! He was
wearing an olive reefer jacket with top-boots, but it
was the face that was unmistakable. It didn't seem
fantastically scary now, not being illuminated in yellow in the depths of a crypt, but it was still a singular
face.

He had thick, bushy eyebrows, a pliable cucumber
for a nose, and his cheeks were covered with pock-
marks. His shoulders and back appeared murderously
strong. Heart beating like a hammer and anvil, I
watched him pass. When he was almost out of sight I

took my leave of the blacksmith and began to follow, keeping a discreet distance. What on earth could he be doing in Mudbury—not even the most optimistic smuggler could think that there was any business to transact here. Had he come to find me? To punish me for seeing him in Dyle? To spy, like Christa said? I decided to do a little spying of my own. Better to find out what he was up to now than have him kidnap me from my bed.

I followed him to the edge of the common land where he paused by a two-story brownstone house. I watched him from the shadow of a weeping willow as he eyed the house speculatively. The shutters were closed and there was no light showing. I knew Dr. Brent lived in this house. Perhaps Mr. Sacre Bleu was going to rob his house in his absence. But no. He began walking again, down the edge of the common land to a stand of trees, and then down the other side of a long flint wall. He was stomping along deliberately in what I assumed was a sailor's walk, and took occasional glances over his shoulder. I was careful now to stay hidden as well as I could behind the flint wall.

He took a sharp turn and took a narrow path into the woods. I followed him, stopping now and then to see if I could still hear his feet shuffling through the leaves. The noise stopped ahead of me and I took it for a sign that he had reached his destination. I crept quietly and low to the ground in a roundabout way, leaving the path and circling, wondering what to do next. A pheasant flushed in front of me, stopping my heart with the commotion of its wings. I waited a few moments and then continued, very cautiously. Between the trees, I could see a small meadow filled with friar's cap and lanky Queen Anne's lace. In the middle of the meadow was a large spreading oak. I crouched down underneath a beautifully delicate group of ferns, and observed as Mr. Sacre Bleu placed something under the gnarled roots of the oak. He turned and left the scene, going down the path again.

I waited for a few moments, getting up the courage to investigate the mystery under the roots. His footsteps faded, and I held back yet longer. I wanted to make certain he wasn't coming back, so I mentally recited all seven verses of "Rise, the Children of Salvation" before I went to look. Having finished the hymn, I crossed the meadow to the oak, to see a corner of what looked like sailcloth sticking out from underneath the roots. I reached down and pulled it out. It felt light in my hands. I had no idea what it contained—smuggled goods, war secrets, or what.

I was never to know the answer, for suddenly I was struck from behind by what seemed a bolt of lightning. I remember thinking, *But it's not even raining*—and falling forward to the ground. . . .

I was dreaming a fitful, fearful dream, in which I was being tossed on the breast of the sea in a very small boat which rode up and down on the waves. I was seasick and vomiting over the side, and was dimly conscious of a cool hand laid on the back of my neck.

"That's the way. Let it all up and you'll feel much better." The voice was gentle, caring. "Here, let's wipe your face and rest a while." I sensed a clean handkerchief being passed over my face, and yes, I did feel a little better. I opened my eyes—the light was much too bright—and saw Lord Dearborne kneeling next to me. He was draping his coat over my shoulders.

"Why did you hit me?" I said to him, weakly.

"I was not the malefactor, although you were up to something which annoyed someone to the extent that he decided to chloroform you. It also appears that you have been struck on the head. Out with it, what mischief were you up to? What was so important that it made you disobey me and go wandering around the countryside alone?"

"You are not my father. You are not even Mrs. Good-body. You have no right to order me to do anything."

"That does not answer my question. What were you doing wandering around in the middle of nowhere?"

I was sick, and he was being entirely too forward in his manner of questioning. This made me angry.

"What were *you* doing out here?" I asked him.

"I was riding. Peterby was showing me this deserted corner of his property, and I was on my way home down the path through the woods. Now if you don't come across with the information I have requested of you I will add to that lump on the back of your head."

He looked decidedly grim. It made me hate him, but I was also afraid, so I told him:

"I was following Mr. Sacre Bleu."

"And who, pray tell, is he?"

"He's an ugly sailor-type person with a cucumber nose who swears in French."

A different look, perhaps of recognition, passed over the marquis's face.

"You followed him here. What was he doing?"

"He was poking around underneath the big oak over there. I went over to look and there was some sort of package there."

The marquis got up and walked to the oak, investigating where I had pointed, under the roots.

"There is nothing here now," he said.

"What does it all mean?" I called to him weakly.

"It means you should do as I say regarding my desire for your protection. It also means that you had better tend to your play-producing and other domestic pursuits and leave off following cucumber-nosed suspicious persons."

"If it pleases Your Lordship."

"It pleases me. Now let's go back to the estate and you can have Mrs. Goodfellow attend to that crack on your head."

"Mrs. Goodbody."

"Whoever. Now let's go, I'll give you a hand up."

This I allowed. But when he put his arm around my waist, I pulled at it with all my strength.

"I may be a slow learner but I am catching on. You may place that arm somewhere else."

"You little fool. Do you want to fall off the horse and break your neck?"

"*Non tali auxilio nec defensoribus istis tempus eget.* That's Virgil. And it means . . ."

"I know what it means," he interrupted. " 'Not such aid nor such defenders does the time require.' What an independent little creature you are. But don't fight me now. You've been hurt and I want to take you home quickly." His voice had softened persuasively and he caressed my face gently with the back of his hand. This time when he pulled me into his arms and lifted me lightly into the saddle, I didn't object. I didn't push him away when he mounted behind me, one strong arm steadying me against his chest. Perhaps it was only the effects of the head injury that kept me leaning quietly on his hard body as the stallion's effortless strides carried us back to Barfrestly.

Chapter Eight

Lord Dearborne created quite a sensation riding up to Barfrestly Manor with me in the saddle in front of him. He ignored me when I demanded to be allowed to walk into the cottage, brusquely picking me up and carrying me straight to my bed, as Mrs. Goodbody came hurrying across the yard, mobcap askew, puffing like a March wind.

"My Lord! Elizabeth! My dear lambkin! Where are you hurt, my love?" asked Mrs. Goodbody, white-faced. "Your head? My word, here's a lump as big as an egg! Was that nasty Plumford boy throwing rocks again? If it was he then depend upon it I shall go straight to his father and give him a piece of my mind!"

"Oh, no, Mrs. Goodbody, it was nothing so bad as that," I assured her. "Only I was following a smuggler, or perhaps a spy, one can't be sure for he swears in French—only that alone doesn't mean he is a spy, er, where was I? Oh yes. I followed him and saw him hide a parcel, probably stolen state secrets, or maybe . . ." I paused to reflect. "Maybe just smuggled gems of great value. Well anyway, he came back around after I thought he was gone and hit my head."

Mrs. Goodbody choked and said she never did, not in all her born days, hear the likes of my story, which was a gratifying response. What was to follow was not gratifying in the least. Lord Dearborne, with an air of paternal solicitude that would have done credit to an archbishop, leaned over me and patted me on the hand.

"Yes, Mrs. Goodbody," he said with the innocence of a suckling babe, "it's a pity that Elizabeth forgot to take an escort with her as I requested. There are a good many rogues about the countryside in these unsettled times."

There, now the fat was in the fire.

"Elizabeth Cordell," exclaimed Mrs. Goodbody, her complexion changing from white to red. "Do you mean to say that the marquis asked you not to go out alone and you never told me of it and then deliberately went and disobeyed him?"

"Talebearer! Snitch!" I yelled wrathfully at Lord Dearborne, who ignored me completely. He told Mrs. Goodbody that he would have a doctor summoned, and left. He was no sooner out the door than I received a snappy lecture from Mrs. Goodbody on the evils of disobedience and ingratitude. Score one for Lord Dearborne. From now on there wasn't a bat's chance in the daytime that I would be able to leave the estate grounds without an escort.

And further, the more Mrs. Goodbody lectured me on the gratitude I owed to Lord Dearborne, the less gratitude I felt. The man could probably have housed and shod a thousand orphans without feeling the slightest pinch. Besides, it was in the will, wasn't it? He had to support us by law. There was no point in arguing with Mrs. Goodbody on this head as His Lordship had already flummoxed her finely. In the time since Lord Dearborne's arrival she had gone from thinking of him as a desperate libertine to regarding him as a paragon among men. I could have disillusioned her by mentioning what he had been about under the honeysuckle bush, had I not been much, much too embarrassed to reveal that to anyone. I shuddered to think of my own response. "You'd be such an easy mark," he had said. I felt my cheeks burn with shame and promised myself to be wary of him and his rakish trickery in the future. There was no desire in Miss Elizabeth Cordell to join the ranks of Dearborne's discarded conquests.

When Dr. Brent arrived, he took a cursory glance at the lump on my head, congratulated Mrs. Goodbody on her excellent good sense in applying cold compresses, advised her to keep me in bed for a day, and predicted I would do very well. (This just shows you what an unsympathetic clodpole of a doctor he was.) The reactions of Christopher and my sisters were more to my taste. They declared me a heroine, and my attacker a villain of the first water.

Christopher, as usual, couldn't be brought to share my reaction to Lord Dearborne's unfair restriction on my personal freedom.

"It stands to reason that I'm not in danger, Kit," I argued. "Why, the fellow would have killed me as I lay there if he had intended to do away with me. He just didn't want to be interfered with at that moment."

"'Lizbeth, I swear you make my flesh creep, prosing on about your own murder like that," groaned Christopher. "Of course Uncle Nicky has to protect you. Dash it all, it's his duty as a gentleman. Tell you what it is, Princess, you're just not used to male authority—didn't have a brother, lost your father when you were a child, and I'll wager the admiral never gave you more than a half hour of attention in all his years as your guardian. And as for that vicar you place so much faith in . . . oh, well, don't flare up at me, I shan't say another word."

That was all that could be had from Christopher on the subject.

The next few days passed slowly, domestic tinkering relieved by visits from the curious. Even the squire came to inquire how I did and to ask the marquis what action to take to capture the villain. Lord Dearborne had told him (as I heard from Mrs. Goodbody, who was present at the time) that there was no need to trouble himself with the matter—the proper authorities had already been contacted. I wondered who the marquis considered the "proper authorities."

Even spending time at home can get you in trouble. One afternoon I had company that I would rather have missed.

I had thought that the squire's ball would be merely a memory and that would be that. It didn't occur to me that anyone would try to further their acquaintance with me. That is why you could have knocked me over with a quill pen when Cecilia Macready paid a call on me, accompanied by a veritable entourage of other people I had no wish to see.

As you have gathered, I was raised to be a country girl, and like any other country girl, I can spin, weave, plate straw, and make black pudding. I don't know if you have had experience with black pudding. To me it is a disgusting concoction, but Mrs. Goodbody is very partial to it. It is a goat's belly stuffed with blood and fat. When preparing this dish, I have no doubt that my face assumes, of its own volition, a harassed and disgusted look. Such a look is what I was clad in, along with a greasy striped calico apron which had been cheerily starched before I began my labors. My hair had become an annoyance to me, so I had bunched it up and put it under a linen mobcap, where it lurked in miserable captivity, to sneak out occasionally and exercise itself in ticklish fashion on the back of my neck until I could find time to recapture it and put it back in its prison. My clothes were sticking to me in the heat from the stove, and I was just about to step out and take some air when there came a knock on the door. I set down my ladle, walked to the door, and opened it.

"Pardon me, girl . . . ," said a vaguely familiar voice. "Oh, Elizabeth, it's you! Such a charming little cottage you have here!"

Cecilia Macready hadn't recognized me out of my ball gown, and feeling like Cinderella at midnight, I cast out for my pumpkin coach, or at any rate, some way to salvage some dignity from the situation. With her were Christopher, Jeffrey, the marquis, a boy I recognized from the ball, and Lady Catherine Doran, of all people, looking like a vision from heaven. What was I to do? The boy from the ball spoke, in his peculiar braying tone:

"Well, being a republican myself, and somewhat of a free thinker, I believe it is laudable for a person of Elizabeth's aristocratic station to live in a hovel like a common peasant."

"Sneck up, Godfrey, you bellow like a cow. *You* are a common peasant." This from Christopher, the friendly face in the crowd. "Elizabeth, you remember Godfrey Woodman from the ball. He thinks he is Oliver Cromwell, don't you, Godfrey."

"Oh dear," said Lady Catherine. "I feel faint." She was holding a delicate lace handkerchief to her pretty nose as the steam from the pudding wafted past her on its way out.

"Elizabeth," said Christopher. "Pay no attention to my companions. Seeing anyone exert themselves upsets them; they feel it is bad form. Why don't you run and put on your riding dress and we shall go riding."

"I really can't leave my cooking right now," I stammered. But then something began to right itself, and I was on my feet again. "I am making black pudding. It is made from goat's blood and fat. It is really quite wholesome." I scooped up some with the ladle and waved it around airily. "Godfrey, you'll surely have a taste, won't you? This is good republican food."

Godfrey turned pale, shaking his head in a vigorous negative jerk. This set the marquis and Christopher to unashamed laughter. When the marquis composed himself, he asked:

"Cat, why don't you try some? You are looking a

mite faint. It might be just the thing to perk you up."

Lady Catherine gave the marquis a look meant to be meaningful.

"What I do need," she said languidly, "is just a brief recline upon a bed . . ."

The insinuation was so strong that its intent was obvious even to me. I felt a warm blush creeping unbidden to my face. Christopher, who had been regarding me closely, hastily intervened: "I can see that we've come pushing in on you at a most inconvenient moment. Cecilia and company just rode over from Macready to pay their respects, but we'll be off now."

And they were off. I went back to my pudding chores, and after what seemed an eternity, I was through. I was sitting in the doorway cooling off, when Christopher rode up again, dismounted, and sat down by me on the step. He was wearing an apologetic air which fitted him stiffly, like a new suit of clothes.

"I'm sorry for bringing that whole crew in on you like that. You weren't really prepared for company and I feel as though I played bad cricket. Cecilia insisted on coming over to pay her respects to you, and Godfrey, bless his meager brain, seems to have developed a *tendresse* for you, but I really think the whole scene was engineered by Lady Catherine. She'll miss no opportunity to get close to the marquis."

"Christopher, you don't have to apologize. How were you to know I was making black pudding? How did the rest of the visit go?"

"Godfrey is learning how to chew tobacco, and he was making everyone sick. He spat, by accident, on the hem of Lady Catherine's gown and that pretty much finished off the afternoon. Imagine a clod like that thinking you would have any time for the likes of him," muttered Christopher.

"Actually, I would rather talk to Godfrey than make blood pudding."

"I would rather make blood pudding than talk to Godfrey," he said.

"That is what you think," I said. And he was off. Christopher is a good friend, I thought to myself as he rode away.

It was getting very close to the time our play was to be presented, and I ceased worrying for a time about smugglers, bodyguards, and other such exciting things. As the time drew near, I wouldn't have noticed if the Corsican Bandit and the entire French army marched right through our cottage and out by way of the chimney, hobnails and all. In fact, I wished that would happen because I could have used them as extras in the play. That's the single-mindedness of an enthusiast for you!

As I surveyed the finished stage on the afternoon before the play, I felt a glow of pride at the results of our labors. We had erected scaffolding that served as the foundation for our sets on the gentle slope of common land next to Mudbury hamlet. The playgoers would bring their own coverlets or stools for seating and the parish ladies had set up a stand that would be stocked with plum cakes and brown ale. Shade for the spectators was generously provided by a holm oak and several pear trees, now in full flower. The huge piece of lumber that the blacksmith had given us had made a most successful transformation into a man-o'-war, circa 1066. My sisters had gotten Jane's brother, who was good at such things, to carve it and then they'd all painted the frame with loving care, right down to the mermaid figurehead who modestly clutched a spray of nodding daisies over her bosom. Caro was just now adding the finishing stitches to the sails, which were made from the same canvas on which we had painted the backdrops.

The *pièce de résistance*, however, was behind the stage foundation. It had been Christopher's inspiration to build a small firework that he would ignite just before the scene in which William was crowned in London, when the Norman army was celebrating. We were enthralled with the idea. Surely the most jaded audience could not help being thrilled by so dramatic a stunt. Christopher assured us that he had made fire-crackers like this many times before and that it could be done with perfect safety. The only thing left for me to worry about was whether or not the noble Norman knight, Sir Hugh of Montfort, the wheelwright's son, could bring himself to the sticking point and plunge his javelin into King Harold. Today, during our final rehearsal, he had broken down at the crucial moment when I, as King Harold, was to die on the battlefield. The ferocious Sir Hugh had flung himself off the stage and cried:

"I can't do it! I just can't stab Elizabeth!"

"You have to stab me. It is very important to the plot that you stab me, or else the Saxons would have won the battle and the Norman conquest would never have been! William the Conqueror would be just plain Bill!"

Sir Hugh evidently had no respect for history. He opened his mouth and wailed, "But I can't stab Elizabeth. She is too sweet!"

It took the efforts of our entire cast, alternately cajoling and threatening, to convince our savage Norman to trod the boards again. Christopher finally won the day by taking the poor boy aside and explaining, "Tomorrow, in the real play, Elizabeth will look like a soldier instead of a girl. She will be dressed in soldier's clothes and will be wearing a fake beard. She will be much more killable." Mrs. Coleman had finished our costumes but she wouldn't let us wear them in rehearsal, as it had been such a task constructing them.

I walked to the back of the scaffolding, to see Christopher standing, hands on hips, regarding his newly finished rocket with great satisfaction. Thomas, the new groom who had been drafted as Kit's assistant on the project, stood nearby with a slightly disloyal look of doubt on his face.

"I don't know," muttered Thomas in pessimistic accents. "You say it'll work but I don't know."

Christopher threw a converting grin his way. "Are you doubting, Thomas? 'Course it will work—just a matter of getting the proper ratio of gunpowder."

"Well, ratios of gunpowder sound very scientific to me," I said, coming up to the two inventors. I handed each a mug of ale, informing them that Mrs. Blakslee had sent down a tray for all the able workers. Kit bore me off to keep him company in the shade while he drank his ale, saying as he did:

"No question of it, 'Lizabeth. We're going to have a hit on our hands tomorrow. Church committee'll erect a plaque in your honor when they count the vast sums brought into the church coffers by the Norman Conquest."

"Right," I said, entering into the spirit of this. "And the plaque will read: 'God makes the bees and the bees make honey; the congregation does all the work but the church makes all the money.' Ah, go ahead and laugh, I hope that we don't both end up in hell for sacrilege."

"Never! Nothing but a rowboat across the River Styx will do for a little heathen like you." Christopher's voice was still unsteady with laughter. "Oh, Lord, what an adorable girl you are. If you could see the look on your face now! You make me want to . . ." He stopped suddenly and flushed. "Oh, dear, you poor little thing. You can hardly help being so beautiful, can you?"

Deeply embarrassed, I begged him to hush again. We sat quietly on the grass for a while then, Kit taking long pulls of ale and I letting a faint rustle of breeze fan the heat from my cheeks. Presently I turned back to my friend.

"Kit, I know you don't like me to bring this up but I can't help worrying that someone somewhere isn't going to like you appearing in a public theatrical. Lord Dearborne may be so angry he won't let us be friends anymore. Mrs. Goodbody told me that the aristocracy considers actors to be, well, disreputable or something like that."

"Don't tease yourself about it, m'dear. Being in one parish play doesn't rank one as a professional actor. It's all for a good cause, right? And, for your information, Uncle Nicky is well aware of the fact that I'm going to be in the play and hasn't made any objection, so you see he's not as top-lofty as you thought. Besides, why should he want to interfere with our friendship?"

"I daresay he thinks you should have grander friends. Ones that he likes."

"He likes you, Elizabeth," Christopher said with a reminiscent grin. "Just the other day he said you have a certain whimsical charm so I shouldn't let myself get carried away and dishonor you, because you were a lady. There, that shows he likes you, doesn't it?"

"No!"

"You don't have to shout at me, I'm not deaf, y'know. Maybe that's not the same as saying he likes you, but compared to Uncle Nicky's usual opinion of women that's pretty high praise, I can tell you. You should hear the things he says about Lady Cat; not but what they are true." Christopher took a long pull from his tankard. "'Sides he didn't ask you to dance at the Macreadys' party. That shows you, doesn't it?"

I grabbed up a handful of convenient grass and tossed it at Christopher. He put a hand hastily over his brew.

"Since when is it customary to express one's liking for another by not dancing with them? I may not know much about the *beau monde* but that is doing it a bit brown."

"It's true for all that." He was brushing the grass out of his soft brown hair. "Young girl, living on his estate, under his protection, as it were; if he started paying attention to you in public it's bound to start the tabbies talking. Lord, all he has to do is look at a woman to get the gossip mills grinding—for you, it would be fatal, believe me. I daresay that he would have liked to dance with you, too, stands to reason. I mean, a dashed beautiful girl and light as a feather in the bargain. See?"

"No, I don't see," I said crossly. "You know what you are, Kit? You are an apologist!"

"No!" said Christopher, revolted.

"Yes," I returned ruthlessly. "And what's more, it won't work. I'll wager that Lord Dearborne has no more liking for me than—than . . . for that wild-looking horse he rides."

"Very fond of his horses, Uncle Nicky is," said Christopher, feeble yet pursuing.

The next morning, the twins had me out of bed before the sun was up. They were shivering with excitement and I made every effort to calm them for fear they would forget their lines in their agitated state. I had little success. They were still chattering nervously when we were backstage donning our costumes, shortly before curtain time. I let my own hair hang down, in the old Saxon way, and put on a false beard. The Saxon women wore pastel gunnas with their hair braided with bits of colored glass. The Norman soldiers were clean-shaven (no false beards), and clip-headed, and wore white tunics with wide sleeves and embroidered edging. Kit made a stunning William the Conqueror. He looked as if he could conquer the whole world, let alone Saxon England.

Caro peeped through the curtain and drew back in openmouthed astonishment.

"There's millions of people out there," she whispered. It was time for the play to begin.

It is impossible to describe the whole play because it lasted over two hours, but I would like to mention some of my favorite highlights.

Christopher exceeded all his rehearsals when he gave his long speech to his army urging them to join him on his voyage of conquest. Then came the voyage of the Norman invasion fleet across the English Channel. This is where the man-o'-war came in. Handles had been attached to the stage side of the "boat" and the feet showing underneath were not too obvious as the "sailors" carried it against an aquatic-blue background. Adding to the illusion was a cutout in the approximate shape of a seagull which was lowered from above the canvas and wiggled back and forth to suggest the illusion of flight. The boat came to a jarring halt at center stage and a ladder was brought up, which the soldiers mounted and then climbed down, thereby disembarking and landing on English soil. A chorus of satisfying boos rose from the audience at this point. This was a tricky maneuver because the soldiers had to climb over the side of the ship by climbing first on the backs of the sailors, who crouched down behind the ship facade out of sight of the audience.

The night before the Battle of Hastings came off even better than I had expected. First we showed the dour Normans, led by a solemn Christopher, spending the night offering fasts and paternosters in pious groupings around an altar of holy relics. On the other side of the stage, the Saxons were whooping it up, draining flagons supposedly full of hard liquor with cries of "Bottoms to the sky!" At one point, I, as King Harold, cried "Bring me my wench," and a soldier led to me a simpering Caro, whom I greeted with a hearty buss on the cheek. I am afraid I maligned poor King Harold, but the scene was a crowd-pleaser. At this point, William the Conqueror buried his head in his hands as if in an ecstasy of prayer, because Christopher found it hard to contain his laughter.

The battle scene went off smoothly, or as smoothly as a battle scene possibly could. Hugh of Montfort managed to cast the fatal javelin and I fell to the stage, twitching and writhing in my death throes, and Christopher cried, "Frenchmen, strike; the day is ours!"

After the battle was over, Mrs. Goodbody made a surprise appearance as Edith Swansneck, Harold's mistress, who was brought to the scene to identify Harold's remains. A roar of appreciation came from the crowd as she took the stage.

I was dragged from the scene in ignominious defeat, and watched the celebrations of the jubilant Normans from the wings.

I was visited there by the Marquis of Lorne. He came up behind me, giving me quite a start. When he spoke, I turned to see a light smile playing over his lips.

"A production worthy of the Globe Theatre in the days of the Immortal Bard," he said.

I curtseyed in my bloodstained battle dress, and said, "I appreciate the compliment from a sophisticated theatergoer like yourself. Wasn't Mrs. Goodbody an adorable Edith Swansneck?"

"Quite charming, really. I saw you open one eye and peek when they were discovering your mutilated corpse."

"I was not peeking. I take great care not to peek. Christopher tried to make me laugh by blowing on my cheek when he leaned over my body, but I wouldn't do it."

"Where is Christopher the Conqueror now?" he asked.

"He's made a firecracker that is going to go off in celebration of William's coronation. I think he went to light it; he wouldn't let anyone else take on that responsibility."

"Where is he?" With lightning speed his hands were on my shoulders. "Quickly."

I was bewildered by his urgency, but I told him as soon as I could choke out the words.

Lord Dearborne left the stage at a run. I followed him, and saw, about twenty yards away, Christopher lighting the firecracker. The fuse had caught. I was now totally confused. The marquis shouted something incomprehensible to Christopher, reaching him in a great bound, grabbing him and pushing him across the yard. I was still following, moving toward Christopher to see what in the world was going on, when the marquis grabbed me too, and pushed us both onto the ground behind a tree with such force that my breath was knocked away.

There was a very loud explosion then, followed by a rain of leaves, twigs, and clods of dirt.

We stood and looked back toward the site of the explosion. The earth was scorched and smoking ten yards in every direction. Far above us was a dazzling display of shooting fire in the sky. The noise of the blast had temporarily deafened me, but I could still make out the cheering of the audience, who naturally thought the tremendous blast was all part of the play. But if Christopher had stayed where he was, he would have been blown to crumbs. There were tears of fright in my eyes as I turned to Christopher and my voice trembled as I said:

"I thought you said that this was perfectly safe, Christopher. If it hadn't been for Lord Dearborne, you would have been killed."

Christopher scrambled to his feet and drew me up beside him. He was looking almost as confused as I.

"I swear that when I checked the thing over yesterday afternoon, it was completely intact. There was enough powder in there to make one-tenth of that blast. Just enough for a loud pop and fizzle." Kit looked up uncertainly into his guardian's eyes. I had never seen Lord Dearborne look so grim before.

"Kit," he said, taking Christopher by the arm, "did you leave that rocket out here overnight?"

"Well, yes, it was on the platform and I didn't want to move it. . . ." The confusion left his face. "Someone must have tampered with it. Someone trying to kill me."

Chapter Nine

Kit was right about one thing—our play was a howling success, if you can measure success in numbers of people telling you that they have never enjoyed themselves more. I had never enjoyed myself less. The blast from the altered bomb was a mere peep when compared to the explosion that came afterward. Lord Dearborne expressed himself with great eloquence on his general impression of our maturity and intelligence, which, I might add, was not favorable. It was a speech that would have done credit to a ship's captain facing a mutinous crew, and Kit and I were effectively cowed, at least until the marquis was out of hearing distance.

That night I was the victim of insomnia again. How could I sleep, worrying who had tampered with our rocket? It had to be someone who knew about the firecracker in advance. Someone connected with the play. Unthinkable. I'd known all those people since I took my first steps. Oh, there was Thomas, of course, but I remembered that he knew nothing about bombs; surely it would have taken someone with a certain skill to make it so deadly? And Thomas was recommended by Dr. Brent. Whatever my personal opinion of the man, there could be no doubt of a doctor's honesty.

My mind kept jumping back to the man that I'd first seen in the church crypt at Dyle, the man I'd christened Monsieur Sacre Bleu. That he was up to no good I'm sure of, but murder? I wondered where he was now.

I discussed all my speculations with Christopher, who listened patiently but told me that I should leave the matter in the hands of Lord Dearborne and the other men from the War Office. A suggestion that we should make a secretive trip to the crypt of the Dyle church to search for further suspicious characters was vetoed with startling vehemence.

"Elizabeth, ain't one crack on the head enough for you? Can't understand how such a gentle girl can be so heedlessly adventurous. These are ruthless men who wouldn't think twice about wringing a neck or three, even as pretty a one as yours. Don't like to tell you things that will frighten you, but you seem to be set on getting involved in this whole thing, and I've got to scare you away for your own good. Whoever fiddled with the firecracker obviously thought it was a golden opportunity, but if they were really serious about knocking me off, they would have waylaid me long ago. They were just taking advantage of my own stupidity."

When I was mulling over his statements that afternoon as I wiped the cottage candlesticks, I was interrupted by a bustling Mrs. Goodbody.

"Oh, there's so much to do, so much to do," she was saying.

"Well, whatever it is that needs doing I will certainly help you all I can," I promised cheerfully.

"I have been to see His Lordship today," she puffed. "We are to pull up tents and go off to London with him."

"London? When? Why?" I gasped.

"We are to leave as soon as we can make ready," she said. "His Lordship only said we are all to have a taste of the Corinthian culture."

"It's probably a hum," guessed Christa, who was seated on our oak table, swinging her legs in the air and munching a peach snitched from the squire's hot-house. "Lord Dearborne isn't going to take an awk-ward squad like us to London with him."

"Off the table, Miss Mischief. 'If you sit on the ta-ble, you'll be married before you're able.' And I can see you've been stealing from the squire's closed gar-den again," Mrs. Goodbody sighed. "You get out the Bible right now and read God's holy Ten Command-ments to see what the Lord has to say on the subject."

"When you say the Lord, do you mean Lord Dear-borne, Mrs. Goodbody?" asked Christa, a perfect pic-ture of pert.

"I've said it before and I'll say it again. There's nothing in the world so difficult as getting decent manners from a thirteen-year-old," said Mrs. Good-body, with resignation.

"But Mrs. Goodbody," I interrupted impatiently, thereby proving that nineteen-year-olds don't always have very good manners either. "Are we *really* going to London? Is Christopher coming too? Are we going to stay there for a long time?"

"Yes. Yes. And no. It's only for a couple of weeks or so. Roger is bringing the admiral's old trunks down from the attic for us to pack in. Oh dear, I haven't had to pack like this since the last time the admiral went off on a sea voyage. Elizabeth, I can see that you have an eager I-want-to-help-Mrs.-Goodbody look on your face, but I promise you that my head's in such a whirl that I'll do better just now all by myself. Why don't you run along outside and get a little country sunshine while you can?"

My head was in a bit of a whirl itself, so I went off in search of Christopher to see what information might be gleaned from him. I tiptoed into Barfrestly through the kitchen door, after assuring myself, as al-ways, that the marquis was nowhere about. I found Christopher quickly. He was stretched full length on a lounging couch in the library, reading a tattered copy of *Turf-side Companion* with rapt interest. He tossed it aside and sat up as I flew in at him.

"Christopher, Christopher! London, London! Is it true?"

"Elizabeth, Elizabeth! Yes, yes! I can tell you are excited because you sound like an echo."

"Why are we going? Why is the marquis making us go along?"

"He got the royal summons from our illustrious Prince Regent. We are to be there for two weeks. He didn't feel that he could leave us alone here under the circumstances, nefarious characters about and all that. You'll love London; a person can have a great many adventures in town. The capital of Western civilization."

"But I won't know anyone there except for you," I said dejectedly. "And you'll probably be out gaming and socializing with the people you already know there. You certainly won't have much time to show me around."

"It's not that I wouldn't love to take you around," said Christopher, "but I do have a more suitable companion for you while you are there. My sister Anne is going to chaperone you. Her husband's out of England on an embassy mission. She's had to stay on their country estate but will come to town to stay at Lorne. She's all the crack in London town, and as thick as grass with Lady Sefton. Just the one to introduce you into society."

"Who is Lady Sefton?" I asked doubtfully.

"She is one of the haughty patronesses at Almack's. Almack's is a private club for the *haute monde*. If they don't give you the nod there you may as well turn in your christening papers and withdraw all pretensions to the smart life."

"I've never had *any* pretensions to the smart life and the thought of it makes me shake to the tips of my fingers. Don't you think that I could just stay here at

Barfrestly? I think that I'll just be in the way if I
come. How will your sister feel, having me foisted
upon her?"

"There's no question of foisting. I told her all about
you in my last letter to her and she's dying to meet
you. But if you'd rather not go, then why don't you
just go and tell Lord Dearborne that you disagree
with his decision . . . ?"

"Yes, and while I'm at it why don't I give him some
advice on national diplomatic policy? You're really a
humorist." The grin that greeted this shot showed me
that Christopher knew very well that I wasn't about to
seek out the marquis and blithely tell him the what-
for. Besides, I harbored no sincere desire to be told to
stay at Barfrestly. I have wanted to visit London all of
my life. Who has not?

I could hardly contain my excitement for the three
days that it took to complete the trip preparations.

It seemed impossible that I could really be going to
London, and I was ready at any moment for some
mischance to intervene that would make it necessary
to cancel the trip. I could hardly believe my senses
when I sat in the marquis's well-sprung traveling coach
on the morning of our departure. My sisters, Mrs.
Goodbody, and I were to ride in this comfortable ve-
hicle while Christopher and Lord Dearborne rode beside us on their overspirited stallions. I watched with
something approaching awe as Lord Dearborne gracefully retained his seat when his mount made a particularly determined effort to rid himself of his rider. Afterward I heard Lord Dearborne casually tell
Christopher that "Jupiter was a bit playful this morning." About as playful as a hell-hag. I'll never understand why people enjoy riding the backs of such skit-
tish, writhing, restless creatures.

In the last century they say the roads were so filled
with potholes and bumplets as to make travel trouble-
some, if not a downright penance. But Parliament has

since permitted turnpike companies to collect tolls in return for maintaining the roads in good repair, so modern travel is quick and comfortable. As I looked out the coach window at the tamed Kentish landscape I felt the thrill of a sightseer discovering new vistas. This was not a feeling that I'd been privileged to enjoy many times before in my somewhat restricted life, and it put me in a state which Mrs. Goodbody rather unflatteringly referred to as a pucker.

My sisters and I bounced around the carriage, pointing out minor landmarks to one another, telling each other riddles, and leaning perilously out the coach window to talk to Christopher. We did suffer a minor delay just outside of Maidstone when a flock of sheep took temporary possession of the roadway, to the frustration of the drivers of several natty vehicles. Mrs. Goodbody asked the marquis if we might have permission to stretch our legs while the roadway was being cleared of the fleecy invaders, so Caro, Christa, Cleo, and I set out on a narrow path through a golden wheatfield.

Cleo led the way and Caro tagged behind, picking quantities of wild plants. Christopher was standing holding the bridle of his horse, talking with Lord Dearborne and Mrs. Goodbody in the shade of the coach, when we returned. Caro laid her collection of foliage down in the middle of this group and demanded that I identify every leaf and blade.

"Um. Let's see . . . This is timothy—it's an edible hay. That is, edible for horses and the like—not for you." I continued my perusal of the wilting specimens. "See this arching stem? 'Tis Solomon's Seal, which has small white flowers when it blooms, which isn't very often."

Christa kicked a large branch with the toe of her new kid boots.

"What's this, 'Lizbeth? Caro certainly did bring a big bunch of it."

I regarded the shiny sinister leaves. "Angels of faith defend us! Caro's been picking in a burnweed patch. Oh, my poor little dear, 'leaflets three, let them be,' don't you recall?"

Lord Dearborne earned Mrs. Goodbody's warmly expressed gratitude by transporting us promptly to an inn where we bathed Caro's skin with gentle industry to arrest the effects of the irritating weed. As the hour passed, it became evident that it was already too late. Caro's arms had become painfully swollen and one soft cheek was slightly puffy where a leaf must have brushed against it. It was decided in a conference between Mrs. Goodbody and the marquis that we would stay the day at the inn and continue on in the morning, after Caro had recovered from the most acute miseries of her botanical malaise.

After Mrs. Goodbody and I shared a lunch in Caro's sunny bedroom, Christa made several praiseworthy attempts to amuse her by tossing her afflicted twin my sawdust pincushion. Unfortunately, they were so noisy as to attract the disapproving notice of the occupant of the next room, who sent us, via a giggling chambermaid, an unfriendly request to quiet down. So Mrs. Goodbody enlisted the offices of Christopher to play a calm game of beggar-my-neighbor with Caro, and sent Christa and me out to take a walk.

I was happy for the chance to explore, and I pulled off my traveling dress and slipped into a powder-blue gown of taffeta gauze. Impatiently threading a fine velvet ribbon through my hair, I hoped that Mrs. Goodbody wouldn't catch me before I got outside and make me don a bonnet on this warm day. I see that I'm a bad influence on my sisters, because when Christa met me at the front door, I saw that she had also shed her traveling bonnet in defiance of Mrs. Goodbody's edict that we should look like ladies at all times. We shared one conspiratorial glance and snuck rather guiltily out the backyard of the inn, past the stone-built stable, toward the blooming cherry orchard. I had just stopped to pat an obsequious barn cat when Lord Dearborne came around the corner of the stables. I suppose that I should be used to seeing him by now, but I'm afraid that his looks still stun me a bit each time. Wishing that Christa hadn't gone quite so far ahead of me, I set the kitten gently on the ground and walked woodenly by the marquis with my eyes focused on the ground, uttering "Good afternoon, Milord," in my most repelling accents. Apparently they weren't too repelling, because Lord Dearborne came to walk alongside me.

"Has Mrs. Goodbody sent you out for a walk? I thought that it would come to that. The good landlord confessed to me that the noise from your bedchamber had gotten so loud that several guests asked of him if he had begun permitting orgies in his chambers. I suppose that I had better accompany you to see that you don't encounter any of the smugglers, spies or corpses who throw themselves at your dainty feet wherever they trod."

I compressed my lips tightly and quickened my pace, still looking downward.

"So shy today, Elizabeth? I remember once under a honeysuckle bush when you were warmer!"

I stopped dead in my tracks and looked straight up into his face, gasping like a grounded trout.

"Of all the unkind things you have said to me, that really takes the tribute! To remind me of something of which I'm so ashamed that I couldn't even tell Mrs. Goodbody."

"I can be thankful for that. I'd really be in the stew if Mrs. Goodbody discovered that I'd been making improper advances toward you." Lord Dearborne looked totally unrepentant, though his eyes were softened by an amusement that was seductively tender. I swallowed angrily and continued walking in silence.

We came out of the orchard onto a daisy-covered

hillside dotted with sun-warmed boulders. I turned to Lord Dearborne again. My voice sounded strange to my ears as I said:

"Is this some game you like to play, seducing country girls in the afternoon? Pray, what do you do with your mornings?"

"Seduce city girls. No, don't run away from me now." I had made a movement away from him, but his arm had shot out to imprison my wrist ruthlessly. "What you'd really like to do is to stay here and tell me what an unconscionable libertine I am. Come, why hold back?"

"Because I don't want to fight with you. How can I fight with you when you're so much better at this than I am? When I like people, then I want to be friends with them. And when I don't like them, then I try to understand why. But you . . . make these complicated approaches filled with innuendos and subtleties that I can't understand and you arouse feelings in me that I don't understand either. All I know is that it's not gentlemanly of you to deliberately try to—well, confuse me in that way when you don't care a pin about me and I'll probably end up being hurt."

"Listen, infant, if I wasn't 'gentlemanly,' you would have been deflowered a month ago."

I am not a great lover of missish behavior, but I must admit that at that moment it would have been nice to faint. I felt the blood come blistering hot to my cheeks.

"For pity's sake . . ." It was a miserable bleat and must have touched him for his face lost some of its grimness. His hands, friendly now, pushed me carefully down to sit on a convenient boulder.

"Pet, I'm sorry. That was ill-said of me. I make a much better guardian for lively youths than beautiful innocents." His voice sounded not unkind; even, to my surprise, a little rueful. "I'm very conscious that if I had encouraged you to trust me you would have taken my advice and not left Barfrestly unprotected on the afternoon that you were struck. It's hardly your own fault that you don't inspire paternal sentiments in me and there is no reason why you should suffer for it." He paused, glancing up the hillside. "Look up there. Your intrepid sister is gathering another armful of plants. I hope to God that she learned to distinguish burnweed this morning!"

For a few moments we sat listening to the light wind whispering through the nodding daisies. A nesting warbler ventured a few bars of tuneful song.

"Elizabeth, was the man that you followed through Mudbury the same man that you saw in the church crypt at Dyle?"

Somehow, the question didn't surprise me. I knew that Christopher confided most things in Lord Dearborne, and would probably have told him about the incident in Dyle. The marquis looked fully capable of putting two and two together.

"Yes, he was the same man. That's why I followed him. I was afraid that he was coming to Mudbury to hush me up so that I couldn't identify him. Everyone says that the smugglers are very ruthless and will murder you without so much as a by-your-leave."

A grin played around the corners of Lord Dearborne's mouth. "So naturally, seeing such a dangerous character, you set off in hot pursuit? Why did you call him Monsieur Sacre Bleu?"

"That's what he said. When I bumped into him in the crypt, he swore 'Sacre bleu.'" I made my voice low and guttural and repeated the curse. "He said it just like that. Do you want to know what I think?" He nodded a respectful assent. "I think that he was French. And what's more, I think that he has something to do with spying for Napoleon because it's said that the smugglers sometimes abet the spies. Henri's death, Monsieur Sacre Bleu and the bomb at the play—I think they're tied together in some way."

"Um, you may be right. I'll pass the information on to the War Department."

"You're laughing at me now. I think this is a very serious situation."

"Exactly, my indomitable infant. Which is why the less you have to do with the whole thing the better."

Christa came down the hill to sit nearby, and began braiding daisies into a crown which she soon arranged into my hair.

"You know what else I think? I think that you've heard of Monsieur Sacre Bleu before, because you didn't seem too surprised when I described him to you after I was hit on the head. Furthermore, the reason that he came to Mudbury wasn't to kill me because he would have done it when I was lying there unconscious if he had wanted to. Which means—"

"Which means you should regard one knock on the head as a warning to refrain from meddling in what you have shrewdly divined to be a very serious business." Lord Dearborne sighed. "It's hard to believe that such a stubborn disposition could lodge in such a sweet little body. Only conceive of my feelings upon discovering you unconscious in the spinny."

"You probably thought 'Aha, an excellent opportunity for some wenching,'" I said as sternly as I could. I slid down to sit at the base of the boulder and curled my knees up under me. "You think that because you are the 'male authority' (as Kit would say), that you can selfishly keep all the mystery to yourself?"

"*Tantaene animis coelestibus irae?*" quoted the marquis with a grin.

"Do you think you can flummox me with a little schoolboy Latin? 'In heavenly minds can such resentments dwell?'" I translated, scornfully. "Yes, they can, except that my mind isn't heavenly in the least. And I am still worried about Christopher. He says that he's not in danger, but I don't know if I can believe him.

You both seem convinced that I am unable to bear the full force of the truth."

"Elizabeth, why is it so impossible for you to place a little faith in my ability to protect you and Kit? You'll be perfectly safe as long as you go nowhere without an escort." He paused to pluck off a caterpillar that had ventured onto the hem of my gown. "I lay the whole problem directly at the door of Mudbury's vicar. He should have spent less time filling you with the exciting adventures of Jason and Odysseus and more time on the virtues of obedience. Did you never learn the parable of Pandora's box? I only want to protect you, Elizabeth."

I felt my old companion, the resentment gargoyle, dig his claws tightly into my shoulder. Before you came to Barfrestly, Milord, I never needed any protection.

Chapter Ten

London, London! It was evening when we arrived and the town twinkled with a million lights. The streets were filled with an astounding array of coaches, wagons, and light sporting vehicles. The chairmen carried flambeaus which lit their faces eerily as they threaded their way through crowds of pedestrians and hawkers with portable stalls. I saw one girl pushing a tipsy cart filled with pots of blooming flowers "all a-blowin' and all a-growin'." The dignified men in plush breeches, tailed coats, and powdered wigs were footmen, or so Christopher informed us. He wasn't so forthcoming with information about an old lady in a long duffle coat with a group of dressed-up young ladies in tow who stood talking to a group of sailors on one street corner. "Shocking," I heard Mrs. Goodbody pronounce, though I saw Christopher hide a smile when Christa guessed they might all be in a "school of some kind."

It seemed incredible to me that there could be such a broad expanse of buildings and people. The same space in Kent would have covered many villages, marsh, thousands of acres of farmland, and a forest or two. But here were just rows of houses and mobs of people, all looking worried and hurried, rushing here and there, and none of them seeming to mind a whit the foul state of the air they were breathing. It made my eyes water.

The whole experience of driving into London made

the possibilities of riots, wars, starvation, and disease so much more real. The walls were covered with posters lampooning people I had only heard about in a very distant fashion, people like "Prinny," whom I had known only as the Prince Regent and "Boney" Napoleon Bonaparte. I had heard how unemployment was a problem, and now I understood. How could there ever be enough jobs to go around among so many people? Indeed, I did see more than a few thin, dirty, and shabbily dressed. And though there were houses row upon row, Christopher told me that he had read once in a republican leaflet that as many as twenty thousand Londoners were without any shelter whatever and slept under bridges and in parks. Some poor families lived in a single room. Families even shared rooms. Christa and Caro were reading out of a guidebook.

"Listen to this, Elizabeth. It says 'a man who saunters about the capital with pockets on the outside of his coat deserves no pity.' What does that mean?"

"He's talking about pickpockets," said Christopher. "They take things right from your pockets while you're not looking if you're not careful."

"Why do they do that?" asked Christa.

"I suppose because they don't have anything of their own," said Christopher simply. "You have to watch out for them all. This includes street thugs, footpads, housebreakers, and counterfeiters. And I do hope to frighten you. Even where we will be staying, at the marquis's house in Mayfair, you are never to go out alone, even in the daytime, without being accompanied by at least a footman or a maid. That is the rule for anyone living in London."

The twins were awed by that last bit of information, but I thought it to be one more of the marquis's surveillance rules.

We were now entering a different area of the city, in which streets were not as crowded, and the atmosphere seemed more sedate. People were moving at not such a rapid pace and the houses were larger and better kept.

"What area is this, Kit?" I asked.

"This is Mayfair. We are getting closer to Uncle Nicky's humble quarters."

The carriage finally stopped in a well-kept square lined with genteel mansions whose windows winked candlelight. We stepped down from the carriage into a spacious forecourt and could glimpse the handsome facade of Lorne House through a beautiful row of plane trees. Mrs. Goodbody looked approvingly up at the trees, murmuring reassuringly to us that if London had such trees then it couldn't be all bad. I needed all the reassurance that I could get because the thought of crossing His Lordship's elegant threshold made me feel like a mule at the milliner's. Just as I was playing about with the idea of crawling back to hide in the coach, the highly finished hardwood door in the mansion's porched entrance flew open and a tall girl wreathed in smiles and jade taffeta came gliding into the graveled courtyard. She dispensed loving hugs to Christopher and Lord Dearborne, who received the embrace in a surprisingly fatherly spirit. Even before I heard Lord Dearborne introducing her to Mrs. Goodbody, I realized that this was Lady Anne Crawford, Christopher's fashionable sister. Their family resemblance was strongest in their manners, which were frank, positive, and unaffectedly friendly. Lady Anne had Christopher's soft sable-colored eyes and shining brown hair. But here the resemblance ended. In Lady Anne, Christopher's classical features were replaced by a wide stretch of mouth and a tiny button nose that seemed totally inadequate for all that girl. Actually, since she's closer to thirty, perhaps "girl" is undignified. But so she strikes one. She took my hands in a kindly grip as we were introduced, continuing with the vivacious chatter that she had begun.

"Christopher, you told me she was a beauty, but there are degrees, you wretch. You should have warned me that I was about to be presented with the task of chaperoning Venus come to earth!" she said. She turned to me. "My dear child, I don't know if you're going to love London or not, but I can quite safely guarantee that London is going to love you!" With this lavish assessment, she swept us into the house with promises of tea, bathing water, and restful bedchambers. We crossed the marble floor of a graceful entrance hall, and climbed the central staircase to the first floor. My sisters leaned perilously over the flow of wrought-iron handrail, the better to view the subdued design in the stained glass fanlight set over the main doorway.

My bedroom matched the tone of the rest of Lorne House, graciously luxurious with an exquisite lightness of detail. The walls were hung in Wedgewood blue and cream damask, and the colors appeared again throughout the room. After my little cot, surely I would be lost in the lovely canopied bed hung in blistered satin! The rest of the room was furnished richly but sparsely, giving an airy, spacious feeling. Even my fantasies of life in a marquis's mansion had not been audacious enough to imagine this.

The greatest hit with the twins turned out to be a little room adjoining their chamber, which someone had discreetly decided to name a water closet. I must say it is a marvelous invention, though I have never heard of such a thing before and if you don't have one, I can heartily recommend its installation!

Also, to my amazement, a friendly lady's maid came to help me prepare for dinner. Imagine, Elizabeth Cordell with a real lady's maid! She helped me to choose a clinging gown of watered bisque silk that she promised was just the thing for "informal" dining, and coaxed my hair into a casual tumble of dancing curls.

"Ooo, miss, don't you look something like!" she en-

thused. Never before had I looked quite so fashionable. I was so excited that I gave the little maid a swift
hug which almost prostrated her from shock.

I was to await Lady Anne's escort to the dining parlor, but decided immediately against so tame a course.
Slowly, and giving myself monstrous airs, I descended
the stairway to the first floor. Smiling and inclining
my head graciously, I curtseyed deeply to the well-
kept portraits that lined the walls. Men in Elizabethan
ruffs, powdered wigs, and sparkling jewels stared
haughtily back at me, with the vivid blue eyes of the
marquis.

Curiously, like an inquisitive mouse, I poked my
head into one high-ceilinged reception room after the
next. Shining velvet and satin draperies, glinting crystal, and islands of exotic carpets set off the delicately
carved and graceful furniture. It was like a place out
of a dream.

The double doors to the grand salon on the first
floor stood open and I ventured cautiously inside,
hardly able to believe that I would not be ejected as
an intruder at any moment. Crossing the high-polish
parquetry floor (much too lovely to be walked on), I
came to the huge bay windows that overlooked the
square, now twinkling with a hundred candlelit windows. I felt rather dwarfed by all this magnificence.
Lord Dearborne came in to join me, the perfect foil
for his exquisite surroundings.

"I was admiring the view, Milord," I offered nervously.

"Yes, the view is enchanting this evening." The
smile that swept me was lazily appreciative. "Were you
shocked by your first glimpse of the wicked pace of
London life?"

"The bustle in the streets, you mean? It made me
dizzy but it's so peaceful here that it might be an evening at Barfrestly. Except that here is rather more . . .
incredible. It's like a palace," I confided shyly. His

smile was, for once, quite kind. I felt my self-confidence increase accordingly. "I've had so much excitement at Barfrestly lately that London may well be dull in comparison. I've been here several hours already without one person trying to knock me on the head, blow me up, or toss me across the front of their saddle," I said, for a little practice at repartee.

"If London gets too dull, let me know and I'll try to arrange some excitement for you," promised Lord Dearborne, giving me a look that demonstrated that it is better to practice one's repartee with less dangerous partners.

Lady Anne joined us then, and Christopher. I had been dreading my first dinner in this exalted company. My sisters were dining in their room tonight with an early bedtime, and Mrs. Goodbody ate be-lowstairs with the marquis's servants. At first I was upset by the notion of taking my meals away from her, but when I suggested that I could eat downstairs too, she vetoed the idea with such horror that I dared not mention it again.

"After all the years I have suffered, seeing you de-nied your true station in life, I'm not going to have you saying anything so silly! Lordy me, whatever would your poor mama say? 'Tis like a wish come true, seeing you in your rightful company," Mrs. Goodbody had lectured.

I remembered an anecdote Christopher had told me about the great Beau Brummell, who is quite the most fashionable man in England. Once, at a dinner party, he had asked a footman to name him his neighboring diners rather than trouble himself to turn his head to discover their identities on his own. Thankfully, I was to discover that affectation due more to avoid the dis-arrangement of the fastidious beau's neckwear than to the formality prevailing at the supper tables of the *haute monde*.

Lady Anne was the liveliest lady imaginable, and

alternately teased her brother, shared the latest political gossip with Lord Dearborne, and upon hearing that I was interested in classical studies, announced that she would take me to see Lord Elgin's marbles on the very next afternoon, though "Nicky disapproves dreadfully of the method of their acquisition."

"Yes, do take her, Anne. I daresay she will regard them as sacred relics," said Christopher, leaning over to tap me on the nose. "Better enjoy your leisure while you can, 'Lizbeth, I daresay m'sister has a million devilish places to drag us to thereafter!"

"Don't I just!" sparkled Lady Anne. "I've only two weeks left before I join my husband in Europe; we'll be gone for four whole months. 'Tis an eternity, I assure you. So I've to pack four months of socializing into a scanty fortnight and that takes a deal of ingenuity. Oh, Elizabeth, there are so many people that I want you to meet and not near enough time. Don't worry, though, for as soon as we are back from Europe we will install in my dear John's house on St. James Square. A mammoth pile I promise you, but the most modish of locations! And you will come and stay with us for an extended visit. No, no, my dear, don't refuse me. Indeed, I would have had you come the moment I learned of your existence from Christopher, but all is at sixes and sevens with us with John suddenly being given that foreign assignment. He left last week for Amsterdam, John that is, and I was so delighted when Nicky sent to ask me to stay here. Ah, speaking of devilish places," Lady Anne continued with a sly glance at the marquis, "Kit, my love, tomorrow night we go to Lady Catherine Doran's for a ball. It will be a dreadful squeeze, I know, but all the world comes."

And, as Lady Anne had promised, it did seem that all the world had come to Lady Catherine's on the next evening. Never before had I dreamed that so many spangled ladies and carefully tailored gentlemen existed. And the names of the guests! We hadn't been there for half an hour before Lady Anne had introduced me to so many notables that my head was swimming. As if it were a mere nothing, Lady Anne had made me known to distinguished generals, intimidatingly famous peers of the realm, and even a royal duke. I was grateful, though slightly overwhelmed, that Lady Anne herself supervised my preparation even to the finishing touch of adding one of her own heart-shaped diamond pins to the shimmering cascade of curls that my ladies had lovingly arranged. The gown I wore was the heavenliest creation of semitransparent silk, smoky topaz with a demitrain. I wore my first pair of long gloves, too, and I was glad to have them for, as I ruefully told Christopher as he led me out for the first dance, my wrists were the only part of me decently covered.

"You mean the neck of your gown? Of course it's decent," Christopher replied reassuringly. "You can depend on m'sister to send you out just right. The girl's got excellent taste, even the Beau says so and everyone knows how finicky he is. 'Sides, it's the style to look as naked as possible. It's considered classical—that should please you. Even the men's trousers are skintight in emulation of nude Greek statues."

"I hadn't noticed any men's trousers," I managed to shoot back primly, if slightly untruthfully, before Christopher and I were separated by a movement of the dance.

It was some time before I was returned to Lady Anne. Christopher had a cadre of his own to introduce me to. Dozens of cheerful, friendly young people swarmed around us in between sets, eager to talk with Christopher after his absence from London. So many of Christopher's friends led me out to the dance floor that at last I had to beg for a rest.

Lady Anne was seated on a crocodile-footed Egyptian sofa set picturesquely near a potted palm. She appeared to be immersed in earnest conversation with a foppish young man, but as I arrived she ousted him promptly and installed me in his place.

"Ah, there you are, Elizabeth. Richard, do run and find Elizabeth some refreshment. I vow this room has become horridly close."

The crowd separated then, and across the room I saw Lord Dearborne. The marquis was beautiful by daylight but there ought to be a law against him in candlelight. The effect is devastating. The gleaming brass buttons of his satin waistcoat seemed almost dull in comparison to the shining highlights of his curling shoulder-length hair. I ascertained with amusement that I was not the only female to notice. A number of ladies cast languishing glances at my "guardian."

I watched in fascination as Lady Catherine came to press herself against the marquis in an unconvincing stumble. "Dreadful!" I ejaculated in an undervoice that Lady Anne, who had followed the direction of my gaze, was able to hear. Then I flushed brightly with the shocked realization that I would have liked to try much the same thing myself.

Lady Anne, thankfully misinterpreting my blush, returned confidentially, "Dreadful is the word for it. But it's not a view that we will have to put up with much longer. Lady Cat's star is definitely on the wane. Already Nicholas is losing interest in her full-blown purring." She tapped her ivory fan on her palm several times before asking casually, "Tell me, what do you think of Nicky?"

I saw Lady Doran say something that produced one of Lord Dearborne's most alluring smiles.

"I think of him as little as I can possibly manage!" I realized that this was scarcely a proper sentiment to express about the man who is at least legally one's guardian. "Oh dear, that makes me sound like the most ungrateful beast in nature and I am fully sensible of all that Lord Dearborne has done for my sisters and me. I don't know what would have happened to us if Lord Dearborne hadn't gone on supporting us after Admiral Barfreston died. Sometimes Lord Dearborne can be the most charming of companions. And then there are times . . ." I stopped. I couldn't bring myself to talk about those times to anyone. Lady Anne regarded me strangely. "Times when he scarcely notices me," I finished lamely.

After a moment she spoke again, though sadly. "It's very tragic that someone with the enormous potential that Nicholas has for real happiness gets caught up in so many meaningless affairs. I've known Nicky since we were children—our families were very close. If you could have seen him as a boy, Elizabeth . . . He was full of life and so idealistic. Then one summer, his family didn't come to visit us as they had every year before. We got a scribbled note from Nicky's mother that said they wouldn't be able to get away from London that year. Later, of course, the whole story came out. Nicky had had an affair with a married woman more than twice his age. Apparently her husband found out and made a bungled attempt at suicide—he even tried to bring a divorce action against his wife, naming Nicky as her lover. Nicky was only sixteen at the time. Nothing ever came of it, and it's ancient history now by London standards of gossip. But when I met Nicky after that he had changed. I mean, he didn't withdraw from the world into embittered seclusion, he had just sort of soured on life. He was harder and there was a streak of cynicism that hadn't been there before. You see, the whole affair wasn't unusually scandalous by society standards, but it was all so sordid. Any woman who cares about Nicky will have to be very patient with him while he learns how to love all over again."

Lady Anne gave me a sidelong glance, then continued: "When it was over, society welcomed Nicky back with open arms—they were willing to accept far worse

youthful peccadillos from anyone with Nicky's title
and wealth. Naturally, Nicky was well aware of the
reason for their broad-minded leniency toward him
and that did nothing to improve his opinion of the human race. He has such contempt for women—he's used
to taking what he wants without needing to ask first. I
think that it would do him an enormous amount of
good to care enough to ask."

I thought of Lord Dearborne on those few occasions when he had unbent with me and his smiles
then—as they were without mockery or contempt. Had
this been what he was like as a young man before
world-weary boredom had eclipsed the sweetness? I
wished suddenly, passionately, that he could regain
whatever it was that he had lost in the process of
growing up. For no apparent reason I suddenly recalled the time he had caressed me in his arrogant,
loveless fashion under the honeysuckle bush, and
again flushed to the roots of my hair. I was glad to
have my wayward thoughts interrupted by Lady
Anne, who drew my attention to a young man elbow-
ing his way impatiently across the crowded floor.

"Oh Lord, Elizabeth, look. 'Tis Godfrey Woodman
coming toward us. Kit says that he's developed the
most profound crush on you while staying in Kent. I
suppose there's nothing for it but you will have to
dance with the tiresome fellow. *Au revoir*, my dear."

To be honest, I didn't think Godfrey a tiresome fellow in the least. True, he had less sense of humor than
a nesting osprey, but then he is a very good poet for
all that he hasn't caught the public fancy. And I was
glad to see a familiar face in the vast sea of unknown
fashionables.

After we danced, Godfrey led me over to a vacant
seat and we exchanged ecstasies over Lord Elgin's
marbles. He was about to quote me a stanza from the
epic poem he was sweating over at present when, very

much to my amazement, we were joined by Lady Catherine Doran herself.

"Ah, Godfrey, prosing on about your poetry again? Dull work for Miss Elizabeth, you may be sure. . . . Run off now and let us chat a bit," said Lady Catherine, gifting Godfrey with a smile that robbed her words of offense. "Elizabeth, my dear, I hope that you don't mind my informality but we hardly need stand upon ceremony, do you think? Nicky and I are such old friends. So, how do you find London?"

"It's very . . . big," I replied foolishly. There was something so intensely suave about Lady Catherine that it left me feeling remarkably gauche.

Lady Catherine laughed as though I had made the cleverest witticism she had heard in days.

"Ah, to think that Nicky has undertaken your guardianship. How delightfully . . . paternal of him! But tell me. My cousin, dear Mrs. Macready, told me that you've had some excitement since Nicky arrived, with the death of the French cook, no less! Here, my dear, let me refill your wineglass and you can tell me about it."

I was so flattered that Lady Catherine was interested in talking to me that I was rendered inarticulate for a few moments. She was so warmly encouraging, though, that I soon lost the shys and gave forth with the full tale of Henri's death, or what I knew of it, anyway. Lady Catherine hung on every word. I finished by telling her that I should dearly love to solve the riddles that I was sure still existed in connection with Henri's death.

"Perhaps you shall, my dear. But how is this? You don't drink! Have another glass of wine. There now. We may be comfortable again. Let me tell you a tale in exchange for that fascinating one you told me."

Lady Catherine went on to relate several very funny pieces of London gossip, what Beau Brummell had said to Lord Alvenley the other evening at dinner, and who Lady Caroline Lamb had tossed a plate of orange peels at during Lady Jersey's *al fresco* picnic.

It is a very special type of flattery that Lady Catherine uses. She is so attentive, and so involved with everything you say that it gives you a marvelous, though false, sense of your own importance. Truthfully, my hostess was a little too attentive. She refilled my wineglass so many times that I was beginning to feel fuzzy. Wine is not my favorite beverage, but I was afraid to offend her by refusing to drink, which just shows you what a wimp I was at the time. The candlelit scene became a soft twinkling blur with Lady Catherine dominating the center. I don't recall how it was that we came to be joined by Lesley Peterby. I only remember Lady Catherine smile up at him in greeting.

"Ah, my dearest Lesley, how charming you are, as usual. Elizabeth, surely you know Lesley Peterby. I can see that Lesley is feverish to have some little chat with you, Elizabeth. You have met before, have you not?" I made an effort at a polite smile which Lady Catherine promptly, if erroneously, interpreted as a signal to play least in sight. There I was, talking to Lord Peterlyn. Peterley? Petersby? The simplest name can become a tongue-teaser if you're tipsy enough. Oh well, choose one and forge ahead.

"How are you this evening, Lord Petersy?"

His rather nasty one-sided grin became even nastier. "Peterby. But why not dispense with formalities? My friends call me Lesley."

I was far from sure that I wanted to dispense with formalities. What I would have liked was a few minutes of country air to clear my head.

"I'm not one of your friends. I'm only your acquaintance—officially at least. So I don't want to call you by your first name, Lord Peter . . . thing. Furthermore, I don't feel like talking, so if you want to sit here, then either you will have to do all the talking or put up with silence."

I was hit by the horrid suspicion that I was even more intoxicated than I thought. Imagine snapping like that at a man I hardly knew, and at a high society ball, at that. Far from minding, my companion threw back his head and laughed.

"Very well, then, charmer. You have merely to sit back and relax while I attempt to carry on the conversation for both of us. Let me see, what can two people discuss on such shallow acquaintance? The weather, perhaps? And do you find the climate to your liking, Miss Cordell? Yes, thank you kindly, Lord Peterby. 'Twas a trifle sultry yesterday, was it not, Miss Cordell? Decidedly, Lord Peterby. But not unseasonably so, I think." He paused to take a quick swallow of wine. "There. You see, there is no need for you to enter the conversation at all. In fact, it would be quite superfluous."

I found myself giggling. "How absurd you are! I'm afraid that I was awfully rude." I leaned toward him confidentially. "You see, this is my first night in London society."

"Excellent. Rudeness is an essential ingredient for a long and successful reign in polite society. Witness the triumphs of Beau Brummell, Lady Jersey, and Lord Dearborne."

The triumphs of Lord Dearborne were not my favorite subject. I drew myself up and said with dignity, "Lord Dearborne is my guardian." I thought this over a moment. "Sort of," I added conscientiously.

"Indeed?" He had a smile like a cat. Do cats smile? Oh, how I wished that I had refused those last three glasses of wine. I rose to my feet with resolution, if not equilibrium.

"I am sorry to have to part company with you, Lord Peterness, but I intend to walk in Lady Catherine's flowers . . . among Lady Catherine's flowers, that is."

The carpeted floor tilted slightly beneath my feet and I was glad to grab hold of Lord Whatever's arm, as he had risen with me.

"Then you must let me accompany you, my fair acquaintance. I know my way around this garden well." He took my arm and escorted me across the room as I muttered crossly, "Well, all right, if you must."

I felt a wonderfully sweet breeze from the large glass double doors at the end of the room, but before we reached there, we were intercepted by my sort-of guardian.

The marquis, at his most urbane, charmingly but firmly dismissed Lord Peterwhat, who left after honoring me with one more predatory glance.

"But I wanted to go out into the garden," I squawked unhappily up at the marquis.

"And so you shall, infant." He led me out onto a lantern-lit stone veranda. "But not with Lesley Peterby."

We descended several steep steps onto an uneven flagstone walkway. I took in a deep breath of floral-scented air and exhaled slowly, feeling my nausea dissipate slightly, though the dizziness remained. I didn't relish the idea of Lord Dearborne telling me whom to go into the garden with.

"Is there something wrong with Lord Peterby?"

"Not if you've a taste for coupling under the shrubbery," he said bluntly.

I wasted about thirty seconds on a choking fit before grinding out, "You are the one with the taste for coupling under the bushes, not I! Of all the hateful, degrading things to insinuate . . ." I returned to choking.

"Gently now, I wasn't questioning your behavior, only Lesley's. He isn't always—let me see, how to put this delicately enough for your ears—shall we say, very gentle with women that interest him."

"You may say anything you like. Anything at all.

Pray don't bother to consider delicacy—I'm sure that it would seem dreadfully provincial for you to do so." I stopped and lifted my hands to my swimming head, shutting my eyes tightly. "Lord Dearborne, I think I'm drunk."

The hands that supported my shoulders had comforting strength.

"Here. Just behind you is a stone bench. That's right. Good heavens, you foolish child, it's nothing to cry about."

"Oh yes, it is! If Mrs. Goodbody could see me now, she'd never speak to me again. And think of my sisters, how will I ever face them?" I recited a melancholy catalogue of all the people that I could never again face. At one point I heard what sounded like a quickly repressed laugh from Lord Dearborne, but when I turned to look up suspiciously at him he was a study in straight-faced sympathy. Sniffing dolefully, I accepted his proffered handkerchief.

"Now listen, my charming little nitwit, there is no need to panic. You're not roaring drunk by any means. You drank a little too much too fast. It happens to everyone occasionally. You are just not experienced enough to know how to hide it."

"You're saying that I can't hold my liquor like a man," I exclaimed. To my helpless surprise, the chill of the night breeze was banished by the warmth of the marquis's arm, which pulled me close against his hard body. The moment lasted forever, as though some giant hand of a time clock had stopped. A concerned call from Christopher brought it screeching back into motion.

"Elizabeth, there you are. I saw her looking a little tippy inside, Uncle Nicky. Need any help?"

"Would you sit here with her for a few minutes? I'm going to slip discreetly into the kitchen and bring a cup of coffee." The marquis grinned at Christopher.

"I'm afraid that your protégée isn't yet used to unwatered wine."

Lord Dearborne melted into the darkness. Christopher took his place beside me and I lay my head rather heavily on his shoulder.

"Oh Kit, I feel so utterly wretched."

"I know exactly how it is," commiserated Christopher in a kind voice. "Too much wine can make one feel sick as a sewer dog."

"Christopher!" I said, rallying at this surprising information. "Do you mean to tell me that you've been inebriated?"

"Lord yes," he said cheerfully. "Been half seas over dozens of times. But you're barely fuzzled, Princess. Never fear, Uncle Nicky and I'll have you right as a trivet in no time."

The marquis returned and, plying me with coffee and comfort, he and Christopher slowly revived me. Lord Dearborne had somehow found my shawl inside and now draped it round my shoulders. Christopher carefully wiped my face with his handkerchief, dampened in the fountain. While I shivered at the touch of his fingers, Lord Dearborne tucked some errant strands of my coiffure back into place.

Finally, Christopher stood back to survey their repairs. "She looks good as new, eh Uncle Nicky? If they ever abolish the aristocracy in England then you and I can become ladies' maids, don't you think? How do you feel now, m'dear?"

"As good as one can who's spent the evening sacrificing on the shrine to Bacchus. I—I want to thank you. You've both been very kind . . ."

"The child's in worse shape than we suspected, Kit," said Lord Dearborne, shaking his head in mock dismay. " 'Thank you' are two words I never expected to hear from Elizabeth."

"Of all the detestable conceited . . . !" I gasped.

"There. Now you sound much more like yourself.

May I have the honor of escorting you back inside?"

Refusing the marquis's proffered arm, I brought my chin right up and marched back toward the house, now much steadier on my feet. The funny thing was that my overconsumption of wine didn't ruin my evening in the least. I was to enjoy three more hours of dancing before I tumbled into bed and slept like a baby until the outrageous hour of nine o'clock in the morning.

Chapter Eleven

I woke the next morning with my mattress swaying under me like the lurchings of a small craft on a rough ocean. With effort I opened my eyes and blurrily beheld one large violet eye, not two inches above my face.

"All right, Christa, you can stop bouncing. She's awake," instructed the eye. Groaning, I thrust my head under a goose-down pillow only to have it wrenched mercilessly from me.

"Go away, you Furies." I rubbed my tender temples. "Christa, stop bumping the bed! If you two had lived during the Spanish Inquisition, they would have given you jobs straight away, torturing Protestants."

"Listen to her, Caro. I'll tell you why she's so out-of-reason cross this morning. Last night she must have got herself glorious oiled," Christa pronounced knowledgeably while propping the pillows into an inviting heap behind me.

"Glorious oiled?" I repeated hazily. "Wherever did you learn that expression?" I sat up and leaned back against the soft mound of pillows.

"From Andy. He's Lord Dearborne's second junior footman, and full of gig too. There's hundreds of servants here. Well, perhaps not precisely hundreds but many, many." Caro came to sit on the other side of me and began to drag a hairbrush firmly through my tangled curls. "If you'd had any sense, you would have brushed this mop last night before going to sleep, then it wouldn't be so hard to comb out now. Have you forgotten that Christopher is going to take us to the Tower of London today?" Caro's eyes met mine reproachfully.

"Er, no, no. Tower of London? What fun." I tried to infuse my voice with enthusiasm. "And isn't that friend of Lady Anne's with daughters your age to come over later this afternoon? Lady Anne is very kind, isn't she?"

"Yes. And yesterday she told us that we were almost family, because Lord Dearborne is Christopher's guardian and he's ours too—so that makes us like sisters to Kit and so to Lady Anne. What do you think of that?"

"I think that's tossing genealogy out with a vengeance," I laughed. "Who was that plump little lady that you went walking with yesterday? I saw you go out with her after we came back from Lord Elgin's, when I was supposed to be resting up for the ball."

"So. You were gazing out the window instead of resting," noted Caro, shrewdly. "That was Mrs. Jameson, who is Lady Anne's dresser. Do you know that all she does is look after Lady Anne's clothes and fix her hair? And she gets paid a monstrous fat salary for it, too. Anyway, she took a liking to us and guided us on a walk through Hyde Park. It was at five o'clock, which is the most fashionable hour, and the park was simply crawling with The Elegant. Do you know that we saw Beau Brummell and Lord Petersham! And guess who was riding with them?" Caro's voice was pregnant with mystery.

"Um, let me see. Napoleon Bonaparte? No? Was it William Shakes— oww! Caro, that's quite a brisk touch on the hairbrush."

"Stop making such foolish jokes then."

"Beg pardon. Who was riding with Beau Brummell and Lord Petersham?"

"Lord Dearborne! And he reined in when he saw us

and came over to ask if Caro had recovered from her poison weed attack. What do you think of that? Everyone about was staring at us in envy, Mrs. Jameson says, because we were talking to such sought-after gentlemen. Oh, and Lord Dearborne introduced us to his companions. I almost fainted when I met Beau Brummell—he is so censorious, they say. I was sure that my bonnet was perched askew or that I had soot on my nose." Christa put one hand up to rub the tip of her nose reminiscently. "Mrs. Jameson assured us later that we looked very well, quite *à la jeune fille*. Did you know that it was Lady Anne herself that bought our clothes and sent them to Barfrestly for us? Mrs. Jameson went with her to help pick them out. Mrs. Jameson said that there was the drollest note from Mrs. Goodbody in with the marquis's letter when he asked her to choose clothes for us. Mrs. Goodbody wrote down our 'specifics' and our coloring—she said that we had 'yaller-white hare and pink eyes'!"

"Pink eyes, indeed!" I exclaimed, laughing. "How I will roast her for that one. Speaking of Mrs. Goodbody, have either of you noticed that—"

"She smells of April and here it is 'most June?" interrupted Christa. "'Course we've noticed. I think her and the marquis's valet mean to make a match of it. Roger is a capital fellow—perhaps he's almost good enough for her. Don't worry about Mrs. Goodbody's amours, Lizzie, we know that you've other things to tease you. You can depend on the offices of Caro and me to further *that* romance."

With that alarming promise, Christa took her twin by the arm, tossed the hairbrush upon my marble-topped dressing table, and left me with the dire warning that if I wasn't ready shortly they'd take me to the Tower in my nightdress.

The next days passed in a whirlwind of sociability. Lady Anne had certainly meant it when she said that she intended to cram four months of "civilized life" into two weeks. Every moment was organized into a social gathering of some kind. Balls, routs, picnics, assemblies, soirées, receptions, and card parties came head upon heel at an alarming rate. I was initiated into the mysteries of hazard and whist by Christopher, who supplemented his instruction with a rule book that advised one (rather shockingly) to sneak glimpses of the opponent's cards to improve one's chances. Lady Anne gave me some very to-the-point counsel concerning the more esoteric conduct required by the *beau monde*—such as a lady may not dance more than two times with one gentleman in a single evening and don't gallop your horse in Hyde Park. I was more than able to reassure her on that head; for all the time and patience Christopher had expended trying to teach me to ride, I was still a losing proposition in the saddle. I wouldn't have nerve enough to walk a horse in the milling, winding traffic in the park, much less gallop on one.

And whenever we were not out or getting ready to go out, we were either receiving visitors or preparing to receive them. One morning, several days later, was particularly trying. We must have had upward of thirty people pay us morning calls. After the first three coachloads, Christopher had suddenly recalled an engagement to ride in the park with his friends, basely deserting his sister and me to the rigors of polite society. Not that Lady Anne minded it. I had swiftly come to realize that she was an indefatigable socializer. Finally we bade farewell to the last of our visitors and walked arm in arm to the dining room for lunch. Lord Dearborne was already there; I had seen him return from his morning's briefing with the P.M. about a quarter hour earlier. We exchanged greetings and I tottered to a Chinese-blue flowered wing chair.

"That was harder than chopping wood! I've never in my life had to be so civil to so many people in so short a time. Lady Anne, that Sir Egbert Mysner must

be the greatest friend of yours. He's been here every
morning this week."

Lady Anne raised her eyebrows. "And I suppose
you think Lesley Peterby, Godfrey Woodman, and
half a dozen others that I can't name off the top of my
head are great friends of mine, too. Elizabeth, you
must drive your admirers demented with your dense-
ness. A good proportion of the company today was
here for the sole purpose of paying suit to you."

My mouth fell open. "You don't say?"

"Yes, I do say. Furthermore, I do wish that you'd
endeavor to rid yourself of your horrid habit of calling
me Lady Anne. I swear you make me feel sixty."

I balanced my elbows on my knees, and rested my
chin on the backs of my fists. "Do you know, Lad—, I
mean, Anne, this is the first time that I've ever had
suitors. I mean, I've had seducers before, but that's
not precisely the same, is it?" I heard a gasp from behind Lord Dearborne's linen napkin.

"Nicky, stop laughing. How can you be so callous?
Poor Elizabeth, I can see that you've been subject to
the most shameful persecution. But pray, never repeat
what you just said in company, or people will get the
oddest notions, I assure you."

Christopher strolled in, deep in thought. "Lord,
there have been some strange characters haunting the
house of late. Was that Egbert Mysner shambling out
of the front just now?"

I answered his question with alacrity. "Yes, it was.
And Anne says that he's my suitor." I spoke with par-
donable pride.

"What!" said Christopher with a grimace. "That
odious little lizard had the nerve to come here making
up to you? My God, I hope that you sent him about
his business with no further ado!"

"Well, not exactly. I mean I didn't want to be uncivil. Don't you like him, Christopher?" I inquired cautiously.

"Of course I don't like him. He's the most self-satisfied, prosy rat I ever met. When we were at Eton he was in the form ahead of me—and continuously stuffing himself with cranberry tarts that his mother sent him." This was delivered with the air of one producing information that would forever rob poor Egbert of any shred of a reputation. "You ought to have more sense than to go encouraging a detestable grab-tart like him!"

Much abashed by this severity, I could only reply meekly, "I wasn't encouraging him."

Christopher regarded me doubtfully. "I suppose that you didn't mean to, but if you sit around peeping up at him through those long eyelashes of yours, I daresay we'll never be rid of him," Christopher sighed. "And watch that you don't go playing off your tricks on Lesley Peterby. He's a deuced fine horseman, but the very devil with women. I saw you about to traipse off to the balcony with him the other night at Lady Doran's. If Uncle Nicky hadn't intercepted you, you might have found yourself in the basket."

That did it! "Oh, I would, would I?" I retorted. "I'll tell you something, Christopher. I may not be quite up to snuff in your eyes, but I am not so wet behind the ears as to be incapable of taking care of myself. There is no reason that I can't go anywhere, at any time and in any company I choose, without suffering the least ill effects." If you discount several bad scares and a lump on the head. Christopher was too polite to say it, but I could tell what he was thinking. At that moment I would cheerfully have handed over my much-praised eyelashes for a chance to prove that I was competent to handle myself from bluff to bottomland. I'll show you if it kills me, I thought recklessly. Of course, I had no idea then that it almost would.

At any rate, I was the victim of so much raillery from Christopher and the twins about my "admirers" that I began hiding in the closet whenever a fresh bouquet of flowers arrived. Caro delighted in thinking up horrible nicknames for every unmarried male under the age of sixty who entered the house. Sir Mysner became "Sir Egbert Eggplant," Lord Peterby was dubbed "Lord Lesley the Loose," and poor Godfrey Woodman was christened "the Chinless Wonder."

After that, probably with the intention of diluting the influence of Egbert Mysner and Godfrey Woodman, Christopher spared no pains to introduce me to his own circle of friends. They formed a cheerful, playfully gallant court; they were always ready to crowd around me at parties, fetching me countless pieces of cake and oceans of lemonade; they argued good-naturedly over the "privilege" of standing up with me; and they took me up beside them at the park, to ride in their dashing high-perch phaetons. However much they might shine in a ballroom though, Christopher and his friends had their hearts in the boxing ring, the hunting fields, and the race-tracks—the boys were sports-mad.

Lord Dearborne, I discovered, moved in quite a different set. His was the world of influence and prestige. His friends numbered among the most celebrated names in England, and his title opened all doors. He was gone from Lorne House often, spending much of his time with the Prince Regent, who doted on his presence both at work and at play. There were times when Lord Dearborne attended the same social functions as we did, though he often came or left with a party of his own. Even when we were home for dinner, which was not often, we rarely saw him—he usually dined out.

When he was around, I enjoyed his ironic view of his surroundings. I would be at a party, someone would make a preposterous remark, and I would find myself wishing for the marquis's acid tongue and quick comeback. Now and then I found myself gazing through the crowd for him when I entered some social function.

Christopher told me that Lord Dearborne intended to attend the Ingrams' garden ball; I had been there for at least an hour and hadn't seen him though, perhaps because there was such a great crush of guests. Lord Ingram's House (for it's much too grand to be called a mere house) is situated on the outskirts of London, in an area still quite rural. The Ingrams' extensive gardens are cut by well-kept terraces and charming promenades that were now strung with Japanese lanterns, in such proliferation that only the more inebriated guests stood in any danger of bumping into any of the pseudo-Roman statues or oversized urns that Lady Ingram thought (mistakenly, in my opinion) added refinement to her grounds.

I had been conscientiously executing a country dance with one of Lady Anne's elderly great-uncles when it came time for the musicians to take their break. My octogenarian gallant escorted me back to the quiet moon-kissed corner in the garden where Lady Anne was chatting with two formidable matrons who patronized me briefly before returning to their interrupted coze. It was some time now since the last of the sun's rays had vanished, and a testy little breeze came to lick at my bare arms and shoulders. Lady Anne, seated next to me on the wrought-iron settee, must have noticed me shiver, for she gave me a quick hug and said:

"Why, I believe that you're chilly, aren't you? One doesn't notice the wind when one is dancing, but as soon as one sits down, it creeps up. Never mind, my dear, I'll run up to the cloakroom and fetch your shawl."

"No, no! I will get it myself, there's not the least need for you to go," I told her hastily, terrified by the prospect of being left to converse with Lady Anne's haughty friends. I would almost rather chat with the executioner's axe as these autocratic damsels. "I can find my way about easily. The gardens are laid out so logically and I'll be back in a flash." One of the ladies lifted her eyebrows in well-bred surprise, which informed me that "in a flash," a tidbit gleaned from Christopher's vocabulary, was a sadly vulgar phrase. The raised eyebrows and an absentminded pat from Lady Anne sped me on my way.

Walking down a white, crushed-rock path through the beautiful flower beds, I found myself with a delightfully free feeling of being let out of lessons. At the end of a path to my left I spied a row of foxgloves nodding invitingly. Why not? What danger could possibly befall me walking alone in the Ingrams' garden? I was soon to find out.

At the curve of the walk was a modern statue of Cupid, one of those chubby cherub types. It's terrible what sculptors have done to the dangerous Greek god of love. Out of impulse I placed a kiss on his plump lips, and pulled a pout back at him. At the other side of the small pathway was a red-brick wall and growing off into the darkness was a line of delicate yellow daffodils. Their coloring seemed to almost match the gown I was wearing and I held out my hem to a petal to compare the two more closely. A melody wafting through the trees informed me that the musicians had resumed their playing. Humming the tune, I swayed from side to side with the music, and curtseyed to the honey locust tree, saying aloud, "Won't you share this dance with me?"

"I would be delighted!" said a deep male voice from the shadow of the tree. I screamed. A form stepped out of the shadow, and it was a moment before I recognized Lord Lesley Peterby.

"Thank heavens it's you," I said, gasping with relief. "You gave me such a fright. Why didn't you declare yourself immediately when I entered this alcove?"

"I would have missed a charming little spectacle." The moon glinted from his wavy dark hair which was falling over one eye in its usual fashion. His eyes traced the neckline of my gown. He came over to stand too close to me, and I backed away from him. The alcove suddenly became very dark and isolated, the music drifting down from the night sky an ethereal orchestra from the dark side of the moon.

"Well, Lady Anne will be expecting me," I said with false brightness. Peterby stepped into the path. I attempted to sidestep him, and with a neat, imperceptible movement on his part, I walked right into his arms.

"You give your kisses freely to a stone Cupid," he purred dangerously. "Why not bestow them where they will be appreciated?"

I disentangled myself and took three rapid steps back. "Lord Peterby, let me correct your evident misapprehension that I came to this alcove for any purpose other than to sniff the flowers and be by myself. Will you kindly step back from the path and allow me to be on my way?"

Now, according to every book I had ever read, that line should have crushed him into submission. Unfortunately, it appeared that Lord Peterby had not read the same books. He walked toward me, I continued to back away, until suddenly—to my dismay—I felt the roughness of the brick wall through the back of my gown. He placed a hand on either side of me, flat on the wall.

"Oh yes, I will let you be on your way, but not just yet, my angel."

"I am not interested in whatever you have in mind," I said tartly. "If you wish to accompany me back to the dance, that is fine. If not, allow me to pass."

His eyes narrowed. "What's the matter? Are you afraid of a real man? Or do you prefer the fumblings of inexpert schoolboys?"

"I don't prefer anyone's fumbling advances right now. If you had any decency, you would desist from your unwelcome attentions."

"By God, when some lightskirt thinks she can lecture me about decency . . . Don't put on a load of innocent airs for me, my beautiful Cyprian. I know Kit Warrington has you in keeping."

I was stunned. "What do you mean, 'in keeping'?" I asked him weakly, hoping I had misunderstood.

He laughed harshly. "Come now, Christopher couldn't be that bad a lover for all his tender years. Especially if that little ballet dancer he supported last year is any indication. She seemed happy with the arrangement."

And then, because I couldn't think of anything mean enough to say back, out of sheer shaking temper I hit him. My novel-reading sisters would have been so pleased to see me imitate the behavior of their favorite heroines, and for a split-second I felt a vaguely surprised pride in myself—I didn't know that I had it in me. My satisfaction lived less than a heartbeat though, dying with one look at Lord Peterby's face. His arm slid down the wall and he grabbed me with iron fingers.

"God damn you, you little slut," he snarled. "I'll break you in half if you try that again."

Tears of rage sprang into my eyes. "Go ahead. I'd rather endure a beating than put up with your hateful advances. If I were a man you wouldn't dare to stand here telling despicable lies about Christopher."

"By God, if you were a man . . . You'd better spend your time learning to be a woman first if you intend to keep Christopher interested. Let me give you a lesson in womanhood." His merciless hands dragged me behind him through the nearby bushes. My heart jumped to my throat, blocking a scream as I realized the peril of my situation. I gathered my breath for another attempt, only to feel Peterby's hands close tightly over my lips.

"Be silent," he growled. We came to a rectangle of light that I recognized as a window in the yellow stone gatehouse that our carriage had passed on the way into Ingram Park.

"Now look in the window and see how a real woman behaves."

Shocked, apprehensive, I did as he commanded. Inside stood Lady Catherine and Lord Dearborne, locked in a torrid embrace. A large ruby winked malevolently on the marquis's hand as he caressed Lady Catherine's bare shoulder. Their relationship was no secret to me, but there was something very powerful about observing it with my own eyes. I turned to look at Peterby, who was leaning against the building, his arms crossed casually in front of him.

"If you aspire to the demimonde, then take a lesson from London's leading strumpet. Lady Cat knows all the tricks." He took my chin roughly between his fingers. "When you decide you've had enough of the adolescent set, look me up. I'll be very generous." He turned on his heel and left me alone and shivering.

Luckily, Christopher and Anne interpreted my stony silence on the way home from the ball as exhaustion. They tactfully suggested that we all retire immediately upon arrival at Lorne House. I lay sleepless in bed listening to the sounds of the great house quieting down for the night. I tossed restlessly for some time before relighting my candle and looking about for something readable. Unfortunately, I had no promising volume at hand and began to think wistfully of Lord Dearborne's well-stocked library downstairs. Crawling out of bed, I hunted through my Hepplewhite tallboy for a warm dressing gown, as my nightdress was one wispy layer of white chiffon.

The house was in absolute slumber as I slipped

down the stairs. On entering the library, I was delighted to find that someone had left a fire burning in the polished steel grate; it had been a chilly evening.

I sat primly on the Queen Anne damask sofa and opened a leather-bound book of Shakespearean sonnets. The words blurred before my eyes and transformed themselves into visions of Sir Lesley boiling in a cauldron of bubbling oil. I relaxed and let my mind flow aimlessly upon that pleasant channel. Before the fire lay a beautiful pelt of an enormous white bear that Christopher had informed me was a gift to Lord Dearborne from a Russian diplomat. I tiptoed over and rubbed my bare toes in the soft fur. I was getting tired now, especially since having my imaginary revenge on Lord Peterby. But I had no particular desire to leave this cozy room and slide between my cold sheets. I slipped out of my heavy dressing gown to lay down on the shaggy bearskin, my loose hair spilling comfortably around me. After all, there was very little chance of anyone coming here at this time of the night, and anyway, if anyone did come, I could hear their footsteps in the corridor and easily hop up and pull on my dressing gown. That was my last thought before I fell asleep.

Sometime later I felt strong arms encircle my shoulders, arms that had an endearingly comfortable familiarity about them. I snuggled closer into them and vaguely heard a low chuckle. I had a sensation of being lifted. Eventually I was aware that the cradling arms had left and I made a whimpered protest. "Time to sleep," whispered a voice. When I awoke the next morning I was sure that it had been a dream, except I had gone to sleep on the library floor. Why did I wake up in my own bed?

Chapter Twelve

At breakfast the next morning I astonished Christopher with a long, impassioned diatribe against the blind prejudice and injustice of conventions that decreed women ineligible to fight in duels. And because men *could* fight in duels was precisely the reason that I didn't tell Christopher the things Lesley Peterby had said to me in the Ingrams' garden. You never know but what Kit might take it in his head to do if he thought my honor had been questioned. Questioned? That adder Peterby had gone further than questioning! My memory dwelt fondly on the slap I had dealt him and I smiled privately at my own audacity.

I looked at Kit across the breakfast table, where he sat in his patterned dressing gown with a Belcher scarf knotted loosely around his neck. He was gazing gloomily at the front page of the newspaper and taking small sips from a steaming coffee cup. I wondered what he would say if I asked him if he'd had a ballet dancer as a mistress last year. Probably spill his coffee, drop his newspaper and stammer, "Well, really," for half an hour. My favorite playmate had some pretty fancy toys. Still, it was none of my business to puff up like a Puritan about it.

Briefly, too, I considered sending a note to Lord Peterby telling him that if he ever decided to jump off a cliff, I, for one, wouldn't die of heartbreak. I abandoned the idea. I could imagine the reaction of the marquis's starchy underfootman if I asked him to deliver a note to Lord Peterby for me.

I knew, somewhere in my heart of hearts, that the most painful shock of last evening had been the sight of Lady Catherine in Lord Dearborne's arms. You have to be an awfully rigid moralist to deprecate a man kissing his inamorata, so I was forced to admit it was not the moral aspect of the sight that had left me with such a queasy feeling in my stomach. There was one logical explanation, but it was just too unpalatable. I wasn't jealous, I couldn't be, it was impossible, absurd. I forced myself to stop thinking about it but I was shaken, nonetheless.

After breakfast, Lady Anne took my sisters and me on a shopping expedition to New Bond Street. I was glad for the chance to go. I wanted to buy a pair of silk stockings for my friend Janey Coleman.

I suppose someone could have slipped the note into my reticule anytime that morning, in any of the crowded shops or busy sidewalks. Anyway, it was there when I got home. On one side of the note was a sentimental ballad, the kind ragged children sell for ha'pennies. But on the other, in a light, backhand scrawl: "Do you want to learn more about Henri's death? Tell no one about this note and come alone to the Cuckold's Comfort gin shoppe at the hour of ten tonight! There is Danger, do not Fail." There was an address at the bottom of the page, presumably that of the "gin shoppe," and it was signed, simply, *Bon Chance*. Good luck?

I thought for a moment of Pandora's box, but admitted I was more influenced by the adventures of Jason and the Argonauts. Could I turn down a teaser like "there is danger"? Not while there is a thimble of spirit left in me. I spent the rest of the day planning my outing.

To get out of the house unnoticed, I devised a master plan of great cunning and verve—wait until no one is looking and sneak out! Rope ladders are strictly for elopements.

The success of the plan hinged upon being able to stay home from the theater that night. As Christopher and Anne were engaged to go with a large group of friends, they could scarcely cancel the entire party to stay home with me if I pleaded ill. I underestimated them. When I announced that I wanted to stay home to nurse a sick headache, they showed such alarming solicitude that if I ever really do get a headache, I'm certainly never going to tell them! I fought off attempts to summon physicians, to burn feathers under my nose, and a dosing with a potion that Lady Anne assured me her mother had sworn by. I finally took the potion to satisfy her and let me tell you that I can see why her mother swore by it. It made me want to swear at it.

Dear Mrs. Goodbody rescued me by chasing everyone out of my room, saying that I was overtired and would do very well if I could have some time to rest. She told Christopher and Anne that they would only distress me if they stayed home too. She didn't know how right she was. If she knew that she was assisting me in a gambol around London at night she would have had a fit.

I chose my attire for the evening with more care than I had expended on the most fashionable gatherings. Deciding that it was best to look as inconspicuous as possible, I donned a battered gray poplin gown of pre–Lord Dearborne days, completing the ensemble with a plain straw bonnet. Whispering a quick prayer, I sneaked down the smooth marble staircase, rather guiltily, with a petition to Vesta, protector of virgins.

Once out in the street it was fairly simple to find a hackney coach to convey me to the address on the note. The jarvey shook his head when he saw the address. He followed the head-shake with a long lecture

on the evils of gin, going on at such length that I
feared I would never reach my destination. Of all the
hacks in London, I would have to get one driven by a
Methodist.

I am glad this Methodist knew the way because I
would never have found it on my own. I stepped
down in front of the Cuckold's Comfort a little early,
and cast about for a while, killing time. It was the
first time I had really been immersed in the streets of
London, and I found it fascinating. I was not frightened, but instead felt comforted by the bustle and
clamor of the crowd, which appeared to be going at
full bore even though it was nearly ten o'clock. I
stopped for a few minutes to watch a Punch-and-Judy
show, but gave up as it was impossible to follow the
action over the full-throated yelling of the throng. Ballad singers were crooning loudly and melodiously;
political pamphleteers were hawking their wares from
street corners and arguing venomously among themselves and with passersby. All sorts of vendors were
selling all sorts of things—cat's-meat, cheese, tissue-
paper flowers—to what seemed to me a largely indifferent crowd intent on brushing past each other in the
greatest hurry to be somewhere else. I was somewhat
shocked at the number of children on the scene,
scampering through the hustle and bustle playing tag,
jump-the-knacker, and threepenny hop. This at an
hour when my sisters were safe and sound in their
beds. I saw one group of naughty boys harassing the
poor lamplighter, who was doing his best to keep the
scene illuminated. Every time he would nearly have
the flame lit on the corner, one of the boys would run
up behind and yank his coattails hard enough to
throw him off balance; he would lose the flame and
have to start over again.

I left this not unfriendly scene with some regrets, to
make my way into the Cuckold's Comfort. The powerful, acrid smell and smoke of the interior set me at

odds for a moment as I peered about. The place was very crowded, shoulder to threadbare shoulder, and everyone was shouting at once, just like on the street outside. The furnishings consisted of long, rough-hewn wooden tables. I peered into the rough, grimy faces of the men and women near to me and received nothing back but a few uncomfortably appraising stares.

It suddenly occurred to me that I didn't have the slightest idea whom I was looking for. The note had been unspecific on this point. I mentally floundered, forcing down a wave of nausea. I suppose I had envisioned a secluded, unfrequented little club, not this raw pandemonium. There was nothing to do but wait for a time and perhaps my correspondent would seek me out. I stood by the door in what I hoped was a conspicuous place. It proved to be too conspicuous. A group of three ragged-looking, odoriferous men soon materialized out of the crowd to stand near to me, leering and talking in low, dirty voices. I made a sign with my fingers at them, something Christopher had taught me, and they took their attentions elsewhere. I made a mental note to learn from Christopher the exact meaning of that handy sign.

The harassment was undeniably making me nervous, so I decided to sit down. Earlier, I had noticed a gabby old woman sitting in a corner who grabbed the ear of anyone who went by and talked to them unintelligibly and interminably. As a consequence, she was eventually left quite alone. I decided it would go easier for me if it looked like I was with someone; this woman was the likeliest candidate. Before joining her, I laid a coin down on the rough bar like I had seen others doing, and the bartender, after some long, jostled moments, responded by desultorily sliding a flagon of gin down to me.

"Little young for the old Blue Ruin, eh miss?" he

said. It was obvious that he would have sold the gin to a babe in arms.

"I appreciate your concern," I said tartly. I couldn't tell if he heard me or not. I picked up the flagon and made my way to the old woman. Sitting down next to her, I copied the slouch of the people around me and unobtrusively let fall some strands of hair from my too-neat coiffure. To pass the time, I began listening with half an ear to my companion, scanning the crowd for my contact all the while.

"To think that I, the illegitimate daughter of Marie Antoinette, would be reduced to selling fish in the market. And damn good fish they are too," she was saying. "Fish is good for a pretty young lady like yourself, ain't that right? Ain't that right, I say?" I nodded vigorously. "Ye're a young woman of sense to treat me so politely. Even though I sell fish in the market I am the illegitimate daughter of Marie Antoinette. I will remember you and when I am restored to the throne of France I will reward you. You can be a lady-in-waiting."

The appointment struck me as being a mixed blessing. Lady-in-waiting to a gin-swilling old fishmonger sitting on the throne of France. I observed the crowd. In some ways it was not very different from those at some of the posh parties I had been to of late. They shouted the toast "bung-ho" with the same amount of rough, brawling energy that the men of my acquaintance would shout "to our gracious monarch," or some such patriotic phrase. They, too, were arguing about politics, though with a slight difference in viewpoint. But their opinions seemed to me just as valid. Everyone argues the same under the influence of hard liquor, regardless of social class. I reflected on how well-rounded this experience was going to make me; I had now observed all facets of English society firsthand, low-life taverns to high society balls.

As time went on, though, my reflections grew more dismal. No mysterious informant appeared and I was beginning to wonder if anyone would show up at all. I knew I had been here at least an hour, for it seemed far longer. Perhaps the writer of the note was unable to keep the rendezvous. Perhaps he hadn't been able to get me a message telling me not to come. Perhaps . . . but my head was aching so from the smoke and the noise that I didn't feel able to sort it out now. I had better just get home before anyone noticed that I was missing.

Having made the decision to leave, I discovered I couldn't wait to get out of the place. I stood up abruptly, and the old woman spilled her flagon of gin down the front of my dress, muttering a drunken apology as she did so. I hastily began to make my way through the crowd.

"Oh, I'm s' sorry, miss, please come back," wailed the old woman. "I am the illegitimate daughter of Marie Antoinette."

Two more steps and I would be out the door. The night air felt good in my lungs. I inhaled it deeply and looked about for a hackney. There were none in sight. Furthermore, the vendors had disappeared and the crowd had thinned out alarmingly. I suppressed an uneasy feeling and decided that my best course would be to walk in the direction the hackney had come and I would eventually run into a main thoroughfare. So I embarked, using as firm a footstep as I could muster. It was best not to look irresolute to anyone who might be observing me. There were a few groups of men wandering about, some of them listing sharply, and before I walked very far, I nearly tripped over what appeared to be a pile of old clothes in the dimly lit street. The pile of old clothes grunted like a sow in the barnyard, and turned out to have human form.

"Oh, excuse me," I said, but the old wreck only looked at me with stark terror in its eyes and shambled down the street, caroming occasionally off a lamppost.

I walked on, hoping my thoroughfare was around
the next bend. The bend turned out to be a twist,
then a jog, and I began to realize it was impossible to
walk directly to anything in this section of London. I
paused for a moment to ascertain my bearings, but
walked on when I noticed a man in a doorway to my
left flipping a dagger over and over in his hand, the
blade glinting in the light from the lamp on the corner. There seemed to be another tavern up ahead; I
could ask for directions there; but when I reached it,
the people sitting on the steps in front formed a wall
with their eyes and I passed quickly without looking
at them. It was getting very dark now. A rat skittered
in front of me and I heard dripping water. It was a
maze. I tried to think clearly. I couldn't bear to go
back to the Cuckold's Comfort and would probably
never find my way anyway; perhaps I should change
direction.

Off to my left was an alley, running downhill; I
peered into it for signs of habitation. Perhaps that
would do. I took off down it, faltering now in spite of
myself as it made another sharp turn. It was so dark
now I could see almost nothing. A feminine voice
spoke in my ear:

"It's a little lost lamb strayed from the flock. Shall
we help it find the way, girls?"

Maybe there were decent people in this horrible
place after all, I thought to myself.

"Where are you?" I said.

"Where are we? Where are you?" echoed another
voice.

"We are over here," said a third female voice. A
hand grabbed my arm and yanked me so violently
into what was probably a doorway that my teeth
snapped.

"Let me go," I begged, unable to scream.

"Don't be loud, little one, we are only going to help
you find your way."

"It would be easier to travel without this," said a woman's voice. I felt my reticule being torn from my hands.

"And this bonnet; no need for that on a lovely night like this one." It was gone. Then to my horror, I felt my gown being ripped up the back and I was standing in my shift. Rough hands frisked me up and down.

"An honest little one," said a voice. "No money hidden."

"Now you can find your way," said one of my tormentors. I was pushed out of the doorway with such force that I fell down hard on my knees. I was too frightened to sob, too frightened to move.

"Run away, little lamb. London is out there waiting for you," said the voice behind me now, and there was a chorus of wicked cackles.

Oh my God, I thought to myself, and I began to make my way down the alley, the pain from my gashed knees making me cry out. I felt the blood running down my leg. I was away from them now and I didn't care what happened to me. I leaned against a cool, mossy wall and realized that I was shaking convulsively.

"Do ye have a sixpence for a poor old beggar?" Someone was begging me for money. Through my haze of agitation I saw a wizened panhandler standing directly in front of me.

"Sorry," I said. "I haven't a farthing." The beggar reached out a hand and pinched my arm.

"Haven't a farthing," he mimicked in a whining falsetto. "Then ye have a wee kiss for a lonely old man."

"I have no such thing." I was dimly aware of a loud shouting and to-do now, echoing eerily from down the alley.

"Ye haven't a kiss for me, eh? Let me tell ye somet'ing, miss. Them's the peep-of-the-day boys acomin', and they'll be wantin' more than a kiss." He gave me a horrid wink. The shouting was very near. "May as

well give me the kiss willingly now because when
they are through wi' the likes of you, you won't be
wantin' to kiss nobody."

"Go away," I screamed, but he was already gone.
Peep-of-the-day boys? I cringed against the wall and
tried to make myself invisible. A group of six or seven
men were coming around the corner, making enough
hue and cry for twenty. I saw a gin bottle go flying
through the air to fragment itself on the pavement.

"Look over there, boys. Something for George to
do." I had been spotted. I pressed against the wall
and hoped that George, whoever he was, was a gentleman. As they came closer I noticed the aristocratic
cut of their clothes, but something about their de-
meanor made me wish I was elsewhere. I was now
close to being surrounded, and a man who appeared
to be crippled in one leg made his way toward me
ahead of the others. In a daze of terror I caught a
glimpse of a curly brown head and a reek of gin as he
pressed me against the wall. A scream involuntarily
forced its way out of my throat as I felt fumbling
hands pushing my shift up from my thighs. "Be good
to Childe Harold, little slut."

"The devil . . . Leave her alone, Gordon. I know
her!" A strangely familiar voice cut through the group.
"I said leave her," and the attacker was gone, skidding
on his face down the side of the wall. That voice. In
the garden. Lesley Peterby.

"You gents go on without me, I'll see to this one," he
said.

"We know you will," they chorused, and I was alone
with him.

His eyes traveled slowly up my quivering frame,
taking in every detail of my miserable condition. He
shook his head slowly.

"I don't know what you're doing here and I don't
want to know." He pulled off his light cape and I felt
it flow about my shoulders.

When he spoke again, it was an impatient growl. "Follow me and I'll take you home."

He started down the alley with a long stride and I followed him, stumbling. Once he stopped to curse, telling me to hurry or be left to the rats. One filthy, narrow street slid into another. Finally, miraculously, the street widened enough to permit traffic and I heard Lord Peterby hail an empty hackney coach. I tried to climb into the coach but the step was so high that my aching knees wouldn't respond. Peterby swore again, then lifted me bodily into the dark, smelly interior. He gave the direction of Lorne House to the jarvey and climbed in beside me, slamming the door with unnecessary vigor.

I made an effort to pull myself together. "I'm very much obliged to you . . ." I stopped, shocked by the whimpering quality of my voice.

"Then for God's sake, don't cry. I have a strong distaste for whining women." Lesley slumped into the corner with his hands crossed behind his neck, surveying me with unfriendly dispassion. "Jesus, you look like someone's set the dogs on you. And you reek of gin. Nicky is likely to put a bullet through me and ask questions later if I walk in the door with you in this condition."

I had hoped somehow to be able to sneak into the house unnoticed; it would be impossible though, because all the doors would be locked, and I was keyless. I shuddered, imagining the scene that would meet my arrival if I waltzed into the house at midnight with Lord Lesley in tow and clad only in a torn shift.

I said miserably, "Perhaps you should have left me back there in the gutter. Considering the humor you were in last night I am surprised that you didn't."

"Ah, last night." My rescuer pulled a small metal comb out of his pocket and flipped it carelessly across the seat to me. "Here, at least comb your hair. Last night I was operating under the misapprehension that you were Warrington's *chère amie*. Lady Cat threw that tidbit my way, the stupid jade. Today I found out, it doesn't matter to you how, that you're not one of the ladybirds that Christopher flies with."

"Lady Catherine!" I ejaculated, my mind fastening on this piece of information. "Why on earth would she tell you something like that?"

"Probably, my innocent, because she hoped that it would give me the incentive to . . . shall we say, force my attentions on you." His face hardened. "I make love to please myself, not to further any of Cat's schemes."

It seemed incredible that Lady Catherine could feel any malice toward me. "But why would she want to harm me? I haven't met her above three times in all my life."

"She's obviously seen you enough to consider you competition for your cold-blooded guardian. The fool is living under the illusion that she'll be able to entice Dearborne into marrying her." He smiled unpleasantly. "Far from showing any inclination to declare himself, Nicholas has become rapidly bored and makes no attempt to hide it."

"He didn't look bored last night in the Ingrams' gatehouse," I said doubtfully.

Lord Lesley shrugged. "That was nothing. One amuses oneself," he replied cynically. I returned the comb to him, too tired to make any further effort with my hair, which fell in a heavy snarling mass down my shoulders.

"But how could I be a threat to Lady Catherine?" I wondered out loud.

"You're not. Dearborne isn't libertine enough to take an innnocent girl under his protection as his fancypiece, nor is he going to marry a country nobody with only her beauty to recommend her. Cat needs somewhere to put the blame for her failure. She could hardly admit that there was a deficiency in her charms."

I felt as though I were smothering in the clinging folds of my borrowed cape, which I had pulled closely about me for modesty's sake. It was impossible to digest Peterby's remarks, so I leaned my face against the greasy window and stared disconsolately out at the dark cityscape. If only, by some miracle, I could manage to sneak into Lorne House without being observed.

Well, miracles will occur only at capricious intervals. I had already had all the luck that I was going to that night, though you would think I deserved some more after what I had been through.

When we reached Lorne House, Lord Lesley dragged the hood of his cape roughly over my hair, telling me it was better to try to prevent me from being recognized. He then hauled me unceremoniously from the hack and rapped sharply on the imposing doorway. The door was opened almost immediately by Roger, Lord Dearborne's valet. Lesley demanded the marquis and Roger led us to the library with a carefully wooden countenance. I was aware of Lord Dearborne but kept my eyes riveted to the floor. Lord Peterby's voice came harshly:

"Before you try to cut out my liver, you might as well know that I'm not the one who's responsible for her present condition. I want five minutes to explain how I found her. After that you can call me out if you still want to."

"As you wish," Lord Dearborne sounded cool, even slightly bored. "Miss Cordell, why don't you sit down? I'll return to wait on you in a moment."

I walked stiffly over to the blue damask sofa, taking meticulous care to avoid glimpsing myself in the reflecting panes of the bay windows. Once seated in the luxurious splendor of the library, I felt even more bedraggled and downtrodden. Wishing I had made more assiduous use of Lesley's comb, I made a few ineffectual attempts to untangle the silky knots with my shaking fingers. Elizabeth Cordell, early Christian martyr, waiting for the arrival of the lion.

When the lion returned to the room, he walked to the ornate Oriental cabinet and poured brandy from its crystal decanter into an elaborate piece of stemware. He placed the goblet on the shining kidney-shaped table next to me and motioned for me to drink. When I lifted the glass to my lips, the scent of the brandy brought back the memory of cheap gin fumes. I set the glass down rather quickly.

"Oh no, my pet, you're going to drink that." Lord Dearborne set the goblet back into my hands. "It's obvious that you are on the verge of vapors. You might find my methods of dealing with hysterical women not to your liking." The words were spoken with an almost cordial urbanity, but I wasn't fool enough to miss the underlying threat. I choked down several swallows of the burning liquid, which brought tears to my eyes in stinging waves.

"What an obedient girl," commented the marquis sarcastically. I could see that this interview was going to be a new low in an already hellish night. "You were limping when you came in. I take it that you've injured yourself? Show me." I pulled back the cape dumbly to expose badly scraped knees.

"Heartrending," said Lord Dearborne in a voice totally devoid of sympathy. He took my chin between his long fingers and turned my face up to look at him. "Lesley tells me that he found you clad only in your shift. Were you hurt in any other way? No, don't jerk your head away. I want an answer."

"No," I snapped, goaded. "I wasn't hurt in any other way, as you so delicately phrase it. But I have been harassed, insulted, robbed, and humiliated in every imaginable manner tonight, on top of getting lost in a horrible jungle of a place that I thought I would never get out of." I rose with what dignity I could muster. "Will that be all, Milord? Because I should very much like to retire." And cry in peace.

"Sit down." His voice cracked like a whip and I sat back down hastily. I watched nervously as he went back to the cabinet to bring out a clean linen napkin and a container of spring water. "Perhaps you'll be so indulgent as to relate the tale of your adventure?" he said, coolly sardonic, and began gently to clean the muck off my knees. The last thing I was in the mood for was a verbal re-enactment of my harrowing experiences, but I could see that Lord Dearborne was determined to drag it all out of me. I might as well get it over with. I told him everything, starting from the time I left the Cuckold's Comfort. I was careful to make no mention of what I was doing there in the first place. The note had been explicit that I should tell no one, and I felt myself bound by it. It had said "there is danger." I had no intention of letting my loose tongue endanger anyone. After tonight danger had a whole new meaning to me.

When I finished my story, I saw that if I had expected to receive any sympathy from Lord Dearborne, I might well have spared my breath. He merely remarked callously:

"Amazing. You've been trotting around in an area of London which no decent woman can enter, even during the day, and a little rough treatment is all that you have to show for it. And if what you've just described includes every 'imaginable humiliation,' then your imagination must be remarkably restrained. Naturally you are aware that you've neglected to mention what you were doing in that part of the city at night alone when the household believes you to be sleeping safely in your bed? I trust you intend to enlighten me?"

If I could have thought of an acceptable lie, I would have told it. What plausible reason could I have

for making a solo visit to the Cuckold's Comfort? I
replied weakly:

"I can't tell you."

"You went there to meet someone, didn't you? Don't
bother to shake your head at me—someone must have
told you how to get there. Who are you protecting? Is
it a lover," he sneered, "or a traitor?"

I think I must have gasped because the marquis
shoved the brandy glass into my hand again—
apparently under the misapprehension that I was beginning to sob. I swallowed the contents of the glass—
I would rather have expired on the spot than let Lord
Dearborne see me cry. He took the glass from my
hand and set it on the side table, then turned to regard me searchingly.

"You know, my little doe, I'm not sure whether you
are a very clever woman or only a pathetic dupe. I
will assume, for charity's sake, that you don't realize
what you're getting yourself into. This won't be the
first time that one of my household has been approached by enemy agents hoping for an inside contact. There are two things that you should know.
First, these are dangerous men who will not hesitate
to get rid of you as soon as you cease to be of use, no
matter what they may tell you now. Witness the fate
of Henri, the cook, the strange accidental death you
have been so interested in."

"Henri? Then he didn't die falling from the roof?
He was murdered?" I roused slightly from my state of
stunned misery.

"Henri was strangled with a dishcloth and tossed
from the roof. A pretty set of fellows you are in with."

"I'm not in with anybody," I objected.

"Secondly," he continued, ignoring my feeble protest, "if you are caught intriguing with the French
government, there is nothing I could do to protect you
from a traitor's fate."

A searing pain began to course through my breast.

"That is the most insensitive, unfeeling accusation I have ever had to endure in my life!" I choked out. I was proven wrong almost immediately.

"I'm making a terrible misjudgment of you, am I? You're wandering around in the stews of London in the dark of night and you won't tell me who you are meeting or why? What kind of lover would ask to meet you in such a place? Even the likes of Peterby can call on you here. I would advise you to examine your associates. I am beginning to think you are a very good actress, Miss Cordell. It takes a definite toughness, not immediately visible in your character, to tryst with somebody in the stews of London."

I was now goaded beyond discretion. "I don't care what you think, Lord Dearborne. You may think me wanton or a traitor, it matters not a whit to me, it does not concern me in the slightest. It is obvious that people in this contemptible town believe what they wish to believe, and if you believe me to be those things, then it comes from your own purposes and desires and not my actions."

My hands were clenched into fists beneath the cloak which rippled from contact with my trembling shoulders. I felt ill. And too angry now to waste energy on tears, though my eyes stupidly persisted in shedding them. I wiped a couple of the obnoxious intruders away with the back of my hand, staring defiantly at Lord Dearborne. Some of the freezing harshness left his face; it was replaced by something more rational, though speculative. He lifted his hands to rest lightly on my shoulders and when he spoke, his voice was gentle.

"My only purpose and desire is to help you. Trust me, Elizabeth. Tell me what kind of trouble you are in."

He made it very tempting. There was a part of me that cried out to clear myself, to deny those bitter accusations. Yet there was another part of me that stubbornly refused to dignify insults with justifications. The hurt was too fresh. If he had so little faith in me, then what was the point of defending myself? I had been tried, judged, and sentenced without a fair trial— I might as well let him hang me, too.

"Would you oblige me by releasing my shoulders," I said. "Immediately!"

"Very well." I was released so abruptly that I almost fell. I turned to walk stiffly to the door, but before I reached it a thought occurred to me.

"If Mrs. Goodbody and my sisters haven't found out that I was out of the house tonight, could you please not mention it? It . . . would be pointless to distress them, don't you think?"

He countered my nervous look with one of uncomfortable irony. "Quite pointless. Your affairs are your own business."

Chapter Thirteen

Last night when I petitioned Vesta, the Roman protector of virgins, I should have remembered that Vesta is also the goddess who punishes virgins. I woke up the next morning with scabbed knees, damaged pride, and the problem of explaining to Mrs. Goodbody the loss of a gown, reticule, and bonnet, all in one swoop. Once you begin lying you have to lie repeatedly to protect the original lie—it's an exhausting business. I reflected bitterly on the simplicity of life before Lord Dearborne had inherited Barfrestly. Ironically, he was accusing me of behavior I hadn't even known about until I had met him and his set, and had been dragged into fashionable London. Prior to that time my behavior had been blameless by many standards; I had never been accused of anything more serious than allowing the tea to boil over.

Nor had I encountered the plotting of tony beauties. If Peterby was to be believed, my Cinderella had the heart of a wicked stepmother. How humiliating it was that I could be so easily cozened into trusting someone. Take one cup of flattery, mix lightly with guile, season with a pinch of feigned deference—oh! and baste with wine; there you have a foolproof recipe for deluding Elizabeth Cordell. What an April fool I must have appeared to Lady Catherine, pouring out my secrets to her while she was thinking of ways to stick in the needle. I had to admit that she had chosen quite a subtle scheme. Instead of trying to destroy my reputation with society in general, she had simply told one potent little lie about me to Lord Peterby and depended on him to do the rest. Men don't seduce pure young woman of gentle birth, but if I was already Christopher's mistress, I became fair game as far as a rake like Lesley Peterby was concerned.

I could have told Lady Catherine that Lord Dearborne, far from admiring me, was convinced that I was either a spy or a Jezebel (probably both!). Lady Catherine ought to conserve her energies for scheming against the "Snow Queen" or whomever.

All women should be as good as Mrs. Goodbody, bless her soul. What can I tell her about my gown? Before bed last night I had taken care to ask Roger not to mention my unconventional outing. He had simply agreed that no useful purpose could be served by telling anyone of it; he neither badgered me nor quizzed me about the incident. Roger is, as Mrs. Goodbody says, a real gentleman.

There was a possibility that the note summoning me to the Cuckold's Comfort had served the purpose of my correspondent. I had been invited to a lonely exploration of the most crime-ridden slums of London. Who could be interested in endangering me like that? It was almost useless to speculate upon. How can you understand so devious a mentality without more facts? The strangest aspect of the evening was that I had gone through such trouble to garner information about Henri's death from a phantom source only to be enlightened by Lord Dearborne. There was nothing said about dishcloths and murder at the inquest. I wondered how the marquis rigged the autopsy. My guardian, Lord Dearborne, was indeed a man of influence.

Just how far his influence could extend became clear a few days later when Christopher and I were making our good-byes to Lady Anne. The footmen were busily passing us, loading the carriage. Mrs. Goodbody was giving orders in her usual bustle, and we were standing to one side idly watching.

"So, Anne, how did your pupil do these last dizzy weeks?" said Christopher.

"I am proud of my little protégée," she said, smiling at me in her warm way. "She received a proposal of marriage, which is doing rather well for a scant two weeks in the metropolis."

"She's jesting," I said. "Don't listen to her, Kit."

"No, actually, you did. The marquis turned it down, of course."

To say I was surprised by this information would be an understatement.

"He turned it down? I didn't know anything about that. What has he to do with marriage proposals to me?"

"He's your guardian," said Christopher. "He is doing his duty. You may not resent his interference when you find out who wanted your hand."

I gaped at him speechlessly.

"Tell her, Anne," he said.

Lady Anne looked as though she were bursting with a secret. "Your radical friend, Godfrey."

"Godfrey?" I said weakly. Christopher threw back his head with laughter.

"Depend upon it, that it's because you're the only one who can stand to listen to his tedious ramblings about what knowing fellows the Romans were."

"Don't heed him, Elizabeth," Lady Anne said, directing a quelling frown at her brother. "Godfrey's too unstable to make anything but the most dreadful husband, besides the fact that his father is running through their fortune so fast that I doubt Godfrey will inherit one single slice of unencumbered property. But we will do better for you later, my dear. You must stay with my dear John and me for the next season.

We must find a husband for you in simple charity to
all other unmarried females!"

I had always suppressed a tendency in myself to
wonder about the future. In this case it was difficult.
I had actually received a marriage proposal which
was refused on my behalf because of the obvious un-
suitability of the hopeful. What if I were to receive a
proposal from someone more appropriate? I thought
of all the men of my acquaintance and was able to
turn up none I could envision marrying. Perhaps, per-
ish the thought, there was a respectable, wealthy, land-
owning bore in my future who would make a proper
proposal to me (ineligible as I am) through the marquis, and I would have to marry him and spend the
rest of my life tending to the needs of a dull M.P.
twice my age.

Lord Dearborne would probably waste no time in
getting rid of me now. I had never meant much to
him. At worst, I was an expense and an annoyance. At
best, I was a casual afternoon's amusement, no more.
Then I realized, frighteningly, that Lord Dearborne
was more than that to me. Far, far more. Strangely,
then, all desire to tell Lord Dearborne the truth about
my night in the London slums died, stillborn. In fact,
it seemed even wiser policy now to avoid all possible
contact, all possible thought of him. I must forget his
efficient compassion when I'd grown tipsy at Lady
Doran's ball; forget the comfort of the iron grasp that
had carried me home after I'd been hit by Monsieur
Sacre Bleu, and, especially, I must forget my numbed
surrender under the honeysuckle bush. I tried to concentrate instead on his high-handed, arrogant ways.
What right had he to assume the worst just because I
came home at midnight, half-naked and escorted by
one of the most conscienceless libertines in London?
After all, there might have been a perfectly innocent
explanation for it. The absurdity of the thought
brought a surprised smile to my lips and I tried to

refocus my attention on Lady Anne, who was speaking to me.

"I'm sorry to see you go, Elizabeth," she was saying. "But I have to take my leave of London as well, to be with my husband. I dislike leaving you in Nicky's hands; although his intentions are honorable, I know he is not cut out for the guardian role. He has always tended to see women as playthings or, at best, playmates. Hold tight till our return from Europe, won't you?"

"It's time to go," said Christopher. The carriage was packed, the driver was in his seat, and Mrs. Goodbody was trying to quiet the twins. I could hear their excited squeals.

"Christopher, you must take good care of Elizabeth. I know Elizabeth will take good care of you," said Anne. She was brushing away a tear. I was touched and shed a tear of my own.

"Elizabeth," said Christopher, close to my ear, "Egbert and Godfrey are here to give their good wishes." He was scowling.

Indeed they were, standing nervously together at a little distance. Egbert was shifting from one foot to the other, clutching a nosegay. Godfrey was clearing his throat. I found myself feeling surprisingly sentimental toward the two of them. They had befriended me even though I was penniless, and Godfrey had even proposed to me. I felt this to be a point in his favor; everybody in London society married for money and status, and as much as Christopher liked to scoff at Godfrey's republican beliefs, they did seem to be genuine. So I tried to be as gracious as possible in accepting the feminist tract, authored by Mary Wollstonecraft, that Godfrey held out to me, and accepted the nosegay from Egbert, and kissed them both. They were brave boys to court me past Christopher's frowns and unkind remarks. When I took my leave, they made a misty pair.

When the petite housemaid came forward bearing a handkerchief she had embroidered, it was all I could do to keep from crumpling into a sobbing heap. She had been so faithful, dressing my hair and seeing to my needs. And how I would miss the house as well. I had been there for only two short weeks and already it seemed like home. (I would especially miss the water closet.)

Dressed in beautifully cut riding clothes, Lord Dearborne stepped out of the house to accompany us. His business had apparently been attended to. He stood by, watching the scene with a discreetly ironic and impatient air.

Just then Mrs. Goodbody came up to me. "You know, Elizabeth, through all the packing, I never did locate that gray poplin frock, your old bonnet, or your reticule. Do you have any idea where they might be?"

I knew I wasn't going to get out of London without Mrs. Goodbody finding out about my adventure. I thought for a moment, and assumed a nonchalant air, though I was quaking inside. With an eye toward the marquis, I said:

"I gave them to a beggar woman who came to the door. They were old, but I thought perhaps she could get some use out of them yet."

"Oh," she said, "that was good of you." I tried to breathe my sigh of relief inaudibly. I could see the ironic look on Lord Nicholas's face deepen.

As we left London. I looked out at the crowds and shuddered when I thought of how well I knew what went on down these streets after dark. And when we reached the country, the air was so clean and easy to breathe, I became quite cheerful at the prospect of being back at Barfrestly where I could pick berries and play with Cleo without fear, if you discount ear-cracking explosions, murdered spies, and roughnecks who sneak up to bludgeon you into insensibility. I wondered how my acquaintances in Kent had fared during my absence. It would be nice to see Jane Colman again, and I would have to tell the vicar about Lord Elgin's marbles. The vicar, while being of the school of thought which decried the forced importation of the marbles from their native land, would nonetheless be interested in anything I would have to say about their artistic qualities.

We arrived late in the evening and hurried the twins into bed. In spite of our exhausted state, Mrs. Goodbody and I were happy to sit out on the steps to chat with Joe Hawkins. We were joined presently by Roger, who sat solemnly next to Mrs. Goodbody and sucked a clay pipe. While the cool breeze soothed our travel-tired bodies, we gazed at the stars, listened to the night birds calling, and caught up on local affairs. Joe Hawkins was somewhat abashed in our presence. He had never been to London and felt ill at ease among "swells," as he called us.

"Imagine our Miss Elizabeth amongst those swells," he said to Mrs. Goodbody, shaking his head in wonderment.

"And a fine lady she made, too," said Mrs. Goodbody. "But tell us what happened in the village whilst we were hobnobbing."

After adoring Jane Coleman silently for years, the wheelwright's son had asked her to marry him, so I had not been the only one to receive a proposal. I would have to get Jane's reaction to that. Mrs. Plumford, the sexton's wife, had a terrible attack of her usual inexplicable illness, but had been cured by Dr. Brent, who gave her some type of wonderful medicine he had invented himself. She took it every day, calling it "Dr. Brent's Healthful Elixir." And someone had seen the admiral walking again. At this bit of information, everyone chuckled cynically and I was glad I had kept it a secret when Christa had seen the ghost.

We talked until night had taken a firm grasp on the countryside and hoots of hunting owls sounded in the

forest. Before I went to bed, I took one last check on
my sleeping sisters. On the small oak nightstand was
Christa's old hand mirror, the same mirror with the
warped glass that made your nose look like it was
planted between your eyebrows. I lifted the glass to
see my reflection in the flickering candlelight—there
it was, distorted as ever. The stylish pale-haired London sophisticate who had looked back at me from the
expensive mirrors in Lorne House was unrecognizable
now. The hazy, confused image in Christa's glass
would always be the real Miss Elizabeth Cordell.

The next few days passed quickly enough as we un-
packed our trunks, dusted the cottage, and made gal-
lons of horsemint tea to refresh the ladies of Mudbury
who came to welcome us home. On our second afternoon back at Barfrestly, we had so many inquisitive
visitors that the cottage buzzed like a London drawing room.

Christopher obligingly carried chairs out of the cottage so the ladies could sit on the lawn and take advantage of the fanning breeze and the shade of an elderly maple. Mrs. Goodbody and the twins recited my
triumphs in the fashionable world (greatly exagger-
ated, of course) while I blushed, disclaimed, and answered dozens of good-natured questions. I patiently
endured Mrs. Plumford's habitual lecture on the im-
propriety of accepting such extravagant hospitality
from Lord Dearborne, and let the innkeeper's wife
twit me on my modish hairstyle. It was just like old
times. My friend Jane's upcoming marriage to the
wheelwright's son was discussed at great length too—
the topics ranged from what to wear on the wedding
day to what to wear on the wedding night. By the
time the ladies had finished their frank conversation,
Jane was as red as I had been earlier and we were
glad to slip off together for a private exchange of
confidences.

It wasn't until late that evening that we had cleared up after our company and got down to some of the real work that needed doing. I donned an old work dress, picked up my hoe from the barn, and went to weed my overgrown vegetable patch. On the way down to the garden I passed several of Lord Dearborne's workmen-guards; they were still around, unobtrusive but plentiful. I set to in the garden with such vigor that I accidentally beheaded a dense bush of basil. What a relief it was to work again after so much exhausting play. When I saw Christopher riding his frisky chestnut across the lawn toward me I waved the drooping basil leaves at him and shouted that I hoped whatever Cook was preparing for his supper could be seasoned with basil.

"Probably! Uncle Nicky had some friends from the War Office call on him today and they'll be here for dinner, so Cook'll likely knock off half a dozen main dishes and a mass of removals. I rode over to the Macreadys' this afternoon—Jeffrey sent his regards to you. Oh, and his sister, Cecilia, too. What a quiz that girl is—you should have seen her gown, she looked like a tube of sausage. How did your tea party go?"

"Dandy. My sisters drew a picture of my London partying that makes the career of the famous Gunning sisters pale in comparison. Everybody thinks I am the queen of the *bon ton*."

"Well, you are on the pathway to becoming the princess of the *bon ton* at any rate," he said, smiling and saluting with his riding crop. "I must be off now, we'll be seeing you. I want to hang about Uncle Nicky's cronies and see what they are all up to today."

I took the basil up to the kitchen to give to the cook. I nodded hello to Thomas, the groom, who was sitting on the counter, swinging his dusty feet, eating some fresh bread spread with red currant jelly he had begged from the cook.

"And how is Miss Elizabeth today?" he said in his cheeky way.

"Miss Elizabeth is fine, thank you. How can she get some of what you are eating?"

"Just have some of mine," he said, tearing off a piece and offering it to me. We munched in silence for a moment, then he said, "The marquis be having company today. A fine carriage with some good horses from London."

"That's right, he is," I said.

"Christopher says they be from His Lordship's office."

"The War Office," I said, enjoying my bit of bread.

"To think that I'd be working for a man in the War Office, who makes important decisions on the fate of the country. Me mother would be so proud of me, rest her soul."

"Your mother is not living?" I asked him sympathetically.

"She passed on some time ago," he said, wiping a bit of jelly from his cheek. "I wager you're happy to be back in your little cottage after that big strange house in London."

"Yes, I am, really. It isn't so luxurious of course, but it is home."

"That's true enough," said Thomas. He let himself down from his perch and walked to the door. "I'm leaving now, Miss Elizabeth. Thank you for having dinner with me. It was a grand occasion."

"Thank you," I said. He let the door slam shut behind him. It suddenly occurred to me that I had never before had such a long conversation with Thomas. He seemed rather familiar, but perhaps that was his manner. He was polite enough to give me some of his bread. I wondered for a moment about the meaning of "politeness." I had been brought up to view polite people as being of good character. My recent experience showed this wasn't always true. Lady Catherine had been charming to me the night of her ball and then told Lord Lesley some unsavory lies about me. And Lord Lesley, who had worse manners than Mohawk, had actually been kind to me, though in his own fashion.

I thought more about this as I lay abed that night. People are not always what they seem. Unfortunately, this new insight into human nature was unaccompanied by any great insight into any of the problems that beset me. There were times when I felt a tremendous urge to run to Lord Dearborne and confide my reason for entering the London slums. It's not that he would approve, but at least some of those ugly suspicions would be banished from his mind. Ever since that evening he had either ignored me completely or talked to me with less warmth than a longshoreman would to a sailor who has just dropped a weighty trunk on his toe. I wanted him to like me again. No, that's not honest. I wanted him to do much more than like me. But I wasn't going to confide in him—if he chose not to trust me, so be it. Such thoughts are hardly conducive to peaceful slumbers. If I had been back in London with a room to myself, I could have lit a candle and read for a while, but that was impossible now that I was sharing a room with my sisters again. They would probably wake up.

There was nothing for it. I could not sleep and I could not read, and I have always hated to lay in bed staring at the ceiling. I must go for a midnight stroll. It suddenly occurred to me what had happened the last time I had gone on a midnight stroll. I had overheard a bit of rude speculation as to my desirability, I had seen a ghostly intruder, and a French cook had been murdered. I paused a moment in debate. I decided finally that this particular set of circumstances would not occur again, so I threw on a shawl and struck out for the open spaces.

I hadn't been two steps out of the door when I saw

something that made me cover my eyes and mutter, "Go away, go away." History was repeating itself; there was a dusky figure flitting silently across the garden not twenty yards from where I stood. This was too much for me to bear. No one else in our household had to deal with such disturbances on a regular basis. I had followed the figure last time, and it had worked mischief when I lost track of it. I resolved to follow it more closely this time.

Something was definitely there. When I uncovered my eyes, the ghost was there all right, so I observed it as carefully as possible under the circumstances. The admiral it was not. I remembered the way the admiral moved: his wide stance; his rolling stride, which slowed down as he got older but never lost its vigor completely. This ghost was being stealthy, running along close to the ground and occasionally lying down behind a bush or a tree. What did a ghost have to be afraid of? Other ghosts? I made the conclusion that I wasn't dealing with the supernatural. My experience in the slums had shown me that live people could be frightening enough.

Now I was left with a whole new set of questions. If I screamed, the intruder would try to shut me up. I had no desire to be another casualty of my guardian's occupation. Screaming could also, perhaps, frighten him away before he had a chance to play his cards; the whole household would be roused for nothing and the intruder would get clean away.

I moved parallel to him across the lawn, staying behind him and stopping when he stopped. After a short time we had worked our way close to the mansion. I watched, my eyes trying to pierce the darkness, as he took a vessel of some kind from underneath his cloak and began sprinkling the hollyhocks with it. Why was he sprinkling the hollyhocks? Why in the name of Zeus would an intruder flit stealthily across a garden in the dead of night only to water some flowers? I crept closer to observe this strange procedure.

My observation was assisted when the stranger struck a light. His face was covered. As the light burned, I realized that he wasn't watering the flowers; he was spreading the unknown liquid onto a large heap of brush which had been piled against the wall of the mansion, and hidden from view by the holly-hock bushes. His intentions suddenly became all too clear when he dropped the light on the brush pile and disappeared, leaving behind what quickly turned out to be a raging hot fire. In just a fraction of a moment, the fire was tall in the night sky and licking across the roofing. The intruder was an arsonist, and Barfrestly Mansion would be a fireball if I didn't do something immediately.

I felt the uncomfortable pounding of my heart beneath lungs that couldn't quite fill themselves with enough air. Mercury gave wings to my heels and I flew, with panicked urgency. There was only one course of action for me, one man who spelled help and comfort in an emergency. I raced to him now. Thank God, Cook had forgotten to lock the kitchen door. I wrenched it open, my blood racing faster than my feet. How long would it take for the flames to reach the main bedrooms and those of the sleeping servants? The fire had started in the other wing; I couldn't even smell the smoke from here. I took the main stairway two steps at a time and pulled Lord Dearborne's door open with a jerk that ripped the skin from my knuckles. Then, even in my nervousness, I stopped and padded quietly into the room. The marquis lay asleep in his bed. The one lit candle beside him gutted, spreading a warmish glow through the gently tangled mane that now curled casually against the white pillowcases. No matter how blasé you are, the sight of that undeniable male beauty could stop you dead in your tracks. If I hadn't been standing in an old building that was well on its way to burning to the ground, I am sure that I would have remained staring at him all night. I sternly called myself to order, thanked whoever might be listening in heaven that the marquis was covered at least to the waist with a sheet, and advanced to shake him gingerly by the shoulders. He woke to pull himself upright with such suddenness that I would have lost my balance and fallen if Lord Dearborne hadn't steadied me by gripping my forearms.

"What are you doing here?" he snapped with amazing crispness for one who had so recently been asleep. Then he stopped and cursed under his breath and patted me gently on the shoulder. "It's all right. I didn't mean to startle you like that. I'm a light sleeper. Something is wrong, isn't it? Well, you can't tell me with your hand over your mouth." He carefully disengaged the clenched fist that I had unconsciously raised to my lips. "What happened?"

"The house is on fire," I said, not mincing words. "Really! I saw him setting it, at least at first I thought he was only watering the flowers but then I thought, How strange, why would a ghost want to water the garden. But when he threw a light at the wall, I understood."

"Well, sweetheart, if you understand that makes one of us," replied Lord Dearborne, who had tossed back the sheet and pulled on a pair of buckskin breeches before I had the time to cover my eyes, blush, or utter a maidenly shriek. He put his hands very firmly on my shoulders, and looked straight at me. "Elizabeth, calmly now, just yes or no. Has someone set *this* house on fire?" I nodded. "Am I the first person you've told?" I nodded again. "What part of the house is burning?" I told him.

He sat down on the edge of the bed and reached for his boots. "The fire won't reach this part of the house for another half hour at least. How did you happen to observe the arsonist?"

It's just like the arrogant marquis to waste time pulling on his boots and engaging in a lot of recriminations with a house burning down around our ears. "Because I was out in the garden trysting with my lover. Would you like me to summon your valet so he can assist you in the arrangement of your cravat?" Have some of your own sarcasm back, Milord.

Lord Dearborne paused, thoughtfully. "Ah, good girl! I was wondering whether to demean myself by shouting through the hallway for him or if I should simply make do without."

Sarcasm is wasted on Lord Dearborne. "Please, N-N-Nicholas, this is no time for stupid jokes," I returned weakly.

Lord Dearborne was gazing at me like one charmed. "You've never called me that before."

"What?" I squeaked.

"N-N-Nicholas. My name sounds rather exotic falling from such lips."

And this after treating me like a leper for days. "Of all the moody, difficult . . . the house is on fire! *Don't you understand?* Burning, flames, heat, smoke! Oh my God, I shall end up in Bedlam, if I don't get burned alive first," I said, a little desperately.

Lord Dearborne finished pulling on his boot and, grabbing me firmly by the elbow, strode purposely through the door and down the corridor. I was amazed by the confidence that allowed the marquis to move so quickly through the dark hallways. When we reached the hallway before Christopher's bedroom, I saw that it was bathed in light from a small ceiling chandelier. There was a man seated on a straight-backed chair next to Christopher's door. The man rose quickly as we approached. Lord Dearborne, now thankfully economical with his words, explained the situation, ordering the man to take Christopher and me out through the kitchen doorway and to keep us out of the way.

The man, whom I recognized as one of Lord Dearborne's "workmen," roused a yawning Christopher and dragged him out of bed, nightshirt and all, while the marquis hastened off through the corridor in the direction of the servants' bedrooms. This time, descending the main staircase with Christopher and the bodyguard, I could smell the acrid smoke twisting ominously through the building.

Once we reached the outside, I heard the urgent shouting of Joe Hawkins, the grooms, and other estate workers who shared the gatehouse. Apparently Thomas, the groom, had seen the flames and rang the stable bell as an alarm. I told my story, which was becoming rapidly more incoherent, to the excited audience. Pandemonium reigned supreme—I've never seen so many grown men behave so much like hens when there was a badger in the barnyard. The marquis appeared and, after surveying the severity of the fire, ordered the men to remove goods from the house. "Personal effects of the servants first!" he was shouting. A pile of household goods grew rapidly in a space a distance from the mansion as the men handed out, in relays, small cedar chests, clothing, and china settings. Huge billowing clouds of yellow smoke were now pouring out of the upstairs windows where the marquis and Christopher had been soundly sleeping just a half hour previously. The fire broke through a large hole in the roof, sending a shower of cinders up into the sky, reflecting brilliantly in the faces of the semicircle of onlookers.

Christopher was hopping about in his nightdress, assisting the men in their labors. "You'll be in trouble if a good gust of wind comes up, my dear boy," shouted the marquis to him cheerily. "You will be causing embarrassment to the ladies present." How could he be cheerful when his house was burning down? I received something of an answer to my question when Joe Hawkins and Christopher hauled out of the house a third soot-blackened man who retched and gasped for air as they dragged him away.

"That's good, boys," he shouted. "Better to leave it alone now. I've other houses. It's not worth anyone getting hurt. Let it burn. Keep watch on the outbuildings; we may as well save them."

The heat of the fire was reaching out to us where we stood. Beads of perspiration were breaking out on Mrs. Goodbody's face. She mopped her brow and said:

"We'd best be watching from the cottage, girls. This is no place for us." The twins were sitting cross-legged on the ground, mesmerized by the sight. I caught their attention, and we herded them away from the fire back toward the cottage. I was depressed about the library; I had spent many a peaceful hour in its musty embrace, and now it was a holocaust. And the admiral's nautical instruments and his old maps. What a tragic loss. We had all spent many years in the benevolent shadow of the admiral and his ugly old house; I felt as though I were watching the funeral pyre of an old friend. A lump rose to my throat as I looked over my shoulder and seemed to see the sad, forlorn face of the old sea dog peering out through the flames that rose laughing toward the heavens.

Good-bye, good-bye, I said to myself as we watched from the stoop of the cottage.

A curricle was being whipped up the drive. It was Wadbury, Lord Lesley's butler, come to help. He stripped off his waistcoat and joined the men who were carrying buckets of water to pour on the roofs of the outbuildings.

"I am here on behalf of Lady Peterby," he was shouting. "We saw the flames from Petersperch and she wished to offer our assistance. Is everyone safe?"

"Perfectly safe, thank you. Come here a moment,

there is something you can do for me," said the marquis. He motioned Wadbury closer and they stood talking, but we were too far away to hear what was being said. Presently the pair made their way toward us, and the marquis spoke in the commanding, peremptory tone that he used when preoccupied.

"I am sending you ladies to Petersperch to stay the night. This is no place for you here. And I imagine the Terrible Two will need their rest," he added in a warmer tone. They squealed in delight as he continued, "I shall have the carriage sent round to pick you up."

"Lord Peterby is there and will see that you are comfortable," added stout Wadbury. And with that, they turned and went back to their labors.

So the performance was over for us, I thought as I helped Mrs. Goodbody pack a bag. The carriage came round and we were helped into it by a tired but still bluff Joe Hawkins.

We were having breakfast with Lady Peterby the next morning when we were interrupted by an exhausted, dirty Christopher. He bore a smoky old crate filled with . . . the admiral's old maps and nautical instruments! My eyes filled with tears of gratitude as Christopher said, his voice hollow and weary, "We thought you might like to keep these."

"And the mansion, in what state is it?" I whispered through my joyful tears.

"Burned to the ground, of course. Leveled. A total loss."

Chapter Fourteen

It was late that evening before Lord Dearborne arrived at Petersperch, disheveled and dirty. He had stayed to make sure the last ember was out. Privately, I observed that even after a sleepless night and strenuous day, he looked energetic enough to take a couple of dragons in hand-to-hand combat. Lady Peterby didn't think so, however. She immediately sent him up to a guest room to rest, promising him a tray with dinner and a footman with bathing water. Roger and Lady Peterby's butler, who had arrived looking dead on their feet with Lord Dearborne, were shepherded off by Mrs. Goodbody to receive much the same treatment.

Lady Peterby had promptly and with endearing graciousness invited us all to stay, at least while Lord Dearborne dealt with the problems attendant to moving the uprooted household to another one of his many estates. He will probably send me to the remotest possible corner of England, I reflected gloomily. I wondered if he owned any property in Ireland. If so, there was probably a place marked out there for Elizabeth Cordell. The temporary thaw, if thaw it had been, in Lord Dearborne's manner toward me in those few moments in the burning mansion had not lasted out the day. His frosty hauteur had returned on his arrival at Petersperch and he didn't even acknowledge my presence in the room as he thanked Lady Peterby for her kindness to us and accepted her offer to house us for the time being.

Belowstairs, as speculation ran rife as to which of his more comfortable houses Lord Dearborne would repair to, I wondered why Lord Dearborne had already spent so much time in Kent. Barfrestly Manor must be the least imposing of his properties. True, at first there had been business connected with his inheritance of Barfrestly that he might have wished to handle personally, but that could have been concluded within a few hours. The rest could have been just as well conducted by one of the marquis's capable lawyers. Certainly Lord Dearborne had shown no interest whatsoever in Barfrestly Estate for the first nine months that he had owned it. What had kept him here among gnarled apple trees, weedy gardens, and leaky old buildings? Not affection for a manor house that he had allowed to burn down without a qualm.

For the present, Petersperch was a more appropriate setting for my elegant guardian than Barfrestly could ever be. The well-kept lawns, trimmed hedges, and clear garden ponds filled with darting gold and silver carp had more in common with Lord Dearborne's life-style than the tumbledown acres he had accidentally inherited from Admiral Barfreston. Conversely, Lord Peterby seemed a natural resident for the ramshackle estate that had been my home. I can't imagine anyone who would look more picturesque pacing through the shabby grounds in brooding solitude. The touch of Lady Peterby was very evident in Petersperch. I was granted the opportunity for a long, friendly coze with Lady Peterby that first afternoon at Petersperch and fell firmly, painlessly under the spell of her delicate charm. Whatever trace of Lady Peterby that exists in her turbulent, dissolute son had never been revealed to me. Still, she calls him "my Lesley" and talks of him in an indulgent manner, as though his libertine propensities were mere boyish mischief. Mothers seem to have a special blindness to the faults of their own offspring. Bravo for that, I suppose.

Life at Petersperch settled into a breezy, pleasant pace. My sisters and I resumed our lessons with Mudbury's scholarly vicar; this took up most of the mornings. On fine days we walked into town, always under some "adult" escort as decreed by our autocratic guardian. Our afternoons were spent in animated conversation with Lady Peterby, gathering flowers from the extensive formal gardens and visiting with any of the neighboring gentry who might happen to come calling. The squire's family came; Jeffrey to renew his casual friendship with Christopher, Mrs. Macready and Cecilia to marvel over the phenomenon of Elizabeth Cordell, lately charity resident of Barfrestly Estate, as visitor and honored guest of Lady Peterby. I could have told them, though I didn't, that they were wasting their awe; old Elizabeth was still as much a charity resident as ever. In fact, and completely by accident, I was made more aware than ever of just how much of a charity resident I was.

On the afternoon of our third day at Petersperch, one of Lord Dearborne's men of business came down from London to go over whatever it is that is necessary to go over when your house burns down. I had seen this lawyer before. He had visited the marquis several times at Barfrestly before our trip to "Loindone" (my sisters' new name for the nation's capital). At any rate, he was a small, fussy man with a beaky nose and tiny glaring eyes that seemed to look right through you and price your underclothes. I studiously avoided his company until that afternoon when I walked blithely into the yellow salon to have tea, secure in the conviction that Lady Peterby and my sisters would be awaiting me there. Unfortunately, they hadn't yet arrived and there sat Lord Dearborne's lawyer, looking for all the world like a crabby, underfed canary that someone had left under the cage cover too long. I would have beat a hasty retreat from the room if I could have without being grossly uncivil. As it was, I sidled nervously over to the waiting tea tray and asked if I could pour him some tea. He pulled down his murky spectacles to peer disapprovingly at me over the rims.

"Ahem. Miss Cordell, isn't it? One of the dependents of the Marquis of Lorne?"

Why not His Majesty, the Marquis of Lorne? But I returned politely, "Yes, sir. Admiral Barfreston provided for us in his will."

"Nonsense. You were definitely not mentioned in the will."

"I realize that. What I meant was that Admiral Barfreston made a verbal request to one of his lawyers that my sisters and I should be supported out of his estate. Which I understand is legally binding on Lord Dearborne, as his heir." I felt an angry flush glaze my cheeks.

The disapproving pout on the lawyer's face intensified. "Not at all. You have a most confused understanding of your position vis-à-vis the Marquis of Lorne. Not only is he under no obligation whatsoever to support your family, he is doing so strictly against my own recommendation. The idea of wasting money on a set of orphans to whom he is in no way related is ludicrous. There are many perfectly good orphan asylums and workhouses in this country and there is no need to carry charity to this ridiculous personal extreme."

The color that had washed over my cheeks a moment ago faded into a chilly numbness. "Do you mean Admiral Barfreston made no bequest to my sisters and me?"

"Nothing. Admiral Barfreston made few communications with his solicitors in the years before his death. He had grown quite vague about his duties as a man of property. The estate business was in a shameful muddle when the Marquis of Lorne inherited. The condition of the land was so poor that it could not even be sold without a good deal of work," he spoke disparagingly. He returned his hard scrutiny to me. "You are a singularly fortunate young lady. You should be grateful that His Lordship is such a generous young man. There are few of my clients who would have so kindly taken on an unnecessary responsibility such as yourself."

Of course I should have known. I don't know habeas corpus from corpus crumbcake, but I should have recognized the line about Admiral Barfreston making a verbal provision for us as precisely the type of courteous pretense one maintains to spare the sensitive pride of a pensioner. Admiral Barfreston had indeed been vague in the last few years of his life. My sisters and I had disappeared behind the foggy visions of sea battles and typhoons.

Anyone with any courage would have gone immediately to her room, packed her cases, and marched to the nearest workhouse, sisters in hand. Vive cowardice! I had been to a workhouse once on a "mission of mercy" with the vicar. The bleak, lifeless faces of the inmates had told a story more eloquent than any pamphleteer's words. The public houses of good works were colonies for the living dead, the hopeless, the forsaken. Never would I condemn my happy little sisters to such a life. And I had recently learned the horrors of setting out unprotected, facing the night streets with all the human predators who prowled there. Probably what I should do was look for some kind of work. As a governess? A nursemaid? Probably what I *would* do was go on as before; pretending belief in the fabrication that Lord Dearborne was under an obligation to support me, that I wasn't just another battening freeloader. Knowing now how fully I was under obligation to Lord Dearborne should have made me all the more grateful to him. It should have, but it didn't. It is hard to feel anything fonder than the utmost pique for a man who persists in treating you (at his most mellow) like a poison-ivy patch.

Whatever anyone else thought of his coldness to me, they said nothing about it. Perhaps they all simply assumed that it was consonant with his usual arrogance, though I noticed Christopher regarding me sharply several times in the evening when the household sat together to dine on Lady Peterby's lace-clothed teak table. Morbidly afraid of revealing my feelings for Lord Dearborne, I adopted a light, Lizzie's-atop-the-world attitude toward life, letting everyone see that there was nothing bothering me. I must have overplayed it because Mrs. Goodbody, Christopher, Christa, and Caro came around separately and in pairs to ask me what in the name of heaven had gotten into me. Life was becoming very confusing. I was keeping so many secrets from so many people that I had to think carefully each time I opened my mouth.

Whenever I could, I escaped from painful adult reality to a world of make-believe with the twins, with their fantastic imaginations and energetic games. On one beautifully alive morning we returned from our lessons to toss our books on a garden bench, tuck our skirts into the tops of our underslips to shorten them to knee length, and race around the formal gardens chasing Lady Peterby's arrogant yard fowl. Black swans, peacocks, and harlequin ducks scattered and barked viciously at our plebeian attack. When we did get close enough, we pulled out tail feathers until we had enough to make colorful plume crowns to decorate our hair, like the American Indians. Whooping and singing, we pretended to be brave warriors, hunters of wild beasts, and enemies of British settlers. We took turns capturing and bringing one another, struggling, to our imaginary village of hide huts. Being the fastest runner, I was the hardest to catch, but in relays Caro and Christa wore me down and dragged me, pleading for mercy between gasps of laughter, to a shallow lily pond where they declared solemnly that they were to drown me. One shove and I was sitting waist deep in water, feathers flopping in my face and faint with mirth.

Now if I had gone into the house for luncheon directly after lessons, I would have known that Lord Lesley Peterby had arrived from London with a determined Lady Catherine in tow. However, since I had not gone into the house, it was a small shock to me when Lady Catherine, Lord Dearborne, Christopher, and Lord Lesley came walking around the curve of the brick wall surrounding the herb garden. I probably would have been embarrassed at being discovered in a lily pond, dripping with moss and leaves, were it not for the flabbergasted look that Lady Catherine gave me. Her face was such a study of round-eyed disbelief that it set me off into peals again. Shaking helplessly, I staggered to my feet and tottered over to mischievously scatter a few droplets of water from my drenched skirts onto Lady Catherine's immaculate gown.

"I vow, the chit's drunk," gasped Lady Catherine.

Indeed, I felt drunk. Or at least light-headed from laughter. "Oh, Lady Catherine, Lady Catherine, I'm intoxicated with life. Have some!" I chirped, waltzing merrily over to send another tiny shower her way.

I flitted over to Christopher. "Oops! Clumsy little me! I must have tripped on my hem." I pressed myself full length against Christopher's tailored finery, leaving wet splotches on his white leather breeches and linen shirt. I looked up into his brown eyes for a responsive smile but saw that his appreciative gaze, instead of meeting mine, was preoccupied with another part of my person. A quick glance around revealed that the other gentlemen present were similarly en-

gaged. Looking down, I saw that my waterlogged
gown was clinging tightly to my figure. I reached out
a muddy fist to chuck Sir Lesley under the chin. "I
don't know what you're staring at. It's nothing you
haven't seen before." Then on tiptoe, I plucked a limp,
bedraggled peacock feather from my sodden curls and
threaded it through Lord Dearborne's buttonhole.
"There," I said, patting his lapel. "I think this belongs
to you, it must have fallen out of your tail."

I turned to my sisters. "Come, girls," I said, holding
out my arms to them. "Assist me to my boudoir. I fear
my attire is too fashionable for this particular company." I was laughing so hard I could not trust my
legs to carry me; the twins came in handy as I took
my leave.

Halfway up the grand stone staircase, we met Mrs.
Goodbody, who hustled me into my bedroom, cluck-
ing that I would catch my death in cold. After the
twins and I had our lunch on gleaming silver trays in
the old nursery (the same one where my mother had
once taught the Peterby daughters), I took a long,
luxurious afternoon nap and awoke feeling depressed
as Hades. There, on the cherrywood étagère next to
the empty limestone fireplace, was the box of old
books, maps, and naval paraphernalia that had been
so precious to Admiral Barfreston. I went over to paw
through them, stopping to polish the tarnished brass
instruments with loving care. The maps were interesting. Some were crazily outdated, a glimpse into another world, with hand-drawn pictures of hideous
dragons, griffins, and demons in the margins. I decided to take the box into Mudbury to show the vicar.
He would appreciate the contents.

I was tucking away an astrolabe, or some such
thing, when a buxom parlor maid came in to inform
me that dinner would be an hour early tonight, so I'd
best start making ready. She added that the Macreadys were to join us; dinner had been moved up to

accommodate the squire, who stolidly kept country hours. In fact, before I had finished dressing, I could hear voices in the entrance hall and knew the company had arrived. I was in no mood to enter the parlor alone, after the way I had misbehaved that afternoon. Still, whenever I thought of how Lady Catherine had looked with her eyes jumping from their sockets, I would almost start to laugh again! I had been dreadful and not even ashamed at the way my dress clung to me. But when I am gripped by the giggles, there is nothing under our bold sun that can inhibit me.

I finished my preparations and knocked on Lady Peterby's door to ask if I could accompany her down the stairs.

"How good of you, Elizabeth. I wish all the young people had your consideration. It is difficult for me to navigate, you know."

I flushed and admitted, "I'm not really as considerate as you think, Lady Peterby. I came to walk downstairs with you because I'm shy of entering the drawing room by myself."

I received a laugh and a quick hug in reply. "A moment, dear," said Lady Peterby, patting the seat of the brocade settee invitingly. "I think that we must talk, just a little."

Obediently, I sat down next to her. Lady Peterby regarded her fingertips reflectively and then turned to look approvingly at me.

"How lovely you are tonight. Well, if you still blush at a compliment from an old lady then the London beaux must be a great deal tamer than they were in my day! Ahem, in fact it is about the London beaux that I wanted to talk to you. Without doubt Anne is a sweet creature and the most well-meaning girl, but she is really too young to have the charge of chaperoning you. Something has upset you."

Lord, is my face as translucent as a window? I shook my head in hasty denial.

"No, no, my dear, do not deny it. I assure you that I have neither the right nor the intention of prying into things that you would not have me know. However, I shall tell you this. Whatever the world may say, I still retain some control over my tempestuous offspring. If he is the source of your distress, I beg you will confide in me because I would not for the world have you plagued by him." She paused to pat my hand and smile again. "I see you are surprised. You think that I've let my partiality blind me to Lesley's faults. He is a wild, unstable boy, I know, bad-tempered, impetuous, and selfish. But beneath that rake-hell, hedonistic crust is intelligence and a great deal of honesty. Adulthood comes more easily to some."

You mean adultery comes more easily to some, I thought. But for all that I was able to assure her that her son was not the source of my distress. In truth, if it hadn't been for Lord Lesley's intervention that night in the slums, might I now be under even greater distress?

"Then it is Nicky." It was a simple statement and it was the simple truth. "You've fallen in love with him, haven't you? I was afraid that might happen. It seems to be a natural consequence of putting any female in contact with him. The boy was always far too easy on the eyes for the comfort of everyone concerned, including himself. And combine that with a set of the most engaging manners, an old and respected title, and a vulgarly large fortune and you will see a far less steady boy than Nicky ruined before he can even appreciate what he has. For all that, though, there's a great deal of sweetness in Nicky, if only someone would encourage him to show it. But what can you expect when the women that he spends most of his leisure with are high-born hussies like Lady Catherine?"

I gave a watery giggle. Probably, had not Lady Peterby's top-lofty dresser come in at that moment to say

Lord Peterby desired speech with his mama, I would have then unburdened myself thankfully before this kindly, sympathetic audience. I had barely time to straighten up before Lord Peterby strode into the room, favoring my sodden countenance with a brief, irritable glance, and said, "Well, don't look with daggered eyes at me, *Maman*. I didn't make her cry!"

"Nonsense. She's not crying. There was a bit of dust in her eye. And you might do me the courtesy of knocking instead of sweeping into the room like a prizefighter lurching into the ring. Just because you will persist in hobnobbing with the horrid fellowship does not give you leave to imitate their manners in this house. You might remember that you were at least born a gentleman. And I want Lady Catherine out of this house by tomorrow afternoon. She is a disgrace to the good name she bears. I will not have you lodging your whores in my home."

Whew! I took one scared peep at Lord Peterby and was surprised to see an ironic grin on his saturnine countenance. He bowed in full court style to his mama. "As you wish," he replied cordially. Much as I relished hearing one of society's dangerous blades being chewed out by his mother, I'm still glad it was she and not I who told him off. It's cornplants to cobwebs he would have blacked my eye.

Dinner went as well as could be expected under the circumstances. I could see that Lady Peterby was trying to keep me out of as much undesirable company as possible, so I was seated between Christopher and Jeffrey Macready, who leaned over me to talk to each other of sport and horses. Anyone in Christopher's set was a safe enough companion for me. It's not that they were so virtuous; but Christopher was so ready to sport canvas in my defense, and his friends had developed a healthy respect for his robust right.

Unfortunately, I wasn't far enough away from Lady Catherine (to be honest, nothing under twenty miles

would be far enough away) to avoid hearing her sala-
cious flirtation with Lord Dearborne. The food turned
to coal dust in my mouth. Everything Lady Peterby
and Mrs. Goodbody said about her was right. She was
a clever, scheming, manhunting coquette. And I wished
fervently that I could be just like her.

Whatever fault the good ladies Peterby and Goodbody might find with Lady Catherine, the marquis
didn't seem to share their negative views. He listened
to her suggestive chatter with casual amusement, a
slow smile often decorating his sensuous lips. All of
the men present seemed to be preoccupied in like
fashion. She would lean over to talk or listen, gracefully managing to make some physical contact with
her conversant, and let the neckline of her gown
droop enough to allow the entire French army march
through on maneuvers. Her conversation may not
have been the most edifying, but the males present
were getting a good lesson in female anatomy. I found
myself wondering if Lord Peterby would obey his
wise mother and send Lady Catherine packing.

At last the meal was over, and Lady Peterby gave
the customary signal for the ladies to withdraw and
leave the men to their talk. We withdrew into a sitting
room, and Lady Catherine turned her charms on us;
she seemed much easier to take without the men
around, confining herself to items of London gossip
instead of flaunting her beauty. Cecilia and I began
to relax under her anecdotes. She really was an interesting and flattering companion on this basis, but her
efforts to get on Lady Peterby's good side were fruit-
less. Her most ingenious tidbits of information roused
nothing more from Lady Peterby than the smallest of
civil exclamations.

The lateness of the hour eventually forced our gathering to a close. Lady Catherine's room was near my
own and I found myself ascending the staircase with
the still verbal beauty. We made our goodnights, and I

had just finished changing into my nightgown when Lady Catherine knocked on my door. She said:

"Elizabeth, do you mind coming to my room for a moment? I want to show you something I recently bought in London. Perhaps your knowledge of classical civilization will help me."

Although I was ready for bed, her invitation was polite and she seemed to desire my help. I was intrigued. I went with her into the room and she motioned me to the bed, and then turned to remove something from her portmanteau. She turned and showed me a cameo, and we held it up to the light to examine it.

"I bought this at Hepworth's," she said. "They told me it was Greek but I wanted your opinion. Could you tell me anything about it?"

"Of course," I said. "That is Eos, the goddess of dawn, pouring the morning from an ewer. I really don't know enough about it to tell you if it is authentic or not. I'm not that much of a scholar, really."

"Now, don't be modest," she said. "You certainly know more about it than I. I had not the slightest idea what this cameo depicted. And neither did the dealer for that matter."

I couldn't help feeling a little proud of myself at that moment. It probably showed on my face.

"I'm so ignorant of classical civilization," she continued. "Why don't you sit and have a glass of wine with me and tell me what you know."

I was hesitant. I didn't like to drink spirits after my experience at that particular ball in London.

"We'll just have a little," she said reassuringly, pouring some for us. To be polite I gave in, feeling that I would just swallow the minimum and then take my leave. To my surprise, the wine tasted not at all unpleasant, and in no time at all, I asked for another glass. It made me feel so relaxed. I had had a hard day of playing and partying, and it was rather pleasant to sit with Lady Catherine and talk about matters that interested me. She paid such rapt attention as I warmed to my subject; we were sitting with our legs crossed, chatting like schoolgirls.

I noticed my tongue beginning to trip while I was making important points about Homer; my eyes were beginning to blur, and my eyelids to droop. I felt so good, but it was time for bed.

"Dear Elizabeth, I feel I have kept you so late. Let me help you to your room," Lady Catherine was saying.

"No, I can make it all right," I said. I was wrong. My legs would not hold me up.

"I'll help," she said. "It's no trouble." I was being supported by Lady Catherine's soft shoulder, making my way down the dark hallway. Now I was being put to bed, at long last. A fire was flickering swimmingly in the fireplace and Lady Catherine was tucking the cover under my chin in a cozy, maternal way.

"Have pleasant dreams, Elizabeth," she said. How could I have ever been so wrong about her, I was thinking. She's really very nice. I was falling and floating into sleep.

Chapter Fifteen

I don't know what it was that brought my mind back to spinning consciousness. Perhaps it was the discomfort of my nightgown which had twisted itself around my body like swaddling bands. The silent room blurred in opaque firelight. Several weak, fretful attempts to free myself from the clinging silk left me panting with exhaustion. My limbs seemed unable to respond to my commands. Was I ill? I certainly felt ill. The fear that I was sick crept over me, the fear that I wouldn't be able to call for help. I would lay here dying, dying alone. Even the bedroom looked strange to me. I didn't remember the heavy mahogany dresser with racing forms tossed casually on it.

Racing forms? I struggled to prop myself up on one elbow just as I heard the sound of voices in the hallway. I concentrated on gathering my energy, to make one great effort to call for help. As I did my eyes focused for one hazy instant on the bedstand and saw there the large signet ruby of Lesley Peterby. In one stricken flash I knew that I had been betrayed. I heard the door handle clunk and Lord Peterby's voice.

". . . and I promise you, Nicky, that it was—" His voice died as he saw me. His expression was filled with such surprise that I wondered if I had become in some way deformed. My hand rose limply to my face.

He spun around to Lord Dearborne and gripped hard at his shoulders. His eyes looked straight and clearly into those of the marquis. His voice was hard:

"God as my witness, Nicky, I swear that she's not here by my design. Seeing her here is as much a shock to me as it is to you."

Lord Dearborne's face seemed as if all emotion were torn from it. The eyes that met Peterby's were curiously blank.

"Don't you think I know that? You wouldn't have let me in here otherwise." His voice was soft but became light and dangerous as he turned his gaze to me. "But I must protest, Lesley. What a churlish way to receive such an exquisite invitation." He walked over to the bed and lifted one of my tumbled curls. "Don't tremble so, sweetheart."

"A mistake," I croaked miserably.

"I do agree that a mistake has been made. It should be my bed that you're warming now and not Lesley's. It seems only fair, doesn't it? *Noblesse oblige* and all that."

He put out one beautiful hand and pulled the sheets back from my body. His breath seemed to stop in his throat. "When I think of how long I've been wanting to do this and held back . . . By God, no longer. After all, if you're handing it out, then I've sure as hell got the right to it since I'm the one who's been paying for it."

Lesley touched Lord Dearborne's sleeve. "She's only a child."

"Then it's time she became a woman. With her looks I'm surprised she made it to fifteen with a maidenhead." He slid one arm under my shoulders and the other beneath my thighs. "Come, my love, and make your offering to Venus."

Struggle was impossible. I had barely the strength to remain awake, and as I was lifted out of bed my head fell back against his shoulder so heavily that my mind seemed to float in a dreary vapor. As my vision cleared, I saw Lesley regarding me searchingly. My lips formed the word, "Help."

"Nicky, don't harm her."

"If you want some hackneyed assurance that I'll be gentle, you have it, but that's all I'm going to promise. Lesley, for the love of God, don't interfere with me now."

My senses all ran together as sluggish as molasses. The world became a blur of shifting movement that ebbed and flowed like powder in a tilting hourglass. Everything leveled for a moment and I realized I was lying on a bed. I saw the Marquis of Lorne standing far, far above. His scrutiny made me feel like I was being caressed by an icy hand. He was loosening his cravat.

"Lord Dearborne . . ." It was no more than a whisper.

"Don't, for Christ's sake, keep calling me that. I hate making love to women who call me by my title."

Another layer of nausea draped itself around my body. All the space in my brain compressed itself into one tiny agonized ball. Defeat coursed through me with such bitterness that I think in that moment I was a bit insane.

"Nicholas, don't—please."

The marquis had been unbuttoning his shirt, but at this he stopped to lean one arm negligently against the bed's rail. "Why so timid, sweeting? A man expects a little more response from his lover." He sounded glib and silky, frighteningly cordial.

I tried to raise my hand to him, I think in supplication, but I felt so weak that the gesture was barely perceptible. I felt suddenly drained of all things save a slithering, mesmerized horror at my own illness.

"Help me, please. I'm so sick."

Suddenly, Nicholas was sitting beside me on the bed, his hands holding my shaking head still. Long, gentle fingers stroked the suffocating hair from my face.

"Elizabeth, what is it?" Then all at once he was lost

in the cloaking fog and I slipped into unconsciousness.

The dearly desired oblivion was not to last long.
What seemed to be only seconds later an intense light
came searing through my closed eyelids. Manipulating
hands tumbled me ruthlessly until a thin liquid filled
every hollow of my head and ran down into my gag-
ging throat, splashing into my windpipe. My desperate attempt to rid myself of the strangling fluid was
cruelly prevented by a pulsing cramp. Convulsion followed convulsion as my tortured body sought to rid
itself of the smothering poison; my blood became a
pricking irritant which throttled each vein in its sluggish path. The sound of my own hysterical sobs was
the last thing I heard before an explosion in my brain
slammed me into blackness again.

I think I woke several times after that because I retain a dim memory of hearing low voices and once
seeing Mrs. Goodbody's frightened face bending over
me. But this time when I awoke the pain had dulled
to a blunt ache and the daylight came in tiny pin-
points. Memory returned slowly, as unwelcome as a
summer drought. I tried to slide back into sleep but
the retreat was halted by the spiteful demons of reality.

My eyes focused on the figure of Dr. Brent, who
was bending solicitously over me as I lay on the bed,
peering solemnly into my face. His previous flirta-
tious, jibing manner was partially hidden by an expression of medical concentration.

"My God, I'm so ill," I whispered. I was gasping for
a good breath as though my lungs were too weak to
inflate themselves. "What have I got?"

"You have been bitten by a bug," he said, feeling
my pulse. His hand was warm on my wrist.

"A bug?" I asked numbly. "What kind of bug?"

"You have been bitten by the green-eyed jealousy
bug, traveling incognito as a randy, though high-born,
London strumpet. She is a good-looking baggage,

nonetheless. If I did not have Medicine as my mistress . . ."

"Would you get to the point," I choked out. "Or I will vomit again." He held the pan for me.

"If only the Hippocratic oath were not my marriage vow," he said. "There now, you must feel a bit better. You were fed too much opium in your nightcap, my dear little girl. Wine with too much of a kick."

I laid back on the bed. "Lady Catherine gave me wine last night. Why would she do that?"

"Confidentially," he said, wagging his eyebrows in his most annoying manner, "I have my own opinion on the reason. I arrived on the scene just when the marquis dragged her out of bed at four o'clock this morning. She says she was just giving you something to help you sleep more soundly, and that she accidentally gave you too much. There seemed to be some question as to exactly where you chose to begin your slumbers."

"What do you mean by that?"

"She was screaming, 'How do I know why the foolish chit ended up in Lesley's bed. You can't hold me responsible for that.' Those were her exact words." The doctor was seated on the edge of the bed now, acting like a goodwife gossiping over the back fence. "You'll feel better soon," he added, patting my hand. "You were nowhere near death."

"Thank you for telling me that," I said. My head was throbbing. "I would not have known otherwise."

"Poor little thing," he said. "I regret that I must leave your side now. I sent Mrs. Goodbody out to get some rest; she was tending you devotedly for a good many hours. I will go and get her now. I myself have other patients to attend to. So just sit tight and your Mrs. Goodbody will be here in a few moments."

He was gone. I struggled to sit up, moving my leaded limbs experimentally. After a few moments of painstaking concentration I was seated on the bed's edge, staring dejectedly at the writhing designs of the Oriental carpet under my bare feet. Though I resisted it with all my will, the full memory of Lord Dearborne's behavior the night before came back to me and I burned with shame. Oh, sweet life, what he must have thought at finding me in Lord Peterby's bed! Lord, it had been obvious what he had thought. What was it that Lord Peterby had said that night he had rescued me from the London slums; that Lord Dearborne wasn't dissolute enough to make an innocent girl his mistress. But if he believed that I wasn't innocent . . . I shivered violently. His casual scorn for me made a mortifying answer to the flowering of my desperately stifled adoration for him. I knew my earlier resentment of him had been my weapon against this stupidly helpless and useless infatuation for Lord Dearborne. If only my armor had not been so weak.

And soon Mrs. Goodbody would come to me, probably frightened and confused by the strange events of the night. She would ask me questions. How could I answer them? How could I tell her what had happened? Startled into panic, I stumbled to my feet and grabbed a foolishly ruffled peignoir from the edge of the divan. I walked unsteadily down the corridor. The Fates alone knew where I thought I was going—*away* was the only destination I was conscious of. Leaning heavily on the balustrade, I had navigated halfway down the main stairway when the frightened energy that had brought me this far deserted me suddenly, like an unfaithful friend. I started to fall foward, half fainting. But instead of feeling the blow of the stone steps I found myself held firmly in a comfortingly strong grip.

"Elizabeth, what in God's name? What are you doing out of bed?"

"Oh, Kit, Kit. Don't take me back upstairs, please." The blood was drumming so loudly in my ears that I could hardly hear his response. The fear in my voice must have been its own message, for he carried me into the serenely sunny sitting room and set me down carefully on the satin daybed.

"My poor girl, you shouldn't be up."

I laughed bitterly. "I'm nowhere near death, Dr. Brent has assured me."

Christopher sat down beside me and placed the peignoir around my shoulders. "You've been very sick, though. Everyone's been up most of the night worrying about you." He slipped an arm around my shoulders and drew me close to him. "My dear, my dear, you look so ill."

I leaned my head back against his arm and, surprisingly, he placed a soft kiss upon my lips. Rigid with shock, I pounded my clenched fists against his chest with all my might. *Et tu, Brute?*

"Horrible, horrible. Y-you are just the same as the other men, wanting to seduce me . . . to treat me like a—a . . ." I stopped to swallow painfully. "I trusted you."

Christopher looked stricken. "No, no. Upon my honor, Elizabeth, I meant no disrespect. I could never do anything to hurt you. Seeing you so pale, just . . . well, that was my reaction. But seduce you . . . ? Good God, what do you mean 'other' men?"

So, for the second time in two days I was to soak Christopher's jacket. Sobbing raggedly into Christopher's impeccable lapel, I told him the full story of the previous evening in all its humiliating detail. I felt the arms that held my shoulders tighten further when I told him Dearborne's part in it. Unburdening myself became such a relief that I went on to tell him of the night in London when I had ventured into the slums and Lord Dearborne's reaction to that.

Christopher gave a low boyish whistle and swore under his breath. He was about to speak when Lady Catherine's voice came fluting down the hall. She

stepped into the sitting room accompanied by Lord
Lesley. I could see that she had on her velvet traveling
dress. Christopher's arm left my shoulders abruptly
and he made a move to stand in front of me as though
to shield me from Lady Catherine.

She laughed shrilly. "It serves nothing trying to hide
the chit. I care not whom she chooses to lace with."

Christopher's lips spared into a thin contemptuous
sneer, one that I recognized only too well. No one
could ever accuse Lord Dearborne of never having
taught his ward anything.

"You doxy, you're not fit to touch her feet. You
should count yourself lucky that we don't bring a
charge against you for attempted murder." I had
never heard Christopher sound so hard. Lady Catherine looked away, but said flippantly:

"My, how dramatic we are today. Murder, indeed.
What I did was in the wretched girl's own behalf, had
she but the wit to see it. So I drugged her and put her
into Lesley's bed, what of it? If things had gone according to plan, Lesley would have come into his
room, assumed her willing and taken her. I daresay
the little idiot would have liked it well enough, Lesley's a charming lover when he wants to be. Then in the
morning, Elizabeth could have gone crying to his
most respectable mama, who would have made all
right by forcing Lesley to marry her. Elizabeth would
have been a wealthy countess; now that is falling
very soft for a penniless girl without name or connec-
tions." Lady Catherine looked up into Lord Peterby's
grim countenance and tittered, "I would hardly be
doing you such an ill turn either, Lesley. Lord knows
the chit is comely enough."

Peterby's face relaxed slightly and one corner of his
mouth quirked. "I've heard all is fair in love and war
but don't you think you've carried things a trifle far,
my love?"

"No!" she snapped. "I'm not to be blamed if the

brat ends up as Covent Garden ware. Oh, she attracts
Nicky, I'll not deny that. I knew that even before I
saw his reaction to her tediously artless play yesterday
afternoon. She fascinates him, yes; with her silvery
laugh and alabaster complexion." She looked at me
and her voice was low and vicious. "But you wait, my
little flower, there are other beauties waiting in the
wings. Your reign may be sweet, but by God, it will
be short. You have managed to arouse Nicky's jaded
senses for now, but that won't lead him to offer you
anything more lasting than a *carte blanche*."

I think I gave a sob, I'm not sure. Christopher's arm
came defensively around my shoulders. I saw that he
was looking at the doorway. I followed his gaze and
saw Lord Dearborne. He had been leaning his shoulders against the wall, but at the end of Lady Catherine's tirade, he straightened himself and spoke softly:

"You're wrong, Catherine. You are speaking to the
lady who is going to become my wife." I think once
before I mentioned to you that I wished I could faint.
Now I was convinced more strongly than ever that it
is a skill that every young woman should cultivate.
The room was so quiet that you could have heard a
feather drop. However, what dropped was not a
feather but an ornate china vase that Lady Catherine
grabbed off the mantel to hurl across the room. The
vase smashed against the floral papered wall, just
missing a mirror by inches. In spite of myself, I found
that I was glad that the vase had been of recent Euro-
pean origin and was not the graceful Greek amphora
that stood on the teak sideboard. Lesley plucked a
porcelain figurine from the top of a Japanese cabinet
and handed it to Lady Catherine with a blatantly pro-
vocative smirk.

"As long as you intend to behave like a melodramatic
bourgeois, then do me the favor of ridding the house
of this ugly little piece."

Lady Catherine glared at him for a moment before

turning to me again. "What a pity you didn't keep your appointment at the Cuckold's Comfort. I was so sure that you would rise to the lure of that one," she spat at me. I saw Lord Peterby's eyebrows shoot up and I think my own eyes must have been as wide as saucers.

"Lady Catherine, how do you know about the Cuckold's Comfort?"

"Because I sent you that note, you fool. I hoped that by having you come alone to the worst section of the city you might have a few . . . experiences that would destroy some of the naive vivacity that Nicky seems to find so enchanting. But evidently you didn't have the nerve to go because you were at a party the very next day, as boringly innocent as ever."

That's all *you* know about it, I thought to myself. Aloud, I asked puzzledly, "But, Lady Catherine, what do you know about Henri's murder?"

"Nothing, you little moron. You so touchingly confided in me that you were interested in the subject, so I used it as candy to draw the baby into trouble. So, you weren't as dull-witted as I thought."

Yes, I am. Call me dull-wit.

"Your carriage has arrived, Lady Doran." Wadbury was standing at the doorway, as impassive as ever. I had seen Lord Peterby give an unobtrusive tug to the call bell only a few moments earlier and here was the well-trained result.

Lady Catherine, whatever else she might lack, had her fair share of audacity.

"Ah, thank you, Wadbury. Elizabeth, may I be the first to wish you happy? What an exquisite couple you and Nicky will make! I vow it will quite take one's breath away. Lesley, I will see you when you return to London?"

Lord Peterby bent to brush his lips fleetingly across Lady Catherine's extended hand. "Assuredly, my love. As long as you leave your boudoir unlocked."

Lady Catherine wrenched her hand away but still kept the uneasy smile. "You were ever an outrageous creature, Lesley. Well, good day to you all, and don't forget to give my regards to Lady Peterby for her kind hospitality." She swept out of the room and Wadbury closed the door quietly behind her.

I sat very still and made a serious study of the toes of my bare feet. I felt Christopher's arm leave my shoulders. He rose slowly to his feet.

"Uncle Nicky, you ought to be shot. I'd call you out myself except that I know you'd never accept a challenge from me. No, that would be dishonorable, wouldn't it? The great Lord Dearborne would never stoop to dueling with his ward, but to attempt an innocent girl and as vulnerable a child as Elizabeth . . . That, I suppose, you think is perfectly within your rights. Do you think that buying her a few dresses gives you the right to violate her?"

Lord Dearborne had the grace to flush. "Goddammit, Kit, I didn't violate her."

"No, because she was violently ill. But you meant to. I would just like to know how you justify yourself. I really am curious. Is it because she's beautiful? She's a temptation to every man who looks at her? What do you think we should do, force her to accept any man who wants her? After all, isn't she tempting them with her beauty?"

The marquis's face was even whiter and his voice even more strained than Christopher's as he said, "I don't justify anything."

Lord Peterby shot out a long arm and grabbed Christopher roughly. "Of course he doesn't have to justify anything. And especially not to you. What do you know about what he feels, what he thinks? Do you think I would have let him carry Elizabeth out of my room last night if I thought he was going to hurt her? Use your head, Kit. He lost his temper for a while last night and gave the child the fright of her life. But he would never have forced her. Dammit, if you don't know that, then you don't know anything about him."

Christopher tore himself abruptly from Peterby's grip. "I don't care. She shouldn't have been put through an experience like that."

Lordy Peterby nodded and grinned. "All right. Maybe not. So Nicky is a terrible guardian. On the other hand, I'm sure that he will make a charming husband."

Visions of Lord Dearborne trying to be a charming husband filled my head. Being a charming husband to a woman he despised, a woman he had been forced to marry through the inept manipulations of his mistress. If I hadn't been such an idiot, Lady Catherine's plotting would have come to nothing and I wouldn't have been forced into this most humiliating of positions. I put one hand to stop the sobs that I could control no longer. Now, on top of everything, I had become a watering can.

I felt someone take my other hand in a light clasp. "Elizabeth," Lord Dearborne said gently. "Kit is right. My actions last night were unforgivable. The only thing I can do in reparation is to offer you the protection of my name."

Terrified, above all things, of betraying my love, I pulled my hand out of his as though I had been bitten by a snake. "No! No! I won't marry you. I won't."

"I am sorry. I realize you are frightened of me, not without cause, I admit. But you need not fear a repetition of last night's events. I promise not to alarm you like that again. Marriage is the only way I can protect you from Catherine's tongue."

"Lady Catherine's tongue won't do much wagging once I've stuffed it down her throat," growled Christopher.

"There would be a certain amount of satisfaction and a lot of justice served by an action like that," said Lesley Peterby. "Unfortunately, justice and satisfaction are irrelevant right now. Any move you make against Cat will create scandal. Kit, you're not wet behind the ears anymore. You know that society will wink away anything that either Dearborne or I did to Elizabeth. And Lady Cat would be in disgrace for a while if the full story came out—when is the jade ever out of disgrace? But the person that will be hurt the most by whatever tale Catherine chooses to tell will be the person you want most to protect. The scandal would ruin Elizabeth Cordell. But as the Marchioness of Lorne, Elizabeth is invincibly protected against Cat's malice."

"I suppose you are right, Lesley," said Christopher. "But it's a damn shame that Elizabeth should be dragged into a loveless marriage through the malicious meddling of an overheated degenerate strumpet like Lady Catherine. I know Uncle Nicky doesn't care. He'll never love anybody anyway. But Elizabeth deserves better."

I couldn't have stated it better myself. Totally overcome with despair, I began to choke on my own tears.

"Damn you, Kit, have your wits gone begging?" said the marquis. Turning to Wadbury, who had returned from seeing Lady Catherine off, he said, "Would you kindly locate Mrs. Goodbody and bring her here?"

"At once, Your Lordship," he said.

Chapter Sixteen

I shudder whenever I think back on the sufferings of the next few days. I was forced to endure the most mortifying of congratulations on my upcoming wedding. Of course, Lady Peterby and Mrs. Goodbody knew everything. The marquis had told them himself and their apprehensive misery increased my own. I knew they both felt that they had failed me in some way. Even my sisters became somewhat subdued, though I tried my best to be cheerful around them.

I was semi-invalided for two days and the forced sojourn in bed increased my sense of isolation and panic. I endured one visit from a withdrawn and stiffly polite Lord Dearborne. The visit gave me such a chilly idea of my married life and later brought on such uncontrolled sobbing that Lady Peterby forbade the marquis to visit me until my recovery was complete.

When Christopher visited, his presence could not be said to be cheering because he was morosely involved in planning a mythical, though horrible revenge on Lady Catherine that could in no way be connected with any of us. Lord Peterby came too. After a short, brutal lecture on the insipidity of virgins in general and weeping ones in particular, he pinched me on the chin and cryptically advised me not to be more of a fool than I could help.

The story told outside the immediate family circle was that I had made myself ill by taking too much laudanum for a toothache. Everyone either believed the story or else had the tact to pretend they did. In the Mudbury area, the news of the upcoming wedding spread rapidly. The reaction was one of amazement, fascination, and pleasure. Our Miss Lizzie was going to marry a marquis. Everyone in the village who had ever spoken to me felt touched by stardust.

At least I was spared the mortification of having it widely known that I "had" to marry. I reflected bitterly that here I was, marrying to defend my good name against compromise and I hadn't even actually been compromised. And if I was miserably unhappy, how must Lord Dearborne feel—being honorbound to give his name to a "penniless little nobody." He must resent and despise me as the foolish child that he had called me on more than one occasion. It was small consolation that he no longer could think I had gone to the Cuckold's Comfort to meet a spy or lover. Now he knew I had gone simply because I was stupid.

My friend Janey Colman came to visit me while I was still abed. She had never been to Petersperch before and it had taken a deal of determination on her part to tap on the grand entrance door, confront the distinguished Wadbury, and ask to be shown to my bedroom. Adding to her natural disinclination to call at so lofty an estate was that some years ago Lord Peterby had found Jane berry-picking alone and had so forgotten himself as to require Jane to make assiduous use of her parasol to protect her virtue. Lord Peterby had laughed and desisted but the memory was kept alive by Jane's mama, who spat on the ground every time Lord Peterby rode by. For all that, Jane arrived at my bedroom with Wadbury as escort and presented me with a cunning bouquet of wildflowers—lily-of-the-valley, star grass, and day flowers arranged with simple ingenuity. But even to Jane, I could not unburden myself. I had exchanged so many confidences with her in the past but here she was powerless to help me. Not Christopher, not Mrs. Goodbody, not Janey, not even Lady Peterby, nor any of my well-wishers could give me the one thing that I wanted more than anything I had ever wanted before in my life—and marriage to Lord Dearborne without it would be torture. It was agony trying to hide my anguished tenderness. I once read some maddeningly eloquent statement on the miseries of unrequited love—no doubt in Shakespeare, who has said a lot of maddeningly eloquent things.

Add to the score, too, the strained relationship between Christopher and the marquis. I knew that Christopher, however many wild oats he might sow, was conservative and romantic at heart and Lord Dearborne's treatment of me had shocked him to the very soul. To be honest, I had been upset by it myself, and perhaps even angered, but now in the light of day, I was not shocked. I would no more expect Lord Dearborne to display conventional manners than I would have expected Dionysus to give up wine or Diana to forego the hunt. I was poor Clytië, the sunflower, rooted in her garden to gaze adoringly at Apollo the Sun in his blazing, compassionless splendor. But Christopher saw only that I was hurt and unhappy, and attributed it to Outraged Maidenhood and Virtue Offended. How could I tell him that it was plain old-fashioned lovesickness? So many times in the past I had complained to Christopher about one petty thing or another that Lord Dearborne had done; Christopher had been his staunch champion. Now, the roles had reversed themselves and to my chagrin I found that I was the one defending Lord Dearborne, trying to soften Christopher's unforgiving outlook on his erstwhile hero.

I stared at the damask wall panels and gold-leaf canopy of my bed for hour after hour, trying to find some way out. All the old questions revolved in my head. All the old fears of being without means or pro-

tection in the world. If I left Lord Dearborne and rejected his plans for me, where would I go? It was unthinkable to ask any of my friends to support me—
with the topsy-turvy economy of the country, even
one extra mouth to feed would be a burden. And I
would have to take my sisters if I left. An existence
without their merry nonsense would be altogether too
bleak. Where could I find a job that would allow me
to bring two boisterous adolescents? And to seek refuge with any of my grander friends, Lady Peterby or
Lady Anne, was impossible. My pride would not allow me to ask them to harbor me, disgraced as my
name would be in the eyes of the *beau monde* if I
refused to marry Lord Dearborne. Even now Lady
Catherine was probably parading around London
whispering that she had seen Lord Dearborne's lowly
bride-to-be in the bed of Lesley Peterby, though Lord
knows how she would disguise her part in how I got
there! I could imagine her sly smile and fluttering
lashes as she told the story, probably punctuating it
with her mirthless titter. Of course, if Lord Dearborne
and I announced our engagement and were married in
all pomp, then her words would be taken as mere
spite—everyone knows about a woman scorned. But if
I failed to marry Lord Dearborne . . .

By the time I was well enough to leave my bed,
banns had already been posted for our marriage and
Lord Dearborne, on Lady Peterby's advice, had written to inform his myriad of relations of the upcoming
change in his estate. It was better that they hear it
from him than Lady Catherine's poisoned tongue.

I was glad that I didn't have to face Lord Dearborne in the breakfast parlor on my first morning up.
Earlier, I had seen him from my window, cantering in
the direction of Barfrestly on his high-life stallion, Jupiter. Thus I was able to enter the breakfast parlor
with a semblance of poise. The whole company was
assembled there, helping themselves to the dishes of

eggs, ham, buttered rolls, and fresh fruit that were arranged on the sideboard. Lord Peterby and Christopher rose to their feet when I came in, a customary courtesy that always managed to make me feel ill at ease, like an impostor. Lady Peterby gave me a warm maternal smile as she looked up from the letter she had been perusing.

"How good it is to see you on your feet again, *cherie*. All goes delightfully for your wedding. Legions of Nicholas's friends and relations are writing to tell how very pleased they are with his marriage. There is even a letter from His Royal Highness, the Prince Regent, who expresses himself at gratifying length and begs that as soon as Nicky has completed his business in Kent he return to present you at Court. As well, the dowager Duchess of Windham (she is Nicholas's grandmother and the matriarch of his family, you know) has written to wish you both well and give her unqualified approval to the match."

"You're dealing without a full deck, Mama. I'll wager that the duchess said nothing of the kind. A more uncivil old woman I've never met!" Lord Peterby twitched the sheet out of his mother's hand. "Let me look. Ha! Here she says, 'I'm glad that Nicholas has finally decided to stop making an ass of himself and put his energies to breeding an heir instead of pleasuring the serving wenches. He had better hurry the business if I'm to bounce my great-grandchild on my knee before I die.' Well, I guess you could call that unqualified approval."

"Imbecile!" Lady Peterby snatched the letter back from her son. "If you intend to chortle like a plowboy than go out to a field and do it! Elizabeth, the duchess always talks like that, it means nothing. Merely, she comes from a franker generation. Now look what you've done, Lesley, you horrid boy."

"Yes, I see. The child is suffused in maidenly

blushes. No, no, don't toss that apple at me, *Maman*. I promise to be good."

"Well, then, cease that dreadful laughing. Poor Elizabeth will be sorry that she got out of bed this morning."

I know that she meant it in the kindest possible way. But I swear to Mars that the next time someone calls me "poor Elizabeth" I will scream my head from my shoulders.

"I'm all right, Lady Peterby. I can take teasing. And I think that frankness is a very good thing. I have the utmost respect for anyone who can be frank." If I had been more open with Lord Dearborne I might never have gotten into this fix. I sat down and began to pick at the omelette that Christopher had put on my plate. Trying to keep my voice light, I asked Lady Peterby if Lord Dearborne had decided on a wedding date.

"Yes, we've agreed that it will be best to wait until fall. Under the circumstances we want to avoid any appearance of undue haste. The duchess has offered to lend her townhouse for the wedding. Nothing could be better, for the approval of the Duchess of Windham will open the highest doors for you, and as effortlessly as a swallow's song. You can remain here with me until the ceremony, though I daresay invitations will soon be pouring in from Nicky's family—all eager to play host to you. You are still looking a trifle peaked, dear. Perhaps you should wait one more day before resuming your lessons with the vicar?"

"Oh no, Lady Peterby, I'm not peaked, really. This is my natural color—I've always been pale." One more day of staring at my bedroom wallpaper would drive me mad. "I feel delightfully fit, honestly, and I'm so looking forward to seeing the vicar today. I have a box of Admiral Barfreston's old maps and such that I want to take to show him. You remember, Christopher, they are the ones you rescued from the fire."

Lady Peterby regarded me doubtfully. "Well, if you have been looking forward to it, I wouldn't want to disappoint you. But I don't want you to tax your strength. You must take the carriage. I won't have you walking so far yet."

"Very well, ma'am," I replied meekly, though it was my spirit alone that was weak. Physically I felt as fit as a freebooter. As I bumped along to Mudbury in Lady Peterby's outdated laudet I told myself squarely that I would have to face facts. The news of my betrothal to Lord Dearborne was already so widespread that it would be impossible for me to cry off now without a truly fearful row. If the Prince Regent had bestowed his blessing on the match, then I knew the marquis would have me to the altar if he had to drug me with Lady Catherine's opium. It was impossible to turn back now without making the marquis look ridiculous, and it's sabers to safety pins that Lord Dearborne wouldn't let that happen. But how could I go through with it, how could I?

I sat back against the worn leather seat and rested my hand on the box of maps that I had brought with me. Closing my eyes, I tried to breathe slowly and deeply, letting the pure country air work its healing magic. Right now there was too much peace and quiet. The twins had walked down to their lessons much earlier, and suddenly I wished they were here to distract me. My dear, dear little sisters. At least I would have them with me through the trials ahead. Christa had told me yesterday afternoon that she had asked the marquis (just to make sure) if he intended to let them come to live with him too. She said that he had told her yes; how else would he keep his peacocks exercised?

It was midday quiet when the coachman set me down in front of the small, modern parsonage with its whitewashed sides and black shutters that the vicar always left closed so no light could enter and fade the bindings of his books. The coachman offered to carry the box of maps inside the house for me, but that would have meant that I would have had to hold the team of horses since there was no one else around to do it. I'd rather lift a box of maps anyday then tangle with one horse, much less two.

So I unloaded myself, told the coachman he could return to pick me up in three hours, and watched the laudet lumber off on the path back to Petersperch. I turned to lug my burden into the house when I heard a low whinny. There was the marquis's stallion, Jupiter, under the varnished leaves of the vicar's holly tree. The reins were looped casually about a nearby bush, which Jupiter had returned to munching after his equestrian greeting for me. Whew! The marquis must be in visiting with the vicar. I set down my box in the dust and dashed over to the inn, where it was a safe bet that I could while away half an hour in conversation with Mrs. Blakeslee, the innkeeper's wife. Perhaps when I returned, Jupiter would be gone and I would be able to put off facing Lord Dearborne for a while longer.

After Mrs. Blakslee had given me the up-to-the-minute details on Janey Colman's wedding and I had reciprocated with all the latest information on mine, I went outside again to have a peek under the holly tree. Yes, Jupiter was still there. But my box, the happily preserved contents of Admiral Barfreston's sea chest, was gone! I tried not to panic—mayhap someone had seen them sitting in front of the vicar's house, thought they must be his, and stuck them inside the vicarage doorway. I was just about to rush willy-silly into the vicar's front door when the squeaking of worn cartwheels caught my attention. There, driving an empty produce wagon, was my old friend from the Dyle church basement, Monsieur Sacre Bleu. And there, on the seat beside him, was the box of Admiral Barfreston's sea gear!

Oh, Ares! Oh, Pluto! Oh . . . hell. I wasn't going to let him get away with it, not if it killed me. You probably recall that each time I say that, it nearly does. You will also probably recall the occasions upon which I've come to grief by setting out on my own in some self-righteous quest or other. So, you would think that I would have learned my lesson by now. Wrong-o! Rome wasn't built in a day and you can't change the stupidly impulsive habits of a lifetime by a few bad experiences. I ran over to Jupiter, mounted with the cooperation of the wicket fence, and took off down the rutted lane after Monsieur Sacre Bleu. Of course I could have gone into the vicarage to get the marquis, and of course I could have told him what had happened, and of course I was to regret that I had not done so a thousand times on that long, long afternoon.

Just because I had successfully attained the back of a horse did not mean that I had magically become a good rider. To be truthful, I wasn't even a competent rider. I think the only reason Jupiter had agreed to leave the vicarage yard in the first place was because the horse was so flabbergasted that I had dared to get on his back at all. He was soon to regain his wits.

We had hardly gone a half-mile down the narrow lane when Jupiter stopped in his tracks and began turning impatient circles, taking great care to brush my legs against the thorny roadside underbrush.

"Whoa, Jupiter, whoa. Nice horsie. Good horsie. No, no, I want to go that way. Listen, you want some sugar? Tomorrow I'll give you some sugar, I promise. Or a nice fat carrot. You'd like that, wouldn't you? Sure you would, you big, beautiful boy." You big dumb brute. I bet you can smell fear a mile away. You're just like your master, ready to take advantage of me at the first opportunity.

It didn't take me long to be convinced that Dyle was the destination of Monsieur Sacre Bleu and the produce cart. That was where I had first seen him and that was where this road led. The only problem now was getting there.

If you had seen Jupiter that afternoon it would have rid you forever of any notion that horses are four-legged creatures. I'll swear I went half the way to Dyle with the cursed animal on his two hind legs. If only I had paid more heed to Christopher's lecture on What To Do If Your Horse Rears. I remember when he had tried to teach me that, I had told him that if he ever so much as put me near a horse that reared it would be the worse for him.

To my great relief, Jupiter stopped his fidgets as quickly as he had started them. He broke into a crisp, steady trot that jarred me to pieces as I couldn't post fast enough, but at least we were moving forward. In fact, suddenly we were moving forward too fast. We cantered around one sharp curve and there was the produce cart disappearing around the bend. I could imagine myself turning to wave airily at Monsieur Sacre Bleu as the stupid horse carried me thundering past. I closed my eyes, dug in my knees and pulled back on the reins with all my might. Jupiter stopped so suddenly that I flew into his neck, and got a mouthful of mane and a stunning blow on the nose. Well, at least we were stopped. And we *were* stopped. The horse refused to budge another inch.

"Come on, Jupiter. He must have gone on a mile by now. What are you standing here for? Do you think a sculptor is going to come and carve your image in marble?" He turned to regard me balefully. Then, as I despaired of ever moving from the spot, Jupiter lifted his shapely hooves and set forward at a fast raking trot. And thus we traveled to Dyle. Stop and start. Turn and twist. Bolt and duck. Christopher says that eventually they are going to replace horses with steam-engine traveling machines. It won't come one day too soon for me.

Mile after exhausting mile we plowed on. Twice I was thrown by some sudden start of Jupiter's, but both times the stallion returned to me, standing restlessly as I made a slow, painful climb into the saddle. He did have an occasional gentlemanly impulse. It seemed like forever until I began to feel the salty breath of the sea. I was staying in the saddle only by clutching tightly to Jupiter's mane and leaning my head wearily against his muscular neck. The ox wasn't even sweating. I knew we had almost reached Dyle when we splashed through a shallow tidal creek and the salt water stung some feeling into my numbed legs. A breeze rustled the salt-marsh cordgrass which stood in tall narrow strips pointing toward the pouting heavens. I eyed the sky uneasily; it looked like it was considering raining. To distract myself I listened for the sound of the timid marsh rail and was rewarded with a fleeting "kek-kek-kek" as the rail went about its feeding. *"Bon appétit!"* I called softly.

When I came to the outlying cottages of Dyle, I decided that it would be better to take the hilly bridle path that skirted the city; if I went through Dyle I would risk being recognized by some of Mrs. Goodbody's Dyle relations. Having come this far, I had no intention of letting anyone steal my adventure. I had seen no evidence of the produce cart for a while now but I knew, without any doubt, that he was heading for the basement crypt. There could be no more perfect place for spies or smugglers. The narrow track was dusty, and set with sharp pebbles that Jupiter's hooves sent sailing into the narrow margins of salt hay. For a while the path climbed and then threaded its way down a steep, chalky cliff. There, on its rocky ledge below, was the church, in all its dour medieval pomp.

I slid off Jupiter's back and patted the velvet muzzle. "Well, at least you didn't murder me, you rascal." I fumbled with the well-cared-for cinches and the sad-

dle came off easily, though I left on the small saddle
blanket. Using the ripped and dirty flounce that I had
torn off my gown, I rubbed down the stallion, the
while plotting my next move. You can plot and plot,
but quite frankly, it's not worth it sometimes. For all
my thinking, it came down to this—there was nothing
to plot until I learned more about what was going forward and so I would just have to creep around the
churchyard and research.

Creeping around wasn't as easy as I had thought it
would be; mainly because I could hardly walk. Whatever skin there had been on the inside of my thighs
was gone and I wouldn't sit down for a month. The
lacy go-visiting gloves that I had worn were no protection for a day of leather assault. My palms looked
like overcooked mutton. In truth there was not one
part of my entire body that did not throb or torment
me.

I considered the merits of waiting for the cover of
dusk to begin my prowl but finally rejected the idea,
deeming it a time-wasting precaution; the area was
spotted with bushes that would be an effective
enough shield. I circled cautiously around the austere
stonework supports of the church. The only eyes that
followed my movements were the glum orbs of the
squatting gargoyles that someone had once added to
the structure under the misapprehension that they
were decorative. Now what? To enter the church,
walk down the long aisle, then penetrate the mysteries
of the macabre basement crypt?

So it seemed. There was no sign of the produce cart
with my box of maps. I wondered if it was hidden off
in the nearby trees or if, despite all, I had beaten
Monsieur Sacre Bleu here by taking the high path instead of coming through Dyle. I dragged open the
heavy oak door which groaned like a grandpa with
gout. The atmosphere of ancient gloom was exagger-
ated by the shadowed twilight of the interior. More

clouds had shrouded the sun so only the thinnest reeds of light filtered through the high windows. Off, far out to sea, I could hear the crotchets of a thunderhead.

I tiptoed across the time-worn flagstones to the passage leading below. There were oil lamps on the table as before, but I boldly opted for darkness. Many times I've heard Joe Hawkins say that if you are ever trying to hide at night, never take a lamp; it will make you an easy target. Sometimes it is better to curse the darkness than to light a single candle. So, cursing the darkness, I began to descend into the perpetual night of the crypt.

I felt my way slowly down the uneven steps, my heart taking up an uncomfortably large portion of my chest. One step at a time, one heartbeat at a time, I found that my exploring toes could discover no more ledges ahead. I must be in the crypt.

It was not even the tick of a timepiece later that I heard the door swing open at the stair head and the sound of rapid footfalls. It took me a few seconds to react, then I ran; no, I flew along the rough perpendicular of the wall, scratching my arms as I brushed its jagged surface. One thing only was important—to get as far away from those invading footsteps as was possible in the moment before they reached the cavern. As soon as I saw the light from the passage, I stopped dead. I could only press myself desperately against the wall and wait with my heart playing a rapid tattoo against my rib cage.

Two men had entered the clammy vault and their voices reached me as clearly as a crystal chime.

"No, don't speak to me in French, Pierre. You will never learn English if you do not persist in practicing it!" His voice was filled with the exasperated patience with which one explains things to a slow-witted child. "I am so busy keeping you and Thomas out of trouble that I have had no time to complete my own work.

Oh, why can they not send me men who have been properly trained?"

"Ah, you are the smart one always, eh? At least give the boy credit. It stands to reason that if the mansion was burning to the ground then the so-conscientious Milord would move his precious documents to a place of safety."

"Imbecile! Is a place of safety the care of a child? Surely the fact alone that she possessed it should indicate that the contents of the box were valueless." The speaker had his back to me but I knew who it was without a single doubt.

"Not necessarily so, my fine buck. Milord is a very subtle man. How do you know that he wouldn't do just that thing to throw us off the scent?"

"Because Milord has real operatives to use. He does not have to work with fools like I do," the familiar voice snapped. "I don't know who is more stupid, Thomas with his midnight flittings and mansion burnings or you with your wild duck chases. You have deserted your post watching the marquis, wasted the afternoon, and risked exposure for a box of useless old maps. How many times must I tell you two to do nothing, no-thing, without my prior consent. This has been the most inefficient assignment I have ever undertaken in England, and all due to the blunderings of two oafs. Napoleon will know why this mission has been a failure. I promise you."

"If you want your missions not to fail then you must tell the general to give you the permission to assassinate Monsieur le Marquis. It is he that destroys all the plans. When I would bribe, then I find he is there first. When I would steal, then I find it has already been removed. He is the devil and smarter than you, though you will not admit it and blame all on your comrades."

"Oaf! Foolish oaf! We are looking for a list of English operatives in France, not a packet of obsolete sea

charts. I know there is such a list. Henri saw it with
his own eyes once, when he cooked in the Warrington
household. We would have had it that night we broke
into Warrington Place had not you been such a fool
and shot the old man before we could force it out of
him. A messy business! And you and Thomas with
your ridiculous playing with fireworks, like children
on Bastille Day. If you would stay away from young
Warrington, he would not recognize you—there is no
need to kill him. Now Henri, he had to die. He was a
good cook and a patriotic Frenchman, and he wasn't
too proud to take my money for his services, but he
wanted too much, he threatened to expose the whole
operation to the marquis and I had to kill him with
my own hands. A most disgusting business, but necessary."

"Ha!" said Sacre Bleu. "What a hypocrite you are!
Killing is necessary only to save your own worthless
neck, but everyone else can just hang."

A circle of light from the area of the steps revealed
that a third person was joining them.

"I agree with Pierre one hundred percent!" said the
new arrival.

"You oafs stick together, right, Thomas?" the other
man replied to the newcomer—Thomas the groom!

"We'll see who's an oaf," said Thomas. "You two
bloody winners are in here jawing like old women and
left it up to me to find Dearborne's Jupiter tied up in
the wood outside. And I found this next to it." He
held up the flounce I had torn from my dress.

"Do you think she saw you?" said Thomas. "Did the
girl see you?"

"*Merde*," said Sacre Bleu. "I hope not."

I realized in that instant that the combined light of
the two lanterns would make me visible to any of the
men happening to look in my direction. I frantically
wished myself invisible, and stood stock-still against
the wall.

"Why don't you ask her yourself?" said the other man, his voice heavy with sarcasm. "She's standing right behind you." Involuntarily, I let out a gasp of fright.

"*Sacre bleu*, so she is!"

"How could she ride the stallion—my God, he is a killer," gasped Thomas. They were all looking at me with speculative eyes. "She can't stay on the tamest nag in the stable."

"She's tougher than she looks." The lantern was brought closer. "Aren't you, Elizabeth dear? If you had stayed in bed a few days longer, you would not now be in a great deal of trouble," said Dr. Brent.

Chapter Seventeen

I stood painfully, quietly numbed with fright. Dr.
Brent; Thomas the groom. It would have been shock
enough to learn these men were spies if I were standing in the town square with the noonday sun streaming down, but here in a dripping subterranean chamber, it was macabre. Spies? They were murderers!
And now I knew and they knew that I knew. And I
was at their mercy.

The man I called Sacre Bleu grabbed my arm ag-
gressively, his calloused fingers pressing hard. "Where
is the marquis, eh? You will not lie to me or I will
make you regret it."

"My dear Pierre," purred Dr. Brent, "if you had not
disobeyed orders, and left your watch, then you
would know where the marquis is. And if you had any
intelligence, then you would guess." Pierre Sacre Bleu
gave a crude curse and released me.

"All right, smart one, where is the marquis?" snarled
Pierre.

"Probably, he is out searching for the mademoiselle
here, which is why, Thomas, you will take the stallion
and lose it somewhere in the countryside. I don't want
the nag found around here. Someone might have seen
the girl riding it." Dr. Brent took one step closer to
me, gathered a lock of my hair between his fingers,
and rubbed it slowly with his thumb. "When one knows
a little of Miss Cordell, all becomes clear. You see,
Pierre, she must have seen **you** in Mudbury and fol-

lowed you here—it's obvious that the marquis knows nothing of her presence here or he would not have allowed it. Ah well, good enough. To search for this little one will keep His Lordship's mind away from us tonight." Dr. Brent turned to Thomas. "Go now, Thomas, take the horse." Into the patter of Thomas's retreating footsteps, Brent called, "And take him far!"

Brent turned back to me. "So, Elizabeth, you have fallen into my lap, if I may be so bold, like a red, juicy little plum. Pray do not cower so. I have no thought of injuring you."

The cruelty in his voice was as unyielding as a granite wall, but I pulled myself up with what I hoped would pass for dignity.

"That's better, although I see you are still as stiff as a corpse, pardon the expression."

I swallowed. "I would rather not pardon the expression, if you don't mind."

"As you wish." He released my hair after giving it a sharp, admonishing tug. "You are an unexpected guest here and it is my place to show you hospitality. I had not expected this pleasure, but I am not too surprised. You have seemed fascinated for some time with Pierre; so much so that you follow him every time you cross his path, like a friendless pup. I myself cannot fathom the attraction, for to me he is ugly. But—to each his own. I apologize for the chloroform last month in the woods, but it was necessary, you see. I was trying to break you of an unseemly infatuation with my homely partner."

In the lamplight, Sacre Bleu was glaring daggers at Dr. Brent.

"What are you going to do with me?" I asked. My voice quivered hollowly in the chamber.

"What are we going to do with you? Pierre and I have often asked ourselves that. Before now, we really had no use for you. You have been so closely guarded that it was difficult to see if you had any say in the matter. But here you are," he spread his hands expansively, "a gift of Lord Dearborne's underestimation of your disobedience."

"That does not answer my question." I tried to keep my voice steady.

"Pardon me. There are two alternatives. One, I could kill you—but what a waste of *très jolie femme*, you are quite a work of art, *n'est-ce pas?*" I wondered if I was going to be sick. It was a possibility, the way my insides were behaving. "Yes, killing would be the easy way out; I am an important operative for His Majesty Napoleon Bonaparte and I really cannot risk being identified. But I am returning to France tonight. I have overstayed my welcome and my adopted motherland awaits me with open arms. So I shall take you with me."

"France? No! Why? Oh, why? If you are leaving England tonight, surely it can't matter to you that I have seen you. I mean, you will have left England. If you leave me here I give you my word that I will say nothing to anyone until you are gone. I swear it." I prided myself on being a much better liar these days. Evidently, Dr. Brent didn't think so.

"My word, what a child," he sneered. "Sometimes, little cherry, you are too disingenuous for belief. There will be other trips to England for me. Napoleon will have more need of information before France has brought England under her heel. France cannot afford to leave alive anyone who could put me out of business, or the only operatives that would remain are clumsy fellows like Thomas and Pierre."

I wondered with surprising dispassion if I was going to be killed instead of merely kidnapped.

"And perhaps Monsieur the Marquis will not be so cool toward us when I hold you in the, er, palm of my hand. Ah, don't look so dismayed, *petite*. Life need not be so bleak for you, I can be a charming fellow and I will teach you how to please me, eh?" He turned to Pierre and ordered him to tie my hands behind my back. "We go to the tower now, such a useful view from there. One can signal to ships far at sea."

I assumed I was to be taken then. To the clock tower, the one I had always found so forbidding, standing like a sentinel gazing for Napoleon's troops.

"Do you have to tie them so tightly?" I said through clenched teeth.

"Pain is good for the soul," said Dr. Brent.

Pierre pushed me roughly in front of him as Dr. Brent led the way. We went deeper into the crypt, round an absolutely black corner, and ducked to the left. We were walking on stone no longer, but on hard-packed dirt. I realized that we were in an ancient smuggler's passageway. We walked in silence for a few moments, the monotonous blackness of the surroundings broken only by the thin circle of light from the lamp and an occasional skittering rat. I began to hear a dull, wooden roar.

"The surf, my dear," said Dr. Brent. "Pierre will steady you from behind; we are about to ascend a ladder." Rather than steady me, Sacre Bleu grabbed me bodily round the waist and lifted me up the ladder.

Suddenly, we were inside the tower and the light from the lamp was superfluous. The thin rays of the late-afternoon sun were attempting to stream through the dusty stained-glass windows.

"Be so kind as to follow with us up the stairs," Brent said. "The view from the top is stunning." I always wanted to see the clock room, but I had never had the nerve to climb up the spiral staircase which wound up the inside of the tower. Now the problem of nerve was taken care of and I would get my wish. One should always try to look on the bright side. I tried not to look down and followed my captors up the steps and through the small doorway into the clock room.

The heat of the place made me feel faint and it was

some moments before I could get my breath. The clockworks clanked and whirred noisily in the golden light. There was a thick covering of dust. I could see a drop of sweat run down Dr. Brent's cheek, leaving a trail behind it.

"Pierre, open the window. Not that one, fool, the one toward the sea." A clean salt breeze swept through the room and I could feel my skin cooling. "Much better, eh, Elizabeth?"

I stepped back uneasily as he advanced to stand in front of me.

"What a shy creature you are." His smile was serpentine. I could see that now more than ever. "Merely, I am going to help you to sit down. Regard the wooden chair to your left. Yes, the appearance may be a trifle unstable, but it should hold your slender form with no trouble." His hands pressed cruelly down on my stiff shoulders until I was seated. "Now," he continued, "you must school yourself to sit quietly while Pierre and I conduct some little business. I must caution you, my dear, to behave very well. If you are a trouble, I'm afraid that it will be more convenient to . . . dispatch you to your Maker. Ah, I see that you can see reason. What a delightfully intelligent girl."

Only for now, you ghoul! The more passive I was now, the less they would be on their guard. Oh God, I had to escape. Please, please, let there be help for me somewhere. Suddenly I thought of Mrs. Goodbody identifying my lifeless body. Her face would be—no, I couldn't imagine what it would be. Where had I been in heaven when they were handing out brains—out picking berries?

Dr. Brent (I wondered what his name really was) and Pierre sat together at the rickety pine table. Brent pulled out some papers and they gazed at them, talking in French, their voices rising and falling rhythmically with the surf washing outside. I watched through the window behind them as a black thunderhead sailed in majestically and began to overwhelm the late-afternoon light, brilliant rays shooting high into the sky as the sun made a futile effort to stay alive. Sacre Bleu lit a candle and the conspirators' faces took on an even more sinister aspect. The bumps and craters in Sacre Bleu's cucumber nose were accentuated in the wavering candlelight, and a gold tooth glinted as he talked. Dr. Brent's face seemed carved out of marble. Their voices were drowned in a clap of thunder, and, as if making amends for my own unwillingness to cry, the sky began to weep torrentially. I sympathized.

The former arid heat of the chamber was soon replaced by a clammy draft and I was to find that cold was added to my other physical miseries. After a while my bound wrists became mercifully numb, but the burning throb in my limbs was increasing. My afternoon in the saddle was catching up to me with a vengeance. I wondered whether the ache in my stomach was hunger or fear. A piercing pain bit at my temples and my stiff neck felt inadequate to hold up the satiny heaviness of my head. With a dismal clarity I recalled the time I had followed Sacre Bleu into the woods, the blow on the head, the aftermath in the arms of Lord Dearborne. I had laid my head against his chest as he carried me home in front of him. Jupiter's strides had slid like silk over silk. I remembered, too, the shamed realization that the marquis's touch had aroused those first stirrings of pleasure in me. His flirtations under the honeysuckle bush, the moment at Lady Catherine's ball when he had pulled me against him, his light friendliness on the hillside on the way to London; these were times of glowing sensation for me, however little they had meant to Lord Dearborne. Heart-stricken, I realized that these might be the only such moments I would ever have. I felt a sudden bright warmth under my eyelids.

A clatter on the stairs far below us indicated the

approach of a visitor. Dr. Brent and Sacre Bleu heard it also, and without a word Sacre Bleu stationed himself behind the door, wielding a wicked-looking truncheon. The steps continued their advance.

"Rest easy, boys, it's only me," said Thomas. Sacre Bleu relaxed his stance as Thomas burst through the door, shaking water from his greatcoat like an unruly dog. "Put down the club, Pierre. If you knock me on the head, you'll get no victuals." He appraised my condition, but made no remark. Placing my box of maps on the floor, he produced a loaf of bread, a wheel of cheese, and a bottle of wine from out of his coat.

"Why in the devil's name did you bring those maps along?" said Dr. Brent.

"I thought we might be able to use them," he said defensively.

"Can't you give the boy some credit?" said Sacre Bleu. "If he had left them someone might have found them."

"Forget it," said Dr. Brent with an impatient wave. "Your methods of operating are beyond me. Let's have the refreshments. Pierre and I have had a hard afternoon of intrigue while you have been running about the countryside getting wet."

The three of them sat down again around the table and began scattering crumbs as I watched. I'd be damned if I was going to ask for any. Suddenly Dr. Brent looked in my direction and feigned great surprise, slapping himself on the forehead.

"Elizabeth, my dear, I completely forgot about you."

"I wish you had," I muttered.

"But you must be starving." He sauntered over to my corner and crouched down beside me, brushing away a strand of hair that had fallen across my face.

"Don't touch me."

"But I was going to untie your hands so you could

eat. Since you wish me not to touch you, I may have
to have Pierre untie you. But Pierre is busily eating, so
I will just ignore your desires. You must eat," he said,
roughly freeing my hands from behind my back.
"That beautiful body of yours will otherwise become
but a fence post." Dr. Brent tore a crust of bread and
a rind of cheese and tossed them into my lap. I
rubbed my wrists and winced involuntarily as the
blood came rushing back. He smirked slyly at my
pained expression.

"I thought you were married to the Hippocratic
oath," I flashed angrily.

"Ha!" Thomas grinned nastily. "He is a hypocritical
oaf and as for his doctoring, I would not trust him to
pull a splinter from the paw of a dog!"

I took a small bite of the bread, though it almost
choked me as it lodged halfway down my dry throat.
"But how did you fool all of your patients? And Dr.
Lindham? You were his assistant."

"Dr. Lindham knows even less about medicine than
I do, for all his distinguished appearance. My father
was a doctor, and I know what a farce it is. All you
have to do is nod your head and look wise, use large
Latin words, and when I ever had to treat anyone, I
just gave them opium. You should be glad the marquis contacted me to treat your overdose, for it is one
thing I am expert at. Any other ailment and he would
have been on to me for sure. Dearborne is no fool."

"But why pose as a doctor?" I asked him.

"Because I get to poke around the countryside and
gain access to people's secrets. Mudbury is centrally
located, close to the coast of France, and populated
with yokels. Who is going to suspect me, no matter
who they see me talking to?" The rain drummed
steadily on the roof.

"Thomas," he said. "Leave off your chompings and
keep watch for the ship. It should be along any moment, and we don't want to miss the signal." Thomas

did not leave off his chompings, but instead took a large hunk of bread and stood by the window. Sacre Bleu and Dr. Brent resumed their desultory French conversation, Dr. Brent keeping an eye on me while I finished choking down my food.

"There now, all finished," he said. "I must tie your hands again, my dear." He stood behind me and performed the task, adding an extra twist before he left off. "Now go back to your corner. I will bring you some wine." I went back to my corner and sat with my back to the wall, so I could gaze enviously at the gulls wheeling in the storm. The cliché "free as a bird" gained new meaning.

"Here you are, dear," said my captor. "The wine I promised you."

"You don't expect me to drink that," I said.

"You'll drink it or I shall require Pierre's assistance to hold open your lovely mouth," he said, affecting a frightening aspect.

"Pierre will be minus his fingers," I shot back at him.

"Such spirit," he said. "No, I was joking. This is just wine. See, I will drink half of it myself." He did so, but I still did not trust him. "So be thirsty," he shrugged, finishing the bottle. "I will talk to Pierre. He is more interesting than you."

Distraught with misery, I gazed out at the storm and wondered if I could reach the window sufficiently ahead of my captors to throw myself out. I tried to imagine what my last moments of life would be like, twisting and turning, the wind rushing through the dark as I plummeted from the tower. There would be a blinding flash of pain as I collided with the rocks far below; then I would be one with the gulls and the storm. I was trying to raise my courage, to shed my hold on life, and was about to make the attempt, when I heard something. Wait and listen, I told my disbelieving ears.

Through the crying of the gulls, the thundering of the wind and surf, the rattle of the rain against the roof, the ticking of the clockworks, and the talk of my captors, came a sound that, thin and low as it was, sounded to me like the clarion call of a thousand bugles. Dear and familiar to me from a hot summer day, it was a sound which brought hope rushing back into my heart like a cavalry charge.

The marquis was blowing a grass whistle, unless my naughty sisters had left their beds to rescue me. It had to be him; only he would know what the sound meant to me, from our moment under the honeysuckle bush. He was close to me, probably in the wood at the base of the tower, and I would bolt from them when we left. Better to die in the attempt than to be dragged across the English Channel with a half-mad spy.

"I see the signal," shouted Thomas.

"He's right, for once," said Dr. Brent, leaping to the window. "We will soon be treading the Champs-Élysées. Pierre, get the pistols."

He turned to me. "And you, my dear. It is time to begin our journey. You will walk behind Pierre, I will walk behind you, and Thomas will bring up the rear, carrying our baggage like the pack mule he is. And one more thing. Don't try to flee. It is a deserted area and no one will hear your screams when I catch you and beat you with the buckle end of my belt."

I staggered to my feet as best I could with my hands tied behind my back. "I can barely walk," I said. "How am I going to flee?"

He gave me an ugly smile and pushed me in front of him. "Let me help you," he said. "Thomas, bring the candle."

We were making our way down the staircase, the sounds of the storm ringing hollow in the interior of the tower. Our shadows cast giant grotesque shapes on the far wall as we spiraled downward. We reached the bottom of the stairs and paused for a moment, Dr. Brent cocking an ear.

"Snuff the candle and we will be out," he said. Thomas obeyed his orders with a quick motion. "As a precaution, we will cock our pistols." Three clicks rang ominously.

"Well, Pierre, open the door. Are you waiting for Christmas?"

We were out in the open, a windy drizzle was prickling my skin. Dr. Brent halted us again. If we could only be underway. He listened and shrugged.

"Let's be off," he said, pushing me again. Five steps, I thought to myself. Five more steps. Two . . . three . . . four . . .

I took a deep breath and ran as hard as I could into the darkness at my left, my bound hands bumping uselessly behind me.

"She's there!" shouted Thomas.

"Elizabeth, get down!" came the marquis's voice. By way of obedience I tripped on the wet grass and fell to my face with such a jar that my wind was knocked out of me.

"Now!" shouted the marquis.

A dozen lamps were uncovered at once, and the three scoundrels were standing in a brilliant circle of light.

"Damn your eyes, Dearborne," shouted Dr. Brent. He crouched down with his companions and a blistering crossfire opened up over my hapless head. The noise was deafening, but in a few moments it was rocketing away over the cliffs and gone, leaving only the plaintive cries of the wheeling gulls.

The three friends of Napoleon had sung their last Marseillaise.

Chapter Eighteen

Before I had even caught my breath, I was dragged ruthlessly to my feet.

"Elizabeth, you little idiot, what in the hell possessed you to gallop across the green like a bolting sheep? Good God, did those bastards tie your wrists? Quit wriggling, damnit! There. You can thank God, whichever one you're worshipping now, that you're already covered with bruises or so help me I'd beat the hell out of you." Lord Dearborne was in a royal temper and it sounded to me like the singing of an angelic choir; under the rough anger there was the pure, unmistakable undertone of a caress. He slid his satin-lined cloak around my shoulders, tying it at the neck with impatient fingers. "Lesley? Good. Take her to the coach and take care that she doesn't break her silly neck tripping over the damned cape." Lord Peterby took my arm and pulled me along behind him.

"Come on, you little wretch, you've only got a few dozen yards to walk." After Dr. Brent, even Lesley Peterby seemed like a pussycat. "What a limp! What in God's name did they do to you?"

"Nothing. At least, not much more than tell me they were going to take me to France. Oh, and they tied me to a chair and gave me rancid cheese and stale bread for supper, though I can't say I felt much appetite anyway." I tried to match my stumbles to Peterby's long strides. We were walking in the direction of the nearby side road.

"I should imagine not," returned Lord Peterby drily. "Why did you tear away from them like that? Don't you realize that was precisely the provocation they needed to gun you down?"

"Of course, but anything was better than going with them to France. And when I heard Nicky whistling on the blade of grass, I hoped . . . I hoped . . ." I broke off in confusion, it was the first time I had ever called my august fiancé by his pet name.

"Nitwit. He whistled so that you would avoid panicking. As though we didn't spend the entire afternoon concocting plans to separate you safely from your so charming companions. There is practically a regiment of soldiers from here to the beach, ready to perform a gallant and safe rescue. Then you ruin the whole thing by taking off like a hare before the hounds. And if Dearborne hadn't been so quick on the trigger . . . Brent almost got the chance to send a bullet through you."

We had reached the coach and I was happy to see it was Lord Dearborne's discreetly luxurious traveling chariot and not Lady Peterby's bouncing laudet. I don't think that I could have endured another jolting trip that day. Lord Peterby lifted me in and I leaned back against the velvety pillows.

"But Lord Peterby, how did you know that I was in there?"

I could see Lord Peterby's grin in the glow of the oil flambeau. "Half the town saw you riding hell-for-leather after a grizzly stranger and a wagon, mounted precariously on Jupiter. Those facts, added to a somewhat rueful knowledge of your generally reckless and impulsive character, led Nicky to the correct conclusion. Unfortunately, by the time he got here, you had already been taken."

There were so many things that I couldn't understand. "But Lord Peterby . . ."

"Lesley," he interrupted.

"Oh, all right then, Lesley," I said with crabby obedience. "How did he know to come to Dyle?"

"Dearborne has known for some time about their rendezvous here. The man you followed here is a notorious agent who was identified several months ago by one of Christopher's servants. We identified Thomas, too, after Christopher's firecracker turned out to have more of a bang than he intended."

"But why not arrest them then?"

"Because Dearborne hoped that they would lead us to their leader. The eel has been slipping in and out of England for years, creating havoc, and it wasn't until this afternoon that they found out that Dr. Brent was the disguise of one of Napoleon's cleverest operatives."

"Lovely. And in the meantime letting Thomas and Pierre terrorize a lot of innocent citizens," I cried indignantly.

"Nonsense. There wasn't any danger if you had only obeyed a few simple rules. Thomas was watched every moment. And there were a couple of full-time men on the trail of your Sacre Bleu."

I gasped. "And which of your wonderful men was watching Thomas the night he decided to burn down Barfrestly Manor?"

Lesley frowned. "Our man had no idea of Thomas's intentions in that instance. He was thought to have been going to another rendezvous with Pierre, so the tail was much too loose. When he finally got down to business, our man was too far behind. Mistakes like that are too common in our business."

"Our business? You work in the War Department as well? I shall never sleep soundly again."

"I am not actually employed in the War Office, so rest easy. I just help Nicky out occasionally. I know my way around London's brothels and low-life casi-

nos. It is a knowledge which Nicky finds useful."
There was some shouting and commotion outside the
carriage. "I should go, Nicky will need some help with
the details," he said. He opened the door.

"Wait, L-Lesley," I reached out and touched him on
the shoulder. "I never did thank you for getting me
out of the slums."

Lord Peterby took my outstretched hand and raised
it to his lips.

"Thank me by refraining from sauntering off on
more perilous expeditions in the future." A bright
ironic smile lightened his features, and he paused on
the carriage steps. "Nicky is getting a rare handful in
you." And he was gone before I could decide whether
or not to acquit him of double-entendre.

Exhausted, I leaned back in the plush seat of the
coach and yawned. My wrists were aching, and far
away I could hear men talking. The rain had slowed
to a drizzle. Through the window of the coach I saw
the clouds part to let through a brilliant full moon,
which seemed to wink at me confidentially. It was
near two o'clock in the morning.

I must have dozed off, for I was returned into half-
consciousness by the forward lurch of the coach.
Careful, efficient hands were propping the pillows
more comfortably beneath my drowsy head and tying
the slipping cloak more securely around my neck. I
peeped surreptitiously beneath my drooping eyelids
to glimpse the pure classical profile and shining red-
gold hair. Lord Nicholas Dearborne, Marquis of
Lorne, was leaning back against the opposite side of
the coach, his long legs stretched out in front of him. I
noticed that his hands were stuffed firmly into the
pockets of his jacket.

Returning my breathing to what I optimistically believed to be the rhythmic cadences of sleep, I leaned
limply over onto Lord Dearborne's shoulder with
what I hoped was the guileless innocence of a slum-

bering child. It was a pretty lame trick, I'll admit, but it was the best that I could think of on the spur of the moment. Lord Dearborne stiffened momentarily, then pulled his hand from his pocket and slid it obligingly around my shoulders. I was lying there trying to think up a way to provoke further action when I felt the back of my wicked lover's hand rubbing lightly against my breast.

I wrenched myself upright.

"Rake! How dare you take advantage of a woman pretending to be asleep? How did you know that I was awake?"

"I don't know—intuition, I guess." I could hear the laughter in his voice. "I'm afraid that I've taken advantage of you in so many situations that I've lost count. How do you feel?"

"Terrible. I hate your horse!"

"If you're sore from the ride, it serves you right," said Lord Dearborne, with something less than lover-like devotion. "Jupiter is trained to take no one on his back but myself or my groom, Jason. I can't understand why that stupid glue bait didn't dump you at the first crossroads. Mayhap your charms work on horses as well as men, my violet-eyed witch?"

"Well, he wasn't charmed at all," I returned crossly. "In fact, I had a more comfortable time of it under the not-so-tender mercies of a bunch of villainous spies. That brutish animal tossed me off twice, conked me senseless by tossing his neck, and carried me under a low-hanging branch that almost knocked my head off. Did you catch him, then?"

"Yes, he came trotting into the Fox and Feathers outside Dyle and demanded his oats as though he owned the place. The stablehands there recognized him and obliged the poor fellow. Lesley is returning to Petersperch tomorrow and will bring him back." There was a low shelf under the seat. Lord Dearborne opened it and drew out a small flask, which he un-screwed and handed to me. "Here, you still feel so cold."

"You are always forcing spirits on me," I com-plained, but took a swallow of the bitter liquid none-theless. The devil take your liquor, Milord, I thought, and looked up at him provocatively. "Now, aren't you going to ask me if I've been, let me see, how did you phrase it? Ah, hurt in any other way?" I laughed.

He smiled at me wistfully and with heart-stopping tenderness said, "I don't know which can move me more, your laughter or your tears. Sometimes at Bar-frestly I would be sitting in the library frowning over pages of Department reports and I would hear you outside in the garden playing at some silly game or other with your sisters or Kit. Every once in a while, then, I could hear you laugh, like sunlight on crystal, fresh, sparkling, innocently alive; all the things that you are and I am not. I tried so hard not to fall in love with you." He brought one finger up to delicately trace the outline of my cheek. The casual affection of the gesture brought tears to my eyes.

When the marquis spoke again, his voice was cu-riously tender:

"God knows that I've made mistakes before, but that night in London when Lesley brought you home, wrapped up in his cloak, you stood there so still and white . . . I almost went out of my mind. I know it was my own fault that you wouldn't confide in me, I've acted like a damned coxcomb since the first day we met. And that night I found you in Lesley's bed, I was so jealous that I lost my control. There's never been a woman before you . . . dammit, you little wretch, will you wait until I finish my sentence before laughing at me? I'm trying to say that . . ."

I knew I should be cherishing this rare moment of humility in my beloved, but it was so out of character that it was too much for me. So I had to interrupt him.

"Nicky," I whispered, twining my arms around his neck, "hush up and take advantage of me."

It was some time before I regained the breath to speak. Then I was sitting curled on Milord's lap with my warmly flushed cheeks leaning against his chest.

"Nicky?" This time I said his name tentatively, savoring it.

"What is it, love?" His lips were in my hair.

"If there has never been a woman before me, then where did you learn all those excellent things?" I asked quizzically.

"Brat. Laugh at my love talk, will you? What I was trying to tell you was that there has never been a woman who has ever meant anything to me. God, I don't know anything about being in love."

"Mmmmm. You seem to be doing all right. My word, what an odd place for you to kiss me. I never realized that people kissed other people in that spot before. N-ick-y . . . ?"

"What is the matter, am I frightening you, sweetheart? It's all right, I'll stop."

"No! Stu-pid. I just wanted to know why you didn't tell me that you loved me before, when you asked me to marry you?"

Lord Dearborne sighed and tilted my chin back so that I was looking directly into his eyes.

"After tumbling you about like a scullery maid, I could hardly brazen out a declaration of love. Especially with Christopher snarling at me and hovering over you like an eagle protecting its only egg. Kit and I made up, by the way; this morning. We had a long talk and he gave me a lot of sage advice. Elizabeth, are you listening?"

"Yes, yes. But, Nicky, I didn't mind being tumbled around like a scullery maid. It was only that I was so sick. Actually, I wanted to be tumbled . . ."

His lips stopped mine with a long, searching kiss, then he said huskily, "I can see that we are going to have to find a very strict chaperone for you until our wedding. What do you say about staying with my grandmother, the Duchess of Windham?"

"If you want a strict chaperone, then not her, Nicky. She's much too anxious to see your heir!"